P9-ELG-334

FEB 2014
Westminster Public Library
3705 W. 112th Ave.
Westminster, CO 80031
www.westminsterlibrary.org
DISCARD

THE
LAST DOGS
DARK WATERS

by

CHRISTOPHER HOLT

illustrated by Allen Douglas

LITTLE, BROWN AND COMPANY
NEW YORK BOSTON

Little, Brown and Company

Hachette Book Group
237 Park Avenue, New York, NY 10017
Visit our website at www.lb-kids.com

First Edition: June 2013

Library of Congress Cataloging-in-Publication Data
Holt, Christopher, 1980–
Dark waters / by Christopher Holt ; illustrated by Allen Douglas.—First edition.
pages cm.—(The last dogs ; 2)
Summary: "Canine heroes Max, Rocky, and Gizmo meet a friendly new community of dogs—and these new dogs have seen humans, who Max, Rocky, and Gizmo thought had disappeared without a trace"—Provided by publisher.
ISBN 978-0-316-20012-7
[1. Dogs—Fiction. 2. Adventure and adventurers—Fiction. 3. Science fiction.] I. Douglas, Allen, 1972– illustrator. II. Title.
PZ7.H7388Dar 2013 [Fic]—dc23 2012030639

10 9 8 7 6 5 4 3 2 1

RRD-C

Printed in the United States of America

For Mom, Dad, and Angel

PROLOGUE

THREE SUNS

Max was running through a city.

The street he ran down was long and empty. People had once swarmed the sidewalks on either side. They'd sat in glass bus shelters beneath advertisements of smiling men and women, or laughed as they went in and out of shops, arms overloaded with colorful bags.

Now the sidewalks were barren. Stray newspapers and plastic bags were blown by a chilly breeze until they pooled next to concrete steps and in doorways. The windows of the stores were shattered, the rooms beyond them dark.

All the people were gone.

Howls and barks echoed around Max, ricocheting among the glass skyscrapers that rose to gray clouds overhead. Max looked back over his shoulder as he ran. Dozens upon dozens of shadowy wolves and dogs chased him. Behind them, a dark storm flooded through the mazelike streets, an inky blackness that blotted out the city in its wake.

Leading the pack of shadow beasts were two enormous creatures—a canine the size of a school bus and a wolf as large as a house. They were all sharp angles, with pointed ears and triangle snouts, and both stared at him through bright red glowing eyes. With each step of their giant paws, windows rattled and the ground quaked. Cracks snaked through the asphalt as if the street itself were being torn apart.

Max knew the two beasts well. The Chairman, an evil Doberman. Dolph, a vicious wolf pack leader.

Run as far as you like. It was the Chairman's deep voice, but it did not come from the shadowy figure; it spoke directly in Max's thoughts.

You will never *escape,* Dolph's voice snarled.

Max wanted to challenge his pursuers, but there were so many, and he was all alone. Maybe if his friends had been here in this nightmare city, they could have faced the rampaging creatures together. But loyal Rocky and feisty Gizmo were nowhere that Max could see.

So instead, he gasped for air and looked forward, away from the cloud of blackness, away from the howling pack.

He veered around the corner of one building, then

another and another. But no matter how many streets he turned down, he never seemed to get anywhere new—each street looked exactly the same. Same darkened storefronts, same two cars parked halfway on the sidewalk, same blank traffic lights swaying as they dangled overhead.

Pain lanced through Max's legs—his muscles were cramping. He couldn't run forever. Already he could feel himself slowing, struggling to catch his breath.

Then he heard it. The sound of rushing water.

A river.

Halfway down the street, Max tried something new: He skidded into an alleyway. It was narrow, grimy, and dim with shadows. Trash was piled along the walls. But this was the way to go—he was sure of it. The gurgles and splashes of the river came from the end of the alley.

Max leaped forward. A break came in the storm clouds, and daylight streamed down from above, sparkling and glinting off the water, which was just coming into view.

As Max reached the end of the alley, a dog stepped into his path. She was a Labrador like Max, only her fur wasn't gold like his—hers was black and specked with white. Her tail wagged when she saw him, though her big brown eyes were sad and weary. Despite being frail and thin, she projected a strength that he recognized at once.

It was Max's friend Madame Curie.

Find the people who made this happen. Her mouth did not move, but her voice echoed in his thoughts. Just as the Chairman's and Dolph's had.

"How?" Max asked. "They all left, and we don't know where they went."

Madame tilted her head, and as she did, something on her collar glinted in the sunlight. There was a golden symbol attached—three linked circles in a row.

Find the three golden rings, her voice whispered. *They will help you learn what you need to know.*

"But what are the rings?" Max barked. "Please, Madame, we don't have much time. I'm being chased. I need—"

But she was gone.

Sadness swelled within Max. He was suddenly overwhelmingly tired and alone. All he'd ever wanted was to find the humans who had raised him and loved him—his family. But the farther he'd journeyed, the more horrible things he'd had to face. Losing Madame and fleeing the snarling dogs and wolves was just the start of it.

He didn't know how much longer he could run.

Just then, the sunlight flared, and Max looked up.

In the sky, three suns hovered side by side. They burned like enormous white holes, and Max had to squint to see them.

Three rings. He had to remember. No matter how tired or sad he was, he had to keep trying. If not for himself, then for his friends.

He had to follow the rings to find the people.

Soon, even squinting was no help against the hollow suns—the searing light grew brighter and brighter until Max could see nothing but white. The alleyway around him disappeared in a blaze, and the ground beneath his feet grew too brilliant to look at. All Max could do was close his eyes and surge forward to the river he knew was close by.

The noisy rush of water filled his ears, drowning out the barks and yips of the pursuing dogs and wolves. Running blind, Max felt the pavement fall away beneath his front paws, and he leaped for all he was worth into the light.

Max awoke.

CHAPTER 1

ADRIFT

Max opened his eyes to a blaze of harsh daylight.

He lay in the bottom of a small boat, the sun's heat warming his golden fur. The little vessel rocked back and forth on the river's current. It was that sound—the sweet soft splashing of the river water against the sides of the boat—that had appeared in his dream.

Water. Max licked his lips. His tongue and nose were achingly dry. Groaning, he got to his feet and crawled to the rear of the boat, then leaned over the edge and lapped up some of the cold, clear river water. The water tasted a little strange compared with what was usually in his bowl or human toilets, but it wasn't bad, just different.

Once he'd slaked his thirst, he sat back on the wooden floor of the boat and glanced up at the wide blue dome of the sky. There was just the one sun, not the three blazing rings he'd seen while he'd slept.

What a strange dream. It wasn't the first he'd had since he and his friends escaped the city controlled by the evil Doberman who called himself the Chairman. The Chairman had led a cabal of vicious dogs called the Corporation, and when Max and his friends had refused to fall in line, the Chairman had tried to lock them up. They'd escaped their cage—helping other dogs flee in the process—but the Chairman and his snarling henchmen hadn't been about to let them get away without a chase. Max and his friends won freedom only when the vicious wolf Dolph showed up and challenged the Chairman to a fight.

Max didn't like reliving those memories, but he never regretted seeing Madame like he remembered her before this began. Even seeing her in a dream was better than never seeing her again at all. The last time he'd been with her in real life, he'd cradled her while she took her last breaths and passed away.

In his dreams, Madame guided Max and gave him advice. Only he didn't know what to make of her words—what did the people's disappearance have to do with the design on Madame's collar?

A honking snore startled Max from his thoughts. He peered beneath one of the two benches in the boat, where Rocky and Gizmo lay curled up in the shadows. It was the little Dachshund who had snored, of course.

How the fuzzy Yorkie beside him could sleep through it, Max could never guess.

Rocky's pack leader was a vet's daughter, and he had helped Max escape from a kennel after all the people disappeared. Together the two fought off a pack of starving wolves, and they'd been traveling companions ever since.

Rocky's stubby black legs kicked. "Come back here, kibble," he muttered in his sleep. "I'm-a-getchoo. I'm gonna eat you up! Stop running." With another honking snore, Rocky smacked his lips and fell still once more.

Kibble.

Max's stomach gurgled. He and Gizmo always made fun of Rocky's love of any and every kind of food, but right then, Max could really have gone for a big bag of beefy bits.

They had been on their boat for three days now, letting the current carry them down the wide river toward the faraway ocean. That was where Madame had said the people had gone. People like Max's family, who had disappeared along with all the other humans when they'd abandoned the cities and left their pets behind.

Why had everyone gone away? Max still didn't know. Madame had said something about a sickness, but she wasn't quite herself at the end, and Max wasn't entirely clear what she'd meant. All Max knew was that he needed to find his pack leaders, Charlie and Emma, and their parents. They must be so worried about him. They would *never* have left him behind if they'd had a choice.

It had been in the frantic rush to escape the Chairman, Dolph, and their packs that Max, Rocky, and Gizmo had found the boat in which they now rode. They'd been in such a hurry to get away from the angry animals and find the humans that they hadn't given much thought to what they were going to eat on the river.

They'd relied mostly on drinking river water to fill their bellies. One time, Gizmo had seen a bright silver fish and dove over the edge of the boat to catch it...but that had just resulted in her spending the night shivering and soaking wet without any fish to show for her swim.

"They're so fast!" she'd said once she'd clambered back into the boat and shaken herself.

"You'll catch the next one we see," Rocky had said. "I just know it."

She was lucky they'd been in a calm patch of water at the time. Max had seen wolves get swept away in the river's powerful current, and he didn't want that happening to Gizmo.

Max knew that if they didn't stop soon to find food, they wouldn't be able to reach the ocean.

He watched the land flow past on either side of the river. Sometimes they saw houses set along the grassy edges of the riverbanks, and sometimes they drifted through small, eerily silent cities. When that happened, the shore would get built up and cemented over and the water would get dirtier until, passing beneath bridge after bridge, they'd reach the city's edge and the buildings would fall away again.

More often than not, though, there was nothing to see: The riverbanks were lined with dark woods thick with shadows, forests filled with creatures. With the humans gone, the wild animals had grown bolder and bolder, leaving the safety of the forests and openly scavenging for food in the cities. Max caught sight of loping deer and darting rabbits and raccoons feasting in garbage cans, nothing dangerous. The only animals he never saw—or heard—were birds. He didn't know where they'd gone. He guessed they'd all flown far away.

But whenever Max thought he should leap into the water and strike out for shore, he would hear a distant howl or catch a whiff of wolf musk on the wind. It wasn't long before he saw gray or white or brown fur slipping between tree trunks, running parallel to shore, almost as if following the boat.

Max didn't know if the wolves were part of Dolph's pack, but it didn't matter. The last thing he wanted was to make enemies of another group of wolves. And so they stayed in the safety of their boat and drifted on.

A fuzzy tan head popped up beside Max. "See anything interesting?" Gizmo asked.

Tail wagging, Max looked down at his little friend, who was blinking sleep out of her eyes. He and Rocky had met her at a small camp of dogs called the Enclave.

It was run by one of the craziest canines Max had ever met, a control freak Poodle named Pinky who insisted he be called Dandyclaw. Despite all that Max and Rocky had suffered through at the Enclave, at least they got Gizmo out of it. The Yorkshire Terrier was small, but she was a smart and fiercely brave companion. She was so endearingly chipper that Max was grateful just to have her around to cheer him up.

"Nothing, really," Max said. "Mostly just trees again."

Putting her paws on the edge of the boat, Gizmo raised herself to get a look. "Trees aren't boring! Especially when they've got squirrels in them."

"Well, just don't go and try chasing any! The river is huge, so it would be a long swim."

Gizmo shivered. "Don't worry, I learned my lesson when I went fishing." She lowered her bushy brows. "I still bet I could have caught that fish if the water wasn't moving so fast. It was just floating there!"

Rocky snored again, then flipped over, his body slamming heavily against the wood bottom of the boat. His front paws swatted at the air. "Kibble?" he muttered.

"Kibble," Gizmo repeated, dropping her paws down again and lying on her belly.

"We need to get ourselves to land," Max said. "Then we can find a human store and drag some food back to our boat."

"Oh!" Gizmo said, her tongue lolling out in eagerness. "That's the best idea. I've been aching to get on dry land again. I feel like I haven't had a good run in *forever*."

Max's own legs felt cramped, especially because he was pretty big by dog standards and the boat wasn't exactly roomy. The idea of racing through grass—for fun, not because he was being chased—sounded like heaven.

"I'm going to start paddling us toward shore," Max said. Holding up a front paw, he spread his toes apart. "See how my feet are kind of webbed? Labradors like me are good at swimming through water."

Gizmo studied her own paw. "Mine are just normal, but my legs are too short to reach the water anyway."

"Don't worry, you can still help." Max gestured toward the bench at the front of the boat. "You take lookout and let me know what you see." Another loud snore rattled out from under the bench. Max chuckled. "I think we can let Rocky keep sleeping. I wouldn't want to tear him away from his dreams. That's the only kibble he's likely to see for a while."

🐾

Max spent the rest of the day clinging to the back of the boat with his front legs while his hind legs were submerged in the river. His back paws dragged through the water as he fought against the current to paddle them to shore.

As he paddled, Gizmo talked about anything and

everything she saw. "That's the tallest tree I've ever seen! Oh, I think I just saw a squirrel! Ooh, *two* squirrels! They look like they're fighting over a nut. They should really learn to share."

"Yeah," Max gasped as he struggled against the river waves. "They probably should."

Gizmo darted to the back of the boat and panted happily as she stood snout-to-snout with Max.

"You're doing really good, Max," she said. "You know, this reminds me of the time I was sleeping in a cardboard box under a bridge. It was raining and cold, and all I had to eat was some old bread crusts that I was saving. Well, this other dog showed up, sopping wet and growling, and he demanded my food."

"What did you do?" Max asked.

"He looked so miserable that I offered to share, but he wanted *all* of it. Just like those squirrels. I tried to be nice, but he just wasn't listening."

His legs aching, Max stopped paddling. The boat slowed, but still drifted toward shore.

"Did you get into a fight?" Max asked.

Gizmo shook her head. "Nah. A duck floated by on a little stream, and while we were distracted, it waddled into the box, took a bill full of bread, and waddled right back out!" She laughed, then stopped suddenly. Her eyes fell. "Oh, we haven't seen any ducks in a long time, have we? Usually they only go away when it's cold."

Max shivered as icy water splashed onto his back. His

legs had grown numb to the chill, but it was still a shock to the rest of him.

"I've been wondering the same thing," Max said softly. "Hey, maybe we'll see some soon, though. Why don't you go check if there are any in the sky up ahead?"

"Okay!" Gizmo said.

She spun around and bounded to the bench at the front of the boat. It wasn't long before she was talking up a storm again. Before finding her way to the Enclave, where she'd met Max and Rocky, the little terrier had been traveling the countryside on her own. She had a lot of tales to tell.

Despite the chatter and the splashes of waves, Rocky kept sleeping.

His strength regained, Max paddled with his hind legs. Slowly but surely, he angled the boat toward shore. Luckily, the flow of the water seemed to help guide them.

Aside from Gizmo's endless chatter, the water lapping against the boat's hull, and the whoosh of the wind, it was utterly quiet on the river. Just like everywhere they'd been since the humans disappeared weeks and weeks back. Max was almost afraid of what they'd find when they finally reached dry land again. More empty, desolate towns filled with sad, starving dogs? More angry bands of canines trying to rule the streets? Wolves or other wild animals with a taste for house pets?

Or something worse?

But the growling in his stomach told Max he couldn't worry. They had to get food. Whatever they'd face on land, they would face it together.

Max wasn't sure how long he'd been paddling, but it felt like ages and his hindquarters burned from the effort. He couldn't see much aside from the dirty floor of the little boat, but he could tell that daylight was fading. Night was on its way.

"Max, I see something!" Gizmo cried out.

"Let me guess," Max said, his tongue lolling out as he panted for breath. "You saw another possum."

"No, silly—something else!"

Max stopped paddling, letting his legs rest, and looked ahead. The little terrier jumped from foot to foot, her stubby tail an excited blur.

"What is it?" he asked.

"It looks like some sort of giant house. It's so pretty!"

Max scrabbled with his hind paws until he managed to heave himself back on board. Water dripped from his fur and made puddles as Max padded to the front of the boat to get a look for himself.

The sun was starting to set, casting a gold sheen across the lapping river waves. His tail wagged as he saw how close they were to the craggy, rocky shore. Insects buzzed over the water, darting shadows in the fading light.

But that wasn't what had Gizmo excited. Farther down the shore was what looked like a fancy white house built atop a platform. Pillars supported wide porches that surrounded each of the building's three levels. Sparkling lights were strung between the pillars, reminding Max of the lights his family put up around the farm during the cold winter months.

Black steam pipes rose from the front of the building, and flags at each corner fluttered in the river breeze. At the back of the strange structure were four giant waterwheels painted red with gold trim.

Dark sludge and debris clung to the slats of the waterwheels—trash that had piled up in the river.

Only then did Max realize this wasn't some fancy riverside mansion after all. It was a boat, and the "porches" were actually decks.

"That's not a house," Max said. "That's a boat!"

"Well, it looks like a floating palace!" Gizmo said. "Have you ever seen anything like it?"

"Never," Max said with a shake of his head.

"Do you think there might be food there?" Gizmo asked.

"I don't know, but it's the first real ship we've seen on the river," Max said. "There has to be *something* on it. We can check it out. Even if there's nothing to eat on board, maybe it's near a town where we can find food."

"Yay! Okay!" Gizmo jumped down from her bench and nuzzled Rocky, who still lay curled beneath it. "Hey, wake up!"

Rocky snorted, then snapped wide awake. "It's a kibble stampede! Watch out!" he cried.

"It's even better than that!" Gizmo said. "Max and I found a big floating house on the water."

Blinking his watery eyes, Rocky looked from Gizmo to Max. "Wait, what? A house? We can't eat a house!"

"No, but we can eat what's inside," Gizmo said.

"You mean food? Did you find food?"

"We hope so," Max said. "Come see."

Rocky went wide-eyed as he climbed atop the bench and got a look. "Oh, it's a riverboat!" he said. "My first pack leader used to put me in her purse and take me to boats like this to play card games. There's always lots of loud noises and flashing lights." Rocky scrunched his nose at the memory. "But there was also people coming around giving drinks and plates of food to the people while they played their games. I bet there's tons of food on board!"

The three dogs barked excitedly to one another as the current carried their small vessel toward the line of mounded-up debris behind the riverboat. But as they drew closer, Max fell silent and the wagging of his tail slowed.

The riverboat sat in the shallows at an odd angle, tilted over, half onshore and half in the water. There was no dock, just a sandbar, as if the enormous vessel had crashed there.

On the side nearest to them, Max could make out a dark, jagged hole just above the waterline. He couldn't be sure if it was just the fading light reflecting off the

water into the interior, but he could swear he saw shadows moving inside.

After all they'd been through, Max felt wary. Someone or some*thing* might have already claimed this ship. Before Max could say anything to his companions, their little boat knocked against the slimy, wood-clogged debris trail that led to the riverboat's paddle wheels.

The riverboat loomed over them, throwing an inky shadow across the water.

Shivering, Rocky looked to Max. "This riverboat doesn't seem near as lively as the one I remember, big guy," he said. "I got a bad feeling."

Just then, a white head quietly appeared over a white-painted railing on the main deck.

"Hey," Max whispered. "I think there's someone there."

The three dogs craned their heads to look. For a long moment, all they saw was the lone white head. With the sun setting behind the ship, the creature was angled in such a way that they couldn't make out its features.

It watched them, unmoving. Silent.

On the second level of the big ship, another head rose into view. This one was mostly white, with two black circles on its face that, from that distance, looked like two hollow, empty eyes.

"I see another one," Gizmo whispered. "Should we say hello?"

"I don't know," Max said. "Just wait."

The two heads twisted, tilting slowly as they took in the three dogs.

Then another appeared, partway down the main deck.

And eight more, one by one, peering through the slats of the painted wood railing. Some had black spots, too, only they were oddly shaped blobs that looked like no eyes Max had ever seen. Others shimmered pure white in the twinkling of the hanging lights and the setting sun.

None of the heads spoke. They just continued to watch.

"Who are they?" Gizmo asked, straining to get a good look.

Trembling, Rocky backed away, almost falling off the bench. "I changed my mind," he said. "I ain't going on that riverboat. I'm not *that* hungry!"

"Why not?" Gizmo asked.

Rocky darted his head back and forth, gaping at both Max and Gizmo. "Can't you guys see? Those are *ghosts*. That riverboat is haunted!"

CHAPTER 2

FIREDOGS

"Ghosts?" Gizmo snickered. "Oh, Rocky, everyone knows ghosts don't ride boats. They like to haunt houses!"

The spectral faces still hovered above them, peering down through the railings. The only sounds were the lapping of the waves against the nearby shore and the whistling of the wind as it rushed past the dark hole in the riverboat's hull. Even the buzzing insects had fallen silent.

Max didn't understand why the heads didn't move or speak—unless Rocky was right and they were ghosts. But that was impossible, wasn't it?

Before he or Rocky could do anything, Gizmo held her head high and leaped atop the bench at the front of the boat.

"Gizmo!" Rocky hissed. "This is a boat that *looks* like a big, spooky haunted house. You can't—"

"Hey!" Gizmo barked loudly up at the unmoving white figures. "Are you guys ghosts?"

"Oh, no," Rocky moaned. Crawling on his belly beneath Gizmo's bench, he placed his paws over his snout and squeezed his eyes closed. "You never ask a ghost if they're a ghost. If they just now realize they're not alive anymore, then they might get really mad!"

A few of the furry white heads twisted and moved, as though looking at one another.

"If you *are* ghosts, you can tell me," Gizmo barked up. "I've never met a ghost before. It would be neat!"

High above them, behind the gold-trimmed railing on the main deck of the riverboat, the nearest figure cleared its throat in a very unghostly way. Then, stepping forward and sticking its snout through the railing, the figure spoke.

"No ghosts here," she barked down, then chuckled. "We're nothing but a bunch of dogs. And I'm pretty sure we're alive."

All along the railings, the other ghostly heads began to laugh—yips and growls and woofs that reminded Max of his dream...only these barks were friendly and filled with an easy warmth. As their snouts opened, he could finally see the shape of familiar doggy heads, and he realized the black eyes he'd seen weren't eyes at all—they were spots on the dogs' foreheads.

Now Max could more clearly see the creature who'd spoken—she was indeed a dog, one with floppy ears and black spots all over her snout. She hopped up and hung her long white paws over the railing and barked.

Rocky peeked out at Max from beneath the bench. "No ghosts?"

Max shook his head. "No ghosts."

"Just us Dalmatians!" one of the dogs on the second deck shouted down.

"We thought *you* were the ghosts for a minute," another one barked. "You look like shadows to us!" All the dogs on the boat laughed.

Rocky crawled out from beneath the bench and strutted over to stand next to Max. "I knew it was Dalmatians," he said to his friends. "I was just trying to scare you guys."

From above came the sound of dozens of paws pounding against wood. All the Dalmatians on the ship raced along the railings; descended stairs, their claws ringing on the metal steps; and came to crowd around the lead Dalmatian on the main deck. They poked their heads through the white wood railing to get a good look at the visitors. One got a face full of flag and, sputtering, pulled his head back.

"I knew a Dalmatian once," Rocky whispered so that the riverboat dogs couldn't hear. "He was the meanest dog I ever met." Rocky's eyes narrowed at the memory. "He would never, ever share his kibble with me. He'd always just bare his teeth and growl, and one time he tried to bite me!"

"That doesn't mean anything, Rocky," Gizmo said, looking back over her shoulder. "You want *everybody's* kibble. Some dogs are bound to get annoyed by it."

"You can't judge all dogs of a breed by how one of them acted," Max said. "I'm sure there are some super-mean Dachshunds out there, even though you're not mean at all."

Raising his snout in the air, Rocky intoned, "I'll have you know that we Dachshunds are a refined, gentle breed."

Above them, the lead Dalmatian cleared her throat once more. "Excuse me for interrupting, but did you folks get stuck there on purpose? Or are you just passing through?"

Max's stomach twisted inside him—hunger. "Actually, we were passing through, but, um, we saw this boat and thought maybe there might be food on it."

The Dalmatians glanced at one another, communicating wordlessly.

"All right, it's decided," the lead Dalmatian barked down. "It wouldn't be very hospitable of us to send you on your way when you need a meal. You see that hole in the hull there?"

The wood around the hole was splintered and jagged, the inside of the ship beyond it pitch-black. It reminded Max of a wolf's jaws opened wide, fangs ready to tear through fur.

"You can use the path of the trash on the water to get up on board," the Dalmatian called. "Sound good?"

"Sounds great!" Gizmo barked, her nub of a tail a wagging blur.

"We'll meet you downstairs." The Dalmatian pulled herself down from the railing, and her pack followed. As they disappeared, she called out, "See you soon!"

"I can't believe we're trusting Dalmatians," Rocky said, shaking his head.

"Aren't you hungry, Rocky?" Gizmo asked, looking down at him from the front bench.

The little Dachshund's stomach growled in response. "I'm superhungry," he moaned, ducking his head. "But I just don't trust random packs of dogs anymore. Not after all we went through back in the city and on the way there! I never thought I'd say this, but I wish we'd stumbled on another house full of cats instead!"

Grunting, Max leaned out and set his front paws on the trash, then pulled the rowboat forward. Driftwood and other debris mounded up around the hull, but the prow was snugged into the trash like it belonged there.

Back inside the boat, Max shook free the gross, stringy garbage that had wrapped around his paws. Turning to his friends, he said, "You two ready?"

"Yup!" Gizmo yipped.

"I guess," Rocky grumbled.

Once more stepping a foot outside the boat, Max's

paw found a stretch of smooth, wet wood. It bobbed a bit as he put his weight onto it, but the trash kept it from moving too much. Carefully, he walked to stand beneath the hole.

"Okay, Gizmo, you first, then Rocky," he called back over the lapping of the water. "Jump onto my back and then through that hole!"

"Aye, aye, captain!" Gizmo barked.

A moment later, Max felt her land between his shoulders. Tiny paws bit into his skin as Gizmo made one more leap—and he saw the fuzzy tan-and-black ball that was his friend fly over his head and disappear through the jagged hole. Soon after, Rocky landed heavy on top of Max's back, then flung himself after Gizmo.

It was Max's turn. Grabbing the slick debris with his front claws, he jumped through the hole and skidded along the cold, wet floor inside the ship. He slid into a wall and yipped, unable to see anything in the pitch-blackness.

Shuffling footsteps met Max's ears: Rocky and Gizmo, turning in place.

"Are you all right?" Gizmo asked.

"Sure," Max said, panting. "No sweat."

"Where are we?" Rocky asked. "Did those Dalmatians trick us? I told you guys that—"

A creak of hinges interrupted him.

In the darkness, a door slowly swung open, red light

streaming out and illuminating the small space. There were shelves stocked with human tools, and buckets with mops, and enormous metal things that smelled of grease and dirt and electricity.

The lead Dalmatian's snout peeked around the edge of the door—Max recognized her now by a great slash of black like a triangle that ran from behind her eye and across her snout. She nudged the door with her head, throwing it wide. Her pack mates crowded in behind her and craned their heads, trying to see past one another.

Tail wagging and nodding approvingly, the Dalmatian said, "You made it!"

"Of course we made it!" Rocky said. "We're no ordinary dogs." Snout raised, he marched up to the Dalmatian. "The name's Rocky. The big guy is Max, and my much-too-eager friend here is Gizmo." Scrunching his brows, he asked, "So what's your game, dame?"

The Dalmatian took in Rocky with amusement. "No games 'round here, son," she said. "Just your friendly neighborhood firedogs."

"Firedogs?" Gizmo asked, wide-eyed. "What's that? You don't set fires, do you?"

The Dalmatian laughed, and her pack mates joined in, their mirth echoing through the bowels of the ship.

"No, ma'am!" the Dalmatian said, still chuckling. "We were bred to help put *out* fires. We help people!"

Gizmo darted over to the Dalmatians and began sniffing them. "Oh, fighting fires! Saving people! How exciting!" Stopping, she looked the dogs up and down inquisitively. "So how many fires have you fought?"

The lead Dalmatian coughed but didn't answer right away. A younger Dalmatian with one ear completely white and the other entirely black nudged past her.

"We haven't fought any yet," he admitted. "We were all raised together on a farm. We were going to be sent to the firehouse at any moment!" His eyes fell. "Or we were before all the people disappeared."

"Hush, Cosmo," the lead Dalmatian said. "We don't want to bring the mood down, now that we've got visitors." She nipped gently at his side, and he backed away to stand with the rest of the pack.

Turning her attention back to Max, the Dalmatian bowed her head. "My name is Zephyr. You three are probably awful hungry, so why don't you follow us up and we'll get you something to eat? The rest of the boys will introduce themselves along the way."

"You've been really nice," Max said. He glared at Rocky. "We appreciate it."

Wagging her tail, Zephyr said, "It ain't nothing. Come on!"

Turning, Zephyr led them through the main level of the ship. To the right of the small room was a big metal bin heaped full of trash bags. Above it was a hatch. Max guessed the people probably threw their garbage down here while sailing and then emptied the bin later.

There were lights on somehow—dim bulbs high on

metal pillars, protected behind cages—but they were all red, casting an eerie crimson glow. Giant pipes rose up from between grates, and there were big metal control panels where humans must have worked to keep the ship running.

Dozens and dozens of paws clanged out on the catwalks as Zephyr wound them through the maze of pipes and machinery. All the floors were at a slight angle, as though they were walking up a hill.

The young dog who had spoken before, Cosmo, hung toward the back, panting happily and trying—and failing—to strike up a conversation with Rocky.

"I've never seen a little dog like you before!" Cosmo said. "What kind of things do you do? Do you fight fires, too?"

With a roll of his eyes, Rocky said, "No, of course not. I was in a fire once, and let me tell you, it was not a good time."

The little Dachshund tried to dart ahead next to Max, but the eager Dalmatian shoved between Max and his friend.

"Yeah, I guess fires aren't for everyone," Cosmo said. Wagging his tail, he asked, "Maybe you like chasing Frisbees? Those are fun! I like to leap in the air and snag them in my teeth." He opened his mouth wide and gnashed his teeth, pretending to grab a flying disk.

"No." Rocky sniffed. "I'm not a Frisbee dog. Much too big for my mouth."

"How about squirrels? Ever caught a squirrel? I love chasing sq—"

"Ha!" Rocky said. "I don't do squirrels. They're almost as big as *me.* Only crazies like Gizmo over there are willing to take them on."

"Thanks!" Gizmo said from the other side of Max.

"No, I don't like having to chase my meals," Rocky said. "I prefer my food from a bag."

"Oh, me, too!" Cosmo said, his sharp tail a blur. "I love kibble. It's the best!"

"Yeah?" Rocky said, looking up at the eager dog. "Me, too. You, uh, don't happen to have any around, do you?"

"Well, no," Cosmo said. "But you're gonna love dinner anyway. We're having biscuits tonight!"

For the first time in days, Rocky's ears perked up. His tongue lolled out of his long snout, dripping with saliva.

"Biscuits?" he yipped. "Oh, I haven't had a good doggy biscuit in ages and ages. I prefer the ones shaped like bones—you get lots of different flavors with those, sometimes beef, sometimes chicken—but I like the softer ball-shaped ones, too. One time I got a bone-shaped biscuit that was *hollow* and had tasty crunchy bits inside. Now, *that* was a good surprise. I mean, I'm a dog who loves his kibble, but biscuits? Those are a rare delicacy."

Cosmo's tail stopped wagging and lowered to tuck between his legs. Embarrassed, he said, "Uh, actually, it's buttermilk biscuits. Like the kind humans eat. We found them in the big freezer and left them out to thaw, so they should be warm.... Maybe a little soggy, but, you know..."

"Oh," Rocky said.

Max lowered his head and nudged Rocky's hindquarters. "Be nice," he said. "We're lucky to have any food at all."

"Yeah, yeah, believe me, I'm grateful! But *real* biscuits..." He shook his head. "You do a trick, you get a mouthful of flavor. I miss training my humans."

The dogs fell silent as Zephyr brought the pack to the base of some metal stairs that rose up to a closed door. But before she could even start climbing them, the door opened suddenly, smashing against the wall with a resounding bang.

Bright white light shone down from the doorway, washing away the murky red glow.

All the Dalmatians stopped and went completely still as the hulking, shadowy figure of a very large dog filled the door frame.

"I'm Boss," the figure's voice boomed. "I'm the alpha of this boat, and no one is fixin' to come aboard without my saying so!"

Clearing his throat, Max held his head high and shoved his way through the Dalmatians so that he could stand next to Zephyr at the base of the stairs.

"I'm sorry," he said with a polite duck of his head. "I

thought Zephyr was the boss. She invited us on board, so we didn't know it would be a problem."

Growling, the dog stepped forward. His face was wide and his ears floppy, like Max's, but he was burlier in the shoulders and chest. Most of his fur was orange-brown and black, with great swaths of white on his snout and his belly and his broad chest. A puffed-out crest of fur ran from his neck down his front.

The big dog bared his sharp teeth and narrowed his icy blue eyes. "Are you questioning my authority aboard this here vessel, boy?" the dog barked.

Max shook his head. "No! I mean, I'm the leader of my friends, but I—"

"You're a leader?" the dog barked. "I've had many a dog come here and try to take over, and I am not having it, no, sir." Taking a menacing step forward, the big dog looked directly into Max's eyes. "If you're fixin' to start something, then I challenge you to a fight!"

CHAPTER 3

CHALLENGED

"I knew it!" Rocky barked. "Those scheming Dalmatians! This is a trap!"

"I am not now, nor was I ever, a Dalmatian," the dog at the top of the stairs growled.

Boss—his name and not just his title, Max guessed—stepped all the way onto the grated landing in front of the doorway. The heavy door slammed shut behind him, bathing him in the unearthly red light of the pipe room.

"My breed is Australian Shepherd. We come from far across the ocean." He slowly walked down the steps, sizing up the newcomers, his mottled, fluffy tail high and still.

"Ooh!" Gizmo yelped, her ears rising, alert. "We're on our way to the ocean. If you came from there, maybe you—"

Boss barked at her from the base of the stairs, the deep sound echoing all around them. The usually fearless Yorkie hugged the ground and backed away.

Zephyr and the other Dalmatians bowed their heads and parted, leaving Max to stand alone in front of Boss. Growling, Boss calmly crossed the empty floor, his icy eyes never leaving Max.

Cosmo whispered to Rocky, "Sorry! We weren't trying to trick you, I promise."

Boss snapped his teeth at Cosmo, and the pup darted out of Max's view.

The Shepherd came to a stop a foot away from Max. There was no mistaking that Boss was the bigger of the two. Even if most of the dog's mass turned out to be from the fluffiness of his fur, Max wasn't keen to go head-to-head with him. He was tired of fighting, tired of being on the run. He just wanted his people, and a meal, and a warm bed.

Deep in Max's gut, his stomach growled. Boss's ears twitched, but the dog's cold gaze did not move from Max's own. Boss's tail wagged slowly, warily, and his brows lowered.

"You heard me," Boss said in a low, threatening growl. "Would you try to control my pack? Do you think you can best me in a fight, boy?" Boss's lips curled back, exposing his fangs.

It wasn't in Max's nature to be anything other than friendly when meeting people and animals. His instincts were to just sniff a new acquaintance, lick him in greeting, and be friends. His wariness toward large packs of dogs was something he'd only just learned during his travels.

But Max wasn't the sort of dog to back down from a challenge.

Max stood still, staring into Boss's eyes without saying anything. He knew that every dog in the room was watching the two of them, knew that no dog would intervene in a fight between two alphas. For a long moment, the only sounds were snorting dog breaths and a distant pinging drip of water on metal.

Max needed to make a move. He could accept the dog's challenge and try to take charge. He'd done so in the past.

But his hunger told him to try something else.

Max tucked his tail between his legs and took a step back.

"I'm sorry we trespassed on your ship, Boss," Max said, lowering his head and scrunching himself down onto the grated floor. "I'm not here to challenge you, and I respect your authority over the dogs who live here."

"Truly?" Boss asked.

The Shepherd's tail had stopped moving, and the dog now looked down at Max with one brow raised, curious.

"Truly," Max confirmed. "We do not intend to live on your ship. We're just passing through. These Dalmatians—

Zephyr and her friends—invited us on board to eat, since we haven't had food for days."

"I see, son, I see."

Boss turned and nosed between the Dalmatians toward Zephyr. As soon as he was out of earshot, Rocky nudged Max's hind leg.

"What are you doing?" Rocky hissed. "Are you going to let that big dog walk all over us, like the Chairman did? He yelled at Gizmo!"

Max shushed him. "Just wait," Max whispered. "I don't know about you, but I'm in no condition to fight."

Rocky growled in frustration, then waddled back to stand next to Cosmo and Gizmo.

"Zephyr," Boss barked as he came to stand in front of the Dalmatian. "You brought these three mutts on board and offered them our food without asking me first?"

"I'll have you know I'm a purebred!" Rocky yelped.

"Keep quiet," Gizmo whispered.

Zephyr nodded solemnly. "Yes. I'm sorry, Boss, it's just you were sleeping, and they seemed like such nice folk...."

"We didn't want to wake you," one of the Dalmatians near Zephyr piped up. "We know how grumpy you get when you're woken up early."

Boss's pale eyes darted between Zephyr and the other Dalmatians. Sighing, the big dog turned and marched back to Max.

"All right, son, untuck your tail and stand tall for me." Boss's voice was still deep and low, but it was suddenly no longer threatening. To Max's ears, the Shepherd sounded old, weary. And friendly.

Max did as he was told. "We didn't mean to cause any trouble."

Boss let out another sigh, then sat down. "You didn't. I can see that." Shaking his head, he looked over at Gizmo. "And sorry, girlie, for shouting at you."

Gizmo wagged her tail and pranced forward, Rocky following. "It's all right!" she said. "I wasn't scared or anything. Loud noises just surprise me sometimes."

Rocky tilted his head, regarding the burly Shepherd with confusion. "Just a minute ago you were barking at us and challenging Max here to a fight," he said. "Now you seem like a completely different dog."

"Well, I reckon I ain't!" Boss bellowed, jumping back up.

Rocky skidded backward and said, "Loud noises scare me—I mean, surprise me—too!"

Clearing his throat, Boss said, more softly, "It's just I have to be careful who I let on board my ship. There are lots of dogs running 'round as wild as roosters in a hen hut these days, and a good many of them want to be top dog wherever they go. I can't tell you how many have come upon our home and thought they'd be in charge." He shook his head. "I'm not fixin' to take any chances."

"I understand," Max said. "We've run into lots of dogs like that. We're from way up north, and there's a whole city controlled by a Doberman who wants to be top dog. It's not a good place."

Boss puffed out his crest of mottled white fur and looked Max up and down. "You have the look of a dog who's seen some battles recently. That's why I had to challenge you, son. See the quality of your inner character and such."

"Hey, buster," Rocky said, waddling alongside Max. "Max is a good dog, you hear? But that doesn't mean he takes any nonsense. You try to mess with us again and *hi-yah*!" Rocky jumped and spun in a full circle, whipping his knifepoint tail through the air. "We'll get ya!"

Barely containing a chuckle, Boss said, "You pack a lot of punch for a smaller pup. I see Max has true companions who will fight for his honor. That says a lot about a dog." Sniffing Max, Boss asked, "I bet you three have a grand tale to tell about the events that brung you to our doorstep."

So the three of them told their story. Max started with the day the people disappeared. As the Dalmatians crowded around to listen, he told them about Madame Curie's strange portents of doom; about how, with Rocky's help, he'd escaped Vet's cage; about fighting Dolph's pack of wolves. Rocky took over from there, recounting the brave way he'd led Max through the woods to Max's old home, and then insisted they leave. "I don't like to toot my own horn," Rocky said, "but if it wasn't for me... well, who knows where we'd be now?" Once he reached the part about the Enclave, Gizmo chimed in and told them about life with Dandyclaw—and how the three companions set off to the city. The younger pups howled in horror when Gizmo mentioned the house of cats, even when Max assured them they were friendly. No one spoke, though, as the tale turned back to wandering through towns full of dogs driven mad by hunger and the loss of their people.

By the time Gizmo got around to the Corporation, Max's stomach growled.

"All right," Boss said, standing and stretching. "That's enough story time. It sounds like our new friends here have been through a lot, and we should finally let them eat."

Max couldn't hide his happiness; his tail started wagging so hard that Boss laughed.

Gizmo asked, "Maybe after we eat we can hear how you came to live here with a bunch of Dalmatians?"

"Oh, it's not just Dalmatians," Boss said. "There's a whole lot of us on board the *Flower*."

"The flower?" Gizmo asked. Scrunching her brows in confusion, she said, "I haven't seen any flowers."

Boss laughed. "This vessel you're on is called the *Flower of the South*," he said. "Hard to understand why it's called that down here, but wait till you see the upstairs. I reckon we live in the lap of luxury here on the *Flower of the South*." Turning toward the stairs, he barked out, "Zephyr! Cosmo! Astrid!"

The two dogs Max already knew by name and a third darted to stand before him.

"Yes, Boss?" Zephyr asked.

"We don't need the whole pack of you spotted pups tearing through my riverboat," he said. "You three will take Max, Rocky, and Gizmo here on the tour." Craning his neck and looking over the rest of the Dalmatians, he said louder, "You all can go get back to whatever it is you were doing before our guests came on board."

The other Dalmatians let out disappointed *Awws*, but they listened to their alpha and filed up the stairs one by one. They shoved open the heavy door at the top and disappeared into the bright light beyond. Soon, only Max, Rocky, Gizmo, Boss, and the three designated tour guides remained.

"All right, pups, have fun," Boss said. "If you'll excuse me, I need to get back to sleeping."

Max ducked his head. "Of course."

The Australian Shepherd bounded up the stairs.

"Well!" said the Dalmatian named Astrid—one of the few firedogs whose heads were completely white—as soon as Boss was out of sight. "That wasn't so bad."

"Oh, yeah, it's gone much, much worse before." Cosmo's head was a blur as he nodded, sending his black and white ears flapping. "I'm just *so* glad you guys are good dogs. If you'd been bad dogs"—he shivered, and a ripple of fur stood up on his neck—"never mind."

Max wondered what would have happened if they'd been deemed "bad" dogs after all. Would they have been locked up in a cage to starve like in the Chairman's Corporation? Or worse?

But the pain in Max's stomach was too much for him to consider such worries right then. Food was so close, and he needed to eat.

He just hoped his stomach wasn't going to lead him—and, more important, his friends—into more danger.

CHAPTER 4

THE *FLOWER OF THE SOUTH*

The three Dalmatians took Max, Rocky, and Gizmo up the stairs, through the heavy swinging door, and into a world awash in light.

So Max squeezed his eyes shut—the ceiling lights were too bright—and his first sensation of the upstairs of the riverboat was of his paw pads leaving cool, grated metal and sinking into tickly plush carpet. Blinking his eyes open, he saw that they were in a short hallway. Save for the ornate diamond patterns in red and gold on the carpet, the hallway was plain—empty white walls and a few doorways.

"This doesn't look as fancy as Boss said it would be," Gizmo said.

"Who cares about fancy? Where's the kibble?" Rocky said.

Zephyr padded along in the lead, straight toward a pair of gray double doors with smudged plastic windows. "Oh, you haven't seen nothing yet," she called back.

At Zephyr's commanding bark, Cosmo and Astrid darted forward, each one nosing inward one of the swinging doors to reveal the room beyond.

More bright lights, made worse because they were glinting off... silver.

The floor of this new room was tiled in a black-and-white checkerboard, but everything else in the room had a shiny glimmer of polished metal. Long rows of cabinets and stoves filled up the entire center and the sides of the large room. Pans and cookie sheets were stacked on countertops, and ladles and pots dangled off hooks. On the higher shelves were hundreds of plastic jars filled with spices, their scents seeping out of their containers, meeting Max's nose, and reminding him of his faraway home.

It was a kitchen—one bigger than any he'd ever seen. Dozens and dozens of cooks could fit in here, preparing hundreds of meals, and Max wanted to eat them all.

"Oh, this place smells great!" Gizmo said, standing next to Max as he gaped.

Snorting and sniffing the ground, Rocky waddled right past the two of them, following an odor. Apparently finding the trail, he shot his head up and darted forward to a nearby oven. Tongue darting in and out and in and out, he licked at a splotch of dried food that dulled the appliance's otherwise immaculate surface.

"Mm," he said. "Grease! A little stale, but not bad! Not bad!"

Snorting, Zephyr walked deeper into the kitchen. Cosmo and Astrid trailed behind her, and the doors they'd held open swung backward on squeaking hinges.

"No need to lick up spills," Zephyr said. "Come this way."

The three turned right, and Max, Gizmo, and a reluctant Rocky followed. Ahead, Max could see a huge room—a wide-open pantry, he realized—ten times the size of the one back home. There were shelves from the floor to the ceiling packed thick with bags and boxes and jars and cans and bottles, and in the middle of the room were more cooking supplies on bright metal racks. Filling most of the floor were giant sacks of powders and mixes, as well as tubs bigger than Gizmo full of bulk food that looked a lot like kibble.

Beside the pantry entrance was an enormous metal door. Like the double swinging doors, it had a window high up, but the glass on this door was frosted over. As they grew closer, Max could feel chilly air seeping from around the door's edges.

Stacked next to the metal door were paper trays inside plastic bags. Inside each bag, arranged neatly on the trays, were doughy white blobs. A few of the bags were torn open, with bite marks on the thawed bread.

"What are those?" Max asked.

"Biscuits!" Astrid yipped. "They only really taste good when they're cooked, but they're still better than nothing!"

And then Max recognized the blobs as sort of wet, pale imitations of the biscuits he'd seen his pack leaders eat. They'd always smelled so good, but these smelled just like—he sniffed heartily—dough. He felt his mouth run with saliva.

His skinny spotted tail wagging, Cosmo darted ahead and stuck his nose inside one of the open packages. Grabbing the tray with his teeth, he shook his head until the plastic wrapping flew free. Then he dragged the tray back to the other dogs and dropped it right in front of Rocky. His jaws parted in a grin.

"See, buttermilk biscuits!" he barked happily. "Go on, try some!"

Rocky crept over and sniffed one of the doughy balls. Crinkling his snout, he backed away. "It, uh, smells a little off."

"Oh, Rocky, don't be so afraid to try new things." Gizmo bit into a biscuit. Wrenching her head, she yanked off a piece, then sat down to chew. And chew. And chew some more. She finally swallowed it down with a grimace, then forced a happy puppy smile. "See? Not that bad."

Cosmo's head fell and his tail stopped wagging.

"Well, maybe tomorrow Boss will bring out some hot dogs or other meat to thaw," he said. "He's the only one who knows how to open the freezer, so he decides what we eat for the day."

Astrid snorted. "Boss isn't here, is he?" she said. "Let's at least give them some of the granola."

"Granola?" Max asked.

Astrid raised her brows and tilted her head at Zephyr. With a sigh, Zephyr waved a paw forward.

"To the pantry!" Astrid said.

She led them around the wire racks toward the big plastic tubs Max had seen earlier. Granola, as it turned out, was some sort of mix of oats and nuts that humans ate. It didn't have the meaty, hearty flavor he was used to, but granola did have that satisfying kibble crunch. Before he knew it, hunger took over and he was gulping down mouthfuls of the stuff, almost forgetting to chew. Gizmo was at the tub next to him, eating her fill as well.

Behind them, Max heard the squeak of a faucet, then a gush of water. Chewing one last mouthful of granola, he turned to see Cosmo atop one of the silver counters, filling up a basinlike sink. On the floor beneath the sink, Rocky sat surrounded by biscuits, in the throes of ecstasy as he devoured the clammy, half-cooked things.

"Whoa, slow down," Max said, walking toward him. "You don't want to get sick."

"You actually *like* those biscuits?" Gizmo asked, staring wide-eyed.

Rolling onto his belly, Rocky used the remaining biscuits as a pillow and closed his eyes in contentment. "You were right, Giz," he said. "I should try more new things. And I thought *doggy biscuits* were good!"

Max hooked his front paws over the edge of the sink and lapped up water from the basin. Rocky and Gizmo climbed to the countertop using a nearby stepladder and drank from the sink as well. Their bellies full for the first time in days, the three dogs sat down at the foot of the sink.

"Time for a nap," Rocky said.

"Nap? Are you kidding?" Panting and eagerly looking among the three dogs, Cosmo said, "You guys have to take the rest of the tour! I've never gotten to be tour guide before, and you can't sleep until I've shown you *everything*!"

Rocky set his head on his paws. "Big boat, blah, blah, blah. Water down below, blah, blah, blah. We get the idea."

All Max really wanted to do now that his hunger was satiated was curl up on a warm patch of rug somewhere and go to sleep. But the young Dalmatian was so eager.

"Come on, Rocky," Max said. "That's no way to treat our hosts." To Cosmo, he said, "Lead the way."

With a huff, Rocky got to his feet and followed Max, Gizmo, and the three Dalmatians to the opposite end of the kitchen. Just beyond a long metal table stacked high with white plates was another pair of gray double doors, behind which Max could distantly make out weird beeping sounds and music. As before, Cosmo and Astrid pushed the doors open to let Zephyr, Max, Rocky, and Gizmo walk through first.

Max stepped out onto plush, burgundy-colored carpet, only this time they weren't in a hallway—they were in a vast room as big as Max's backyard at the farm.

The room was filled with wide round tables covered with lacy white tablecloths. High-backed chairs surrounded them, and a glass vase with a dead, dried flower sat at the center of each table. Golden chandeliers dripping with sparkling crystals dangled overhead. The walls were lined with booths, their red leather seats set into polished, dark-brown wood.

"Dining room," Cosmo said. "For the people."

Zephyr led them past a wood-paneled wall and into a still bigger room, the music and trilling sounds growing louder and louder. This one was even brighter and, like the dining room, was filled with tables in neat rows. But these weren't tables for eating. Max recognized the stacks of red, white, and black circular chips scattered on the green felt tops and on the dark carpet: These were card tables. His pack leaders' father used to watch men and women play games at tables like these on the TV.

Deafening music came from machines all around the right side of the room that looked like TV sets built into booths, plastic benches set in front of them. There were three rows of these booths, all flashing lights and screeching with noise.

"What's with all the noise?" Max called over the sounds.

Zephyr ducked her head. "It's those slot machines, some of the other dogs called them. We tried to turn them off, but we couldn't figure out how."

Cosmo panted at Max. "You get used to it after a while."

Max wasn't sure what he'd expected to find inside the *Flower of the South*, but this was nothing like he'd imagined. He stepped in and stopped when his foot landed on slick plastic. He looked down: a red poker chip.

To the right, near the flashing slot machines, there was a long countertop with glass bottles of all shapes and sizes sitting on shelves in front of a big mirror. To the left was a booth enclosed in glass. There were tall gold cabinets protected in the room behind the glass, filled with small rectangular drawers. One of the cabinets didn't gleam gold like the others—it was wide and a matte black, and it looked like it was made of some sort of thick, heavy metal. On its front was a silver handle and a round black dial.

"What's that big metal box?" Rocky asked the Dalmatians. "Is there more food in there?"

"We don't know," Cosmo answered. "We tried to

open it, but it's locked shut. I wish I knew what was in there!"

"Oh, I bet it is food!" Rocky said. "Humans always keep the best stuff locked away."

Zephyr said, "Come on," and led the group beneath the gaming tables. "This is where we all sleep," she said. "Some of us sleep below, and some of us sleep up top. The tables make good beds."

"There's nowhere else to sleep but in here?" Max asked, gesturing with his snout toward the slot machines. "What about the other decks?"

Astrid shook her white head. "Well, it gets cold up on the top deck, since it's outside. And the deck above us is quiet, I suppose, but it's also so... dark and empty. Most of us kind of enjoy all the lights and sound. It makes it seem almost like our people are still here, you know?"

"And like I said," Cosmo added, "you get used to it! Everyone else here did."

Only when he said that did Max realize that there were other dogs in the room, many of them deeply asleep. On one long table lay an exhausted Golden Retriever, her head tucked under a pair of oversize red dice set into one corner as she tried to sleep. Curled in a blanket next to her were five puppies, so small and new that their legs were tiny nubs and their eyes seemed unable to open. They shivered and squirmed, mewling softly.

"That's Gloria," Astrid whispered as they walked

past. "She found us last week about ready to burst. The little pups don't have names yet."

"Aw," Gizmo said, craning her neck to try to see. "Maybe we can help her name them!"

A woolly Sheepdog lying beneath a table wagged his tail cordially at them as they passed. A few mutts of breeds Max didn't recognize conversed among themselves while casually spinning a puppy around on a gold wheel inlaid with red and black. The puppy barked in delight. None of them seemed to notice or care about their new guests.

At the back of the room was a pair of doors made of the same gold-accented dark wood as the rest of the game room. Right beside the doors was a big circular table, around which seven dogs sat on chairs, studiously looking over scattered playing cards.

"How's the game going, Earl?" Zephyr asked.

A stocky gray Bulldog, chewing on what looked like an old breadstick, glanced down at the Dalmatian.

"Eh, still trying to figure it out, Miss Zephyr," he grumbled. "Sherlock over there still insists we're not supposed to use the cards with the little hearts on them."

"No, no, no," a tawny, droopy old Bloodhound said. "It's not a heart! I'm telling you, my pack leader played these games all the time. When you see this half-diamond with the two lumps, you're supposed to yell and toss the chips everywhere."

"That doesn't sound right, Sherlock," a dark-furred Collie said, using a paw to rearrange the piles of cards closest to him. "I think you're supposed to make 'em go red, black, red, black, till there are no more cards, then you yell 'Bingo!' "

"Hmm?" said a squat Bull Terrier. "What was that?"

"Not you, Bingo, the game."

Sherlock *tsk-tsk*ed. "I'm telling you boys, this is how you play."

All seven dogs started yipping at once, trying to talk over one another. As Cosmo and Astrid shoved open the fancier—and, judging by how they strained, heavier—wooden double doors, Zephyr said, "Have fun, boys!"

"They've been at it for weeks," she added as she sauntered out onto the riverboat deck. "Still haven't come up with any rules. But I think they're having fun anyway."

A warm breeze rose up off the river as Max and his friends stepped outside. The colorful flags snapped in the wind. It was fully dark out now, and beyond the rail Max could see the glittering reflections of the white lights strung between the supports of the awning above them. The glow cast through the casino window and from the twinkling lights was dim but pleasant.

Unseen crickets chirped and bullfrogs croaked, and Max closed his eyes, sniffed in the damp air, and just enjoyed the feeling of the river without being trapped in a tiny rowboat. Maybe he could find his friends their own riverboat to take them the rest of the way to the ocean.

Zephyr led them up a flight of stairs to the second deck, then another until they'd reached the roof deck of the entire boat. Distantly, Max heard an echo of human voices and was confused.

"This place is amazing," Rocky said, gaping at what lay before them.

"I'll say," Gizmo added.

The boat had a pool set into its roof. Max had never seen such a thing, but there was no mistaking the chemical smell of chlorine wafting off the blue water—glowing thanks to lights embedded in its tiled, underwater walls.

Surrounding the pool were white deck chairs and round tables and tall red and yellow umbrellas. More dogs were there, curled up in the chairs, quietly watching the source of the voices Max had heard. On a flat, blank wall on the opposite side of the pool, a human movie was projected. In the movie, an angry woman slapped a man. They glared at each other—then, weirdly, started kissing.

"A lot of us come up here and relax before bed," Zephyr explained, sitting down next to a bar similar to the one down in the game room. "You can't really see the movie during the day, but it can be nice to come up here and get some exercise by swimming."

"You have movies?" Rocky asked, tail wagging excitedly. "Oh, I've missed movies so much! I used to watch tons of them with my pack leader while I snacked. Say, do you got that one with the yellow bricks?"

"Nope," Astrid said. She'd lain down with her head on her paws, the movie images reflecting in her big eyes. "Just this one, playing over and over."

Max sniffed in the direction of the screen. "You watch the same movie all the time? Doesn't that get boring?"

"Maybe," Cosmo said, too enraptured by the people on-screen to look at Max. "But it reminds me of my people. I miss them."

Max turned his attention to the screen as everyone went quiet. The man from before was with two children, and they were running toward a car, afraid. They didn't look anything like Max's pack leaders—Charlie and Emma were younger and had different hair—but he couldn't help thinking of them all the same. He wondered if they had looked just as afraid when they'd been forced to leave him behind. He wondered if they were still afraid.

He hoped not. He hoped they were sleeping safe and together, dreaming of him like he always dreamed of them. He swore to himself that he'd see them again, and soon.

Max heard one of the dogs on the beach chairs sniffling. He didn't blame whoever it was. He didn't know what was going on with the story, but just hearing human voices again...

Max, Rocky, and Gizmo all lay down to watch the movie.

"I miss the *nice* people," Cosmo said wistfully.

"Me, too," Gizmo said. Then she asked, "Wait, *nice* people? Are there any other kind?"

The Dalmatians shifted where they lay as though suddenly uncomfortable. They cast uneasy glances at one another.

"There are bad people," Astrid whispered nervously. "Very, very bad people."

Her expression stern, Zephyr looked straight at Max. "You don't want to know about the bad people."

Max opened his mouth to ask what sort of bad people she meant, but Zephyr turned her head away. Before he could say a word, she said, "We don't want to talk about that. You've had a long trip. Just watch the movie and rest."

Max *did* want to rest, but now he felt wide awake. The dogs on this boat were afraid.

Even though all the people were supposed to have disappeared, Max couldn't help but get the feeling that it hadn't been that long since the Dalmatians had had a run-in with some humans. Some very *bad* humans.

CHAPTER 5

THE STORY OF BOSS

Max closed his eyes many times during the course of the movie, but sleep wouldn't come.

It wasn't that he was uncomfortable—his belly was full, the night was warm, the air was fresh except for the traces of chlorine, and he was surrounded by other contented dogs. And it wasn't the voices from the movie screen that kept him awake, either—he hadn't realized how much he'd missed the reassuring tones of human voices.

But an hour and a half later, after the screen went black and people words scrolled by and then the movie started all over again, Max was still wide awake.

Quietly, Max rose to his feet and stretched his legs. The lapping of the water in the pool was overshadowed by a chorus of doggy snores and the sounds of the movie—all of it noisy enough to cover his retreat. He wasn't worried about waking anyone up. Walking slowly and quietly, Max made for the stairs.

He was halfway down when Rocky came bounding down the steps after him.

"Where you going, buddy?" he panted. "You ain't leaving us, are you?"

Max wagged his tail. "I would never do that," he said. "I just couldn't sleep. I thought I'd go for a walk." Looking back up at the top deck, he asked, "Is Gizmo coming?"

"Nah," Rocky said. "She's completely out. Me, I slept all day. I'm too antsy to sleep yet."

Moments later, Max and Rocky were on the quiet second deck. They hadn't toured these rooms, and Max was curious. Rising on his hind legs to glance through windows, all he saw were still, shadowy shapes. Human furniture, most likely.

Then one of the shapes moved.

Max leaped back from the window, so far that his hindquarters and tail smacked against the white wood railing. Good thing it was there, he thought, or he might have gone tumbling to the deck below.

As he watched from the railing, the hulking shadow disappeared from view.

"Whoa!" Rocky said, startled. "What's going on, big guy? You all right?"

The door next to the window creaked open. Max tensed, ready to fight if needed. Were the bad people here?

"Oh!" Boss said, slipping through the door and onto the deck. The dangling lights illuminated his glossy fur. "Hello, boys. How was the tour?"

Max relaxed as Rocky crept out from underneath him, waddling casually, as though he hadn't been afraid at all. "Oh, it was fine. Nice digs you got, big and spacious, lots of room. And those biscuits you brought out for dinner weren't half bad."

Boss thumped his tail against the deck. "You liked them, too, huh?" he asked. "See, I got nothing but complaints, even though I thought they were sort of tasty. But you know dogs—everyone wants meat with all the trimmings. Thing is, we got to ration the good stuff, or we won't have any left to look forward to when we're stuck with just the boring food."

"That makes sense," Max said.

Boss's ears drooped. "I try to be a practical sort. Most dogs don't know the meaning of the word."

"That's probably why you're the alpha," Max said. He was beginning to like this dog. Despite that first uneasy confrontation in the pipe room, Boss seemed to be a greater leader than either Dandyclaw or the Chairman had ever been. A better dog all around.

Rocky said, "Oh, yeah—you've got to be practical where food is concerned. That's what I always say."

"So how did you get to be alpha dog of a riverboat in the middle of nowhere, anyway?" Max asked.

Boss turned away, a distant look in his eyes. "We're not in the middle of nowhere," he said, sighing. "You boys follow me. Might as well tell you my story, since you told me yours. Fair's fair."

Yawning, Boss loped along the silent deck and around the front of the ship to the side facing land. As they did, Max got his first look at where they'd come ashore.

The riverbank was broad and flat and covered with tall, slender trees. But there were signs of humanity—broad avenues with lit streetlamps, shadowy houses set back across wide lawns. Farther upshore, Max could make out boathouses and docks where dark, abandoned skiffs bobbed on the waves.

And beyond the immediate shore, not very far off, was a city.

It was smaller than the Chairman's city—the buildings here weren't spaced so close together. There weren't as many sleek, glass skyscrapers; in their place were redbrick structures with arches and pillars and other unique stone details not quite like anything Max had seen before.

The biggest difference, however, was that in this place *all* the buildings were lit up, as though the city were still alive. Windows were like little square stars on the horizon, and storefronts cast a bright yellow glow on the empty streets. The tallest buildings had neon signs on top that glowed red and blue, and even from this distance the crimson and teal light trickled over the river waves, which lapped against the sand and rocks of the shore.

"Oh," Max gasped. "The lights. They're so pretty." Realizing that because there was electricity, there might be people in the city—real live people!—he turned his head to look at Boss. "If there's lights on, does that mean…?"

Boss sat back and bit at something in his paw. "I'm afraid not, son. No humans left. We checked. I don't know why they left all the lights on when they evacuated. Maybe they thought they'd be coming home soon."

"Eee-vack-cue-what?" Rocky asked.

"Evacuated," Boss repeated slowly. "That's the word the people used. I think it means the order to leave everything right away. Or at least my pack leaders did."

"So you were in the city when the people left?" Max asked. "That's why we're here, actually. We're searching for our families, but I'm also supposed to find other people who can help us along the way. Maybe if you saw where all the people went…"

Turning from the view, Boss curled up and lay down, facing the dark wall of the riverboat. "No, sir, I am not from around here," Boss said, staring at nothing but seeming to see *something*. "I come from down south, a place called Baton Rouge. Lived there my whole life, from the day I was weaned and given to my pack leader to the day a month ago when my pack leaders headed out of town.

"I had to leave behind everything I ever knew and loved. It can near 'bout turn the heart of a dog to glass and break it, I tell you." He closed his eyes and breathed out slowly. "I grew up next door to a beautiful caramel Collie named Belle. Finest companion I've ever known. She was my best friend."

"*Was?*" Max asked, a nervous lump in his throat. "Did... did something happen to her?"

"I don't rightly know, son," Boss said, his voice dropping so low that Max almost couldn't hear him. "Last I saw her, I was being loaded into my pack leaders' truck after they got their evacuation notice. She was waiting on my porch—we had us a great porch, sort of like the decks on the *Flower*, in fact—just sitting there, watching me go. As pretty as the day I first laid eyes on her. After that, I can only guess what happened to her." He shivered. "But she's a smart lady. I'm sure she's fine." He swallowed loudly. "I'm sure of it."

"So her people just left her, huh?" Rocky said, coming to sit in front of Boss and Max. "That's rough. But why didn't your people take her with you?"

"I bet they would have if they could," Boss said. "But they were risking enough taking me. We left at night, driving without headlights, heading up the road in the opposite direction the big trucks were going."

"Trucks?" Max asked.

A breeze rose up, rustling Boss's thick, mottled fur as his stare went distant once more.

"Those trucks with the men in the green uniforms. I remember a few days before we left, they came banging at our door, telling my pack leaders they had to go and that they had to leave me behind. My pack leaders complained—they are awful stubborn, those two—and the men in the uniforms were nice about it, but they made it clear that my pack leaders didn't have a choice in the matter.

"But like I said," Boss continued with a chuckle, "my pack leaders are old and stubborn in their ways, and they weren't going to take orders from nobody. So they grabbed me and we fled under cover of darkness, as they say.

"We drove and drove, always at night, always on twisty roads that no other cars used. During the day, my pack leaders would sleep in abandoned motels. And then we'd set off again once night fell."

"Is that how you ended up here?" Rocky asked.

Boss nodded. "Pretty much. No one wanted to come near the city you see yonder, since it was deemed especially dangerous. We were nearing downtown when the truck ran out of fuel. One of my pack leaders tried to sneak some gas from a station near a highway, but the big trucks were there, and they nabbed him."

"Do you know why?" Max asked.

"I don't know for sure. Seems there weren't any people left in this city at all but the men in the uniforms, so my pack leaders stood out. The uniformed men wondered why we were going in the wrong direction. Then they found me and all tarnation broke loose. Next thing I know, they were waving these metal sticks over my pack leaders and shooing me away.

"And then I was alone, until I discovered this riverboat. Other dogs started coming 'round, and soon enough—well, I was running the place."

It was a lot like the stories Max had heard from other dogs—as well as the house of cats they'd come across outside the Chairman's city: people in uniforms and masks tearing humans and their pets apart. Sometimes the people were in baggy white suits that covered their whole bodies, sometimes they just wore gloves and masks that covered their faces. Not that it mattered much. For some reason, a whole bunch of people decided that animals were bad and the only way to keep humans safe was to run far, far away. But why? He wished again that Madame were here to explain these things to him. She was so much smarter than any other dogs he'd met, almost as smart as a human herself.

"What kind of metal stick was it?" Rocky asked. "Like a catching stick? Maybe... maybe you were supposed to try to grab it from the uniformed guys?"

Boss shook his head. "They were attached to machines,

little metal boxes. The boxes beeped and made all sorts of noises. Whatever the boxes and sticks were, afterward, they seemed to think my pack leaders were okay. It was me they didn't want anywhere around."

"They thought you were bad for some reason," Max said softly. "But bad how? Why did the people in uniforms make all the humans evacuate?"

"I reckon that's the question of the century, son," Boss said, and grunted. "I wish I could tell you the answer. Whatever they're afraid of must be really, really bad, worse than we dogs can imagine." Glancing back at the glittering city skyline over his shoulder, Boss's tail drooped. "Don't let those bright lights fool you—the people are never going to come back."

All three dogs fell silent at that. Max poked his head partially through the railing and looked at the shining, empty city. He could hear the faintest murmur of human voices—the movie on the top deck playing over and over, a reminder of what they'd lost.

Boss stood and stretched, then yawned. "All right, boys, I think it's my bedtime again. Don't let my sad stories get you too down. We've got a good thing going here on the ol' *Flower of the South*. You boys and your lady friend seem like nice sorts. You can stay here with us for a spell, if you want."

Pulling his head free from the rail, Max peered up at the alpha dog. "Which direction were all those trucks going with the people?" he asked.

"South," Boss said. "Same direction as the river flows. Straight to the ocean."

"Then that's where we're going, too," Max said. "No matter what happened, no matter how afraid the humans are of us, we can't give up on finding our families."

"Max is right!" Rocky said. "We just need to make them understand—we're not bad dogs!"

Boss's jaws parted in a sad smile. "I don't blame you. I just hope once you find them . . . Well, I just hope those uniforms aren't around."

With that, he wandered off into the shadows. Max thought about heading back up to the pool, but exhaustion had finally overtaken him, and he wasn't in the mood to keep walking.

"You all right, buddy?" Rocky asked as he curled up against Max's belly to go to sleep.

"Yeah," Max said. "Good night."

" 'Night."

Moments later, Rocky was snoring and kicking his legs, chasing his dream kibble.

It took Max longer, but he finally started to doze off. The last thing he thought before finally falling asleep was, *Of course my people will be happy to see me. They'd never be afraid of me.*

But even as he thought the words, he realized he had no idea if they were true.

CHAPTER 6

DREAMS AND MEMORIES

Max was floating in the small rowboat.

He was all alone, lying on his side and looking up at the sky. The boat rocked gently, and the babbling of a small stream met his ears. Distantly, he could hear birds calling to one another, though none flew above him.

How strange, he thought. He hadn't seen or heard any birds in weeks and weeks.

Fluffy white clouds drifted across the blue canvas of the sky. They shifted and transformed into shapes that looked vaguely like his friends—squat, sausage-shaped Rocky and short, fluffy Gizmo. But then the clouds parted, revealing the sun—no, the *three* suns. They blazed bright and gold, but somehow Max could look directly at them without his eyes hurting. They sat in a neat row high in the middle of the sky, connected at their edges. In the center of each bloomed a dark hole, transforming the blazing suns into rings.

Max, a voice echoed in his head.

Jerking up, Max saw Madame sitting tall and regal at the front of the boat. Her body was slightly plump, her nose wet—she looked healthy. The plain wooden bench had transformed into a plush doggy bed—a red cushion set inside polished brown wood with intricate gold details. Madame smiled down at him.

Max, she said warmly, though her mouth did not move. Her white-streaked black fur rustled in the gentle breeze. *Have you found the people, Max? Are you looking?*

The light from the three bright suns glinted off her collar—the symbol of three golden rings, which he'd also once seen tattooed on her back.

Searching for the people was so hard, and so dangerous. He didn't want to think about it. They were happy in this rowboat on this gentle stream, drifting away together on a warm summer's day.

"I've been looking," Max said to her, rising to sit at attention. "But this place is so nice, isn't it? Maybe we can stay here awhile, just you and me."

Madame's tail wagged.

I do so enjoy our time together, her voice echoed. *But please don't ever give up, Maxie. You're stronger than that.*

Mist rose up off the water, like an early-morning fog. It swirled around Madame, and dots of sparkling light appeared within the haze, as though it were filled with stars. The mist ruffled Madame's fur and tickled her chin, and she laughed.

And as the mist surrounded her, she began to fade from view.

"Madame!" Max barked. "Please don't go yet. I want to spend more time with you."

Don't worry, Maxie. Madame's voice was distant, muffled. *I'll always be here in your dreams when you need me. But you can't give up on your journey yet. Follow the symbols. Find your people. And spend time with those you love in the real, waking world, too.*

The mist twisted around Madame until she was fully enveloped in a cloud of glittering white. The cloud floated up to the bright blue sky, toward the three gold rings. Max howled softly as he watched Madame drift away.

Suddenly, something heavy bounced off his ribs.

Max awoke.

🐾

Max's eyes snapped open, his lips parting as he softly yowled. Catching the sound in his throat, he blinked to collect his bearings.

He was on the wood floor of the riverboat's second-story deck. A cool morning breeze took hold of the flags hanging off the railing nearby, making them lazily billow out. Beyond the edge of the boat, misty morning light spread across the water and the sandbar, the trees and the docks, and the big buildings of the city on the horizon.

The rowboat was still moored in the debris trail. Madame was long gone.

Just a dream. Another vivid vision of his old friend.

And something heavy slammed into his side once more.

"Ow!" Max yelped, jerking to sit up.

Rocky sat next to Max, head tilted.

"You all right, buddy?" he asked. "You were making strange noises and shaking like you were cold. Bad dream?"

Yawning, Max got to all fours. "No," he said, though he could tell he sounded sad. "It was a nice dream, actually. I just wish I could spend more time in it."

Rocky's brows narrowed in concern. "You okay?"

"Definitely," Max said. Brushing past the little Dachshund, he headed toward the stairs that would lead them to the rooftop pool. "It's a nice morning. How about we go find Gizmo and get some breakfast?"

Perking up, Rocky's tail became a blur. He powered his little legs to match Max's longer stride. "Biscuit time?" He licked his lips. "You don't have to ask me twice!"

Max and Rocky found Gizmo lounging on one of the deck chairs in the shade of a colorful umbrella, happily chatting with four of the Dalmatian firedogs and a gray Cocker Spaniel with long, curly fur–covered ears and fluffy legs. They all listened intently as Gizmo regaled them with tales of her adventures. Some other dogs splashed in the pool—including the young Dalmatian Cosmo—while the human movie continued playing the same scenes that it had all night.

Max and Rocky pulled Gizmo away from her fans, then made their way down the two flights of stairs, through the noisy gaming room, and into the kitchen. The gleaming room was empty, save for dozens of plastic bags and cardboard trays that had once contained biscuits. The other dogs had already eaten and were now out entertaining themselves elsewhere on the *Flower.*

Rocky dove directly toward the last tray of biscuits and began gobbling up the doughy morsels. Max and Gizmo headed to the pantry—and almost tripped over a dog lying in the entrance, gnawing on an old bone.

"Oh!" Gizmo yipped in surprise. Composing herself, she smiled. "Hey, I remember you. We saw you last night."

She was right. The dog was the large, woolly Old English Sheepdog who had wagged his tail at them from beneath a gaming table as they took their tour. His eyes were small, friendly, and mostly hidden behind fluffy brows, and a big, bushy mustache covered his face. The dog had the air of an old-timer about him.

"Well, hello again," the dog drawled, letting the

bone drop from his mouth to land on his paws. "Glad to see you're making yourselves at home on my ship. The name's Twain."

"Nice to meet you," Max said. "I'm Max, and this is Gizmo. Our friend Rocky is currently occupied eating biscuits."

Twain guffawed. "I declare, seeing all you dogs run in here to choke down people food has been the funniest thing I've witnessed in ages." He winked at Gizmo. "Maybe if you folks stick around, I'll show you my secret stash. In the meantime, have at the human chow."

The Sheepdog sat up, making space for Max and Gizmo to walk by and head to the bulk tubs filled with granola and nuts. Max took a big mouthful of the granola and started to chew, trying not to eye the tasty beef bone Twain had been gnawing.

"So this is your boat, huh?" Gizmo asked after swallowing down her first bite. "Did you always live here?"

"That I have, youngun'," Twain said. "I've lived on the *Flower of the South* my whole life, riding up and down the river with the wind in my fur and listening to the sounds of the paddle wheels slapping the waves. All the humans that used to come here would rub my head for good luck before they played their people games." He chuckled. "I can't say it worked much, but it worked enough that I was always getting petted."

"Oh, that sounds so pleasant," Gizmo said, bouncing from paw to paw. "This is my first time traveling on a river, but I bet you have tons and tons of river adventures to share."

Claws clacked against the black-and-white tiles of the floor. Pulling his head from the granola bin, Max turned to see Rocky creeping around the wire racks, a grumpy expression on his face.

"I've got lots of stories, you bet," Twain went on. "But most of the craziest stuff has only happened recently."

"Humph," Rocky said, forcing past the mustachioed Sheepdog and plopping himself in the center of the pantry floor. Eyeing Gizmo, he asked, "You want to hear a *real* story? I got one for ya—one with monsters. There's these big, gray creatures with floppy wings for ears and a long nose like a snake. They've got huge, flat feet that could squash you like *that*." He slapped his paw against the tile to illustrate. "I saw them through a window." He laughed nervously. "Sort of a window."

"'Sort of' a window?" Gizmo asked.

Rocky sighed. "All right, fine, it wasn't a window. It was a TV. I saw the monsters on TV. But I thought they were right there in the living room, and I wasn't scared at all!"

Twain chuckled. "I think you mean you saw an *elephant*. Boss knows one of them. He told us all about the creature when he first got here. Said it was really smart, not scary at all."

"They're a *little* scary," Rocky grumbled.

Eyes drooping and serious, Twain said, "Actually,

there are some things 'round these parts you *should* be scared of."

His belly full, Max turned away from the bulk food tubs and sat next to Gizmo and Rocky. "Like what?" he asked.

Twain peered back over his shoulder. Certain no one was listening, he crept forward and spoke in a quiet voice. "None of the other dogs want to talk about it," he said. "But even though all the humans left, sometimes there are boats other than the *Flower* out here on the river."

"Boats sailed by animals?" Max asked. "That's not that scary. We got here in a little rowboat, actually."

"That's not what I mean." Twain shook his fluffy head. "For a time, the *Flower* drifted on the river just fine even without any humans to steer it. We were anchored farther upriver, and we had a big ramp we could use to get down to the docks so we could explore freely. That's how we found some of the other dogs and brought them on board. We made it a safe haven, a lit-up beacon for all the abandoned dogs.

"But then, late one night, other boats appeared. There were shadowy people on board, and they had great bright lights that they shone in through the windows. We all hid when they came by, but they must have seen the casino on the main deck. Before we knew what was happening—*Bam!*" He barked the last word so loudly that it echoed throughout the kitchen. Lowering his voice, he continued. "They rammed into us. They made a great big hole back near the waterwheels and broke the chains connecting us to the anchor.

"All of us scrambled on deck to try to find a way to keep from being swept downriver, but the current caught the boat and there was nothing much we could do. Our ramp cracked and broke free, falling into the water and disappearing. We pressed all sorts of levers in the steerage cabin, but by the time we figured out what the controls did—*bam!* Again! We crashed into the sandbar and rammed into a big boulder. We were grounded—and we had a matching hole on the front side of the boat to go with the one in the back."

"What's a casino?" Gizmo asked.

"That's what the humans call places like this, where they come to play games," Twain explained. "And they don't just play for fun. Those colored chips they use are exchanged for real people money. That's what the bad people on the other boats were after: money."

Shuddering at the memory, Twain continued on. "Those people on the boats followed us and came on board through the holes. They were dressed all in black, and they wore masks over their faces and leather gloves. Most of the other dogs hid on the upper decks, but me and Captain went to check it out. When we got near the people, though, they threw all sorts of heavy things at us—one of them threw chairs! So we joined the others in hiding and waited for them to go away.

"They stormed in and went straight for the big metal box in the money booth," he said. "Tried for ages to get inside the thing, but they had as much luck as we did. They all started yelling at each other and then left. They went upriver, oh, must have been a couple weeks ago by now. All I know is that other dogs we've taken in since then have seen them, too. And we all agree that those people don't seem friendly, not one bit."

"That metal box," Max said. "There must be something important inside if they went through so much trouble. But what?"

Twain didn't get a chance to answer.

A chorus of panicked, loud barks came from beyond the double doors that led into the casino. More joined in, then more and more.

Max didn't hesitate. He leaped over Twain and raced across the tiles to the front of the kitchen. He could hear Rocky's and Gizmo's footsteps as they followed him.

They had almost reached the doors when one flew open and slammed against a metal cabinet. Panting, Zephyr darted through, skidding to a stop as she saw them.

"They're here!" she gasped out.

"Who's here?" Max asked.

"No time to explain," Zephyr barked. "If you value your lives, hide. Now!"

CHAPTER 7

THE BAD PEOPLE

"Hide from what?" Gizmo asked.

Rocky gasped. "Is it... is it... monsters?"

But Zephyr was already gone, racing through the kitchen toward the back hallway that led to the bowels of the ship.

"It must be the bad people," Twain said gravely, coming to stand behind them. His expression was serious as he met Max's eyes. "You should see. Follow me."

The stench of fear flooded the air, overtaking the smells of oats and raw dough and ancient grease in the kitchen. Max didn't ask any questions. The dogs of the *Flower of the South* knew the dangers of this place better than he did—if they were afraid, then he knew he should be afraid, too. With a wordless jerk of his head toward his two small companions, he followed Twain out into the casino.

Three dogs shoved past them as they entered the casino's dining room—the notch-eared Dalmatian Max recognized as Zeke and two other mutts whose breed he couldn't identify. They reeked of terror, their tails slung between their legs, as they darted, frantic, through the swinging kitchen doors.

Barks echoed throughout the casino as Twain led Max, Rocky, and Gizmo onto the gaming room floor. The warnings were so loud they even drained out the cheerful, whooping strains of music coming from the slot machines.

The Golden Retriever mother raced to carry her puppies by the napes of their necks one by one behind the bar. The curly gray Cocker Spaniel whom Gizmo had befriended earlier in the morning helped.

The card-playing dogs let their cards and chips scatter as they scrambled down from their felt-covered table. They ran in circles, banging into one another, howling in terror.

"Put a lid on it!" Twain hissed as he raced past them. "We don't need to be drawing attention to ourselves!"

The stocky Bulldog, Earl, nipped at his friends' sides until they clamped their jaws shut. "You heard him! Pipe down!"

Twain led the three companions outside. Most of the barking had fallen silent, and though a few stragglers bounded desperately past them to run to the safety of the ship's underbelly, all the dogs appeared to have hidden.

Fear still overwhelmed Max's nostrils. He could only imagine what these dogs had seen to make them so afraid.

Quietly, Twain led Max, Rocky, and Gizmo up the first flight of stairs to the second deck. Max could hear a loud buzzing and splashing from the opposite side of the boat, but he didn't dare ask questions.

"This way," Twain whispered, glancing back over his shoulder. He guided them to a slightly ajar door at the front of the riverboat. The Sheepdog held it open while Max, Rocky, and Gizmo slipped through.

They entered a small, wood-paneled room with a giant window spanning the front, showing a view of the river and the nearby docks. The room smelled of oak and greasy furniture polish, and a pair of wide leather chairs sat front and center.

There were plaques and framed photos on the wall, and in the center of the room, between the chairs, was a big wooden wheel with polished spoke-like handles jutting out. Next to the wheel were strange metal devices with numbers on them.

And sitting on a stool in front of the wheel was Boss.

The Australian Shepherd spun to face them, his body tense and his teeth bared as he growled. Seeing that it was just Max and his friends, the dog relaxed.

"Shut the door," he barked. "If you're going to come in here, get inside quick and make sure no one sees you."

"Either of you big guys gonna finally tell us what's going on?" Rocky asked as he waddled toward a leather chair opposite the door.

"Take a look for yourself," Boss said, gesturing with his snout toward the front windows.

Max padded forward, then leaped up and placed his paws atop some of the machinery so he could get a clearer view. Only then did he realize one of the windows had been smashed out. Tiny slivers of glass lined the frame. A gust of wind rushed through the cabin before fading away.

Rocky jumped onto the leather chair, followed by Gizmo. Together, they all looked out, and Max finally saw the source of the splashing and buzzing noises.

A sleek gray boat, half the size of the riverboat but still huge, was slowly cruising alongside the *Flower.* The front half of the boat was taken up by a multilevel cabin. The inside was lit up bright, illuminating a man in black clothing who stood in front of a gleaming metal steering wheel. Unlike the brown, wooden steerage cabin on the riverboat, the inside of the people's cabin was all sleek white couches and tables. Colored bottles lined the tables, and strange equipment—backpacks with hoses snaking out, elaborate masks—rested on the seats.

For a moment, Max felt a pang of longing. There, so close, so very, very close, was a human. A real live human, not one projected on a screen that repeated the same words and actions over and over every two hours. It had been so long since Max had seen a human, felt the touch of friendly people rubbing his fur and patting his head, heard voices calling him "good boy," that he almost wanted to leap out the broken window and go chase after the human's boat.

But the stench of the dogs' fear still hadn't faded, despite the wind rushing into the room. And all it took was a look at Boss's and Twain's bared teeth and raised hackles to know that this person, whoever he was, wasn't likely to play fetch with Max anytime soon.

Max turned his attention to the rest of the bad people's vessel. On the back half of the boat, two boxy, shiny black vehicles sat side by side. Max had seen cars like them before—his pack leaders' parents had one that was similar, in fact, and they always seemed to refer to it as the "Essyouvee."

As the dogs watched, the boat veered left toward the docks and boathouses just south of the beached riverboat. A woman in baggy pants and a sleeveless shirt appeared from a door in the back of the cabin. She shouted orders as the man steering the big boat brought them in next to the dock.

Then the ship's engine grumbled and shut off.

"It's people," Gizmo whispered. "Real live people! They aren't all gone!"

"Shh," Twain whispered. "Don't get yourself too excited, little pup. Just watch."

Two men emerged from the doorway the woman had come out of. They were big, muscled men with serious expressions on their faces—one with a shaved head and one wearing a baseball cap. Dangling from their necks were plastic, transparent masks. The capped man held another mask out to the woman, and she snatched it from him. She gave the men commands as she put the mask's straps over her head.

Her words carried easily over the water, now that the boat's engine was turned off. Max could hear everything the humans were saying, though he understood only a few words here and there. "Down." "Get." "Yes."

Grumbling, the two men walked to the side of the boat nearest the dock. Both men planted their feet and, muscles straining, pulled on leather straps that stuck up from the deck. A wide metal ramp rose up, which the men then heaved over the side, forming a bridge onto the dock. The ramp slammed down on the dock with a loud metal clang.

While the woman watched with crossed arms, the men carried out square red-and-black jugs from the boat's cabin and loaded them into the open trunks of the vehicles. That done, each man climbed inside an SUV. The car engines roared to life, and one by one the men drove the two vehicles down the metal ramp and onto the docks. They continued onto the asphalt road that ran in front of a boathouse, then into a gravel parking lot to the side of the boathouse. A line of trees stood at the edge of the gravel lot.

The man whom Max had seen steering the boat came out the back door. He was skinnier and had a large backpack slung over his shoulders. He tossed the woman an empty duffel bag, and she caught it.

And then the skinny man looked up at the riverboat—right at the room where Max, Rocky, Gizmo, Boss, and Twain all sat watching.

"Get down!" Boss hissed.

No one hesitated. Max ducked his head, his heart pounding as he wondered if any of the people had seen them. He strained his ears, listening.

The man's voice wafted through the open window, then the woman's. They didn't sound excited or scared. Still, he waited until he heard the clang of their boot steps against the metal ramp before he dared to finally jump back up and look out the window once more.

The skinny man gestured at the *Flower* while he talked with the woman, his hands flying wildly as though he were mimicking billowing clouds. He made a strange sound when he did this, whooshing air through his lips. It seemed familiar somehow. It reminded Max of the noise his pack leader Charlie used to make when crashing toy trucks against each other.

The two people were interrupted by shouting.

In the gravel lot, the driver's-side door of each SUV was wide open. The burly men had stepped out of their vehicles and were yelling and waving their arms toward something in the trees. Straining his eyes, Max could barely make out two skinny, mangy dogs. They looked up at the men with sad, desperate eyes as they crept forward out of the underbrush and onto the rough gravel.

"Food?" one barked weakly. "Any food, nice men?"

The big men kept shouting, not understanding the dog's words. "Go!" Max understood. "Get!" They pulled their masks up over their faces, still shouting even though their voices were muffled.

"Oh, those poor dogs," Gizmo whispered.

Hearing the commotion, the skinny man and the woman pumped their arms and ran off the docks and around the side of the boathouse.

"Run," Rocky said, hushed, even though the dogs couldn't hear. "Come on, run away and hide!"

As Max watched, helpless, the bald man stomped forward, leaned down, and picked up a rock as big as his fist. Hefting his arm back, he threw it at the nearest dog. The dirt right next to one of the dog's feet exploded into a cloud of pebbles as the rock thudded hard against the gravel. Yelping, the two starving dogs raced back off into the woods behind the boathouse.

Gizmo growled. "Those are bad people," she barked. "Bad, bad people!"

"That they are," Boss said solemnly.

Yelling at the bald man, the skinny man waved his hand above his head. Peering back over his shoulder, he called out to the woman, who was occupied on the side of the boathouse. She held a can of spray paint and had a mask covering her face. A cloud of inky black spurted from the can as she moved her arm in big circles, leaving behind a drawing on the boathouse's red wall.

Finished, the woman shoved the spray-paint can into her duffel bag, then strolled over to one of the SUVs. She hopped in, and then both cars roared to life. Seconds later, they had reached the road at the front of the parking lot, and disappeared through the trees in the direction of the distant city.

"Where are they going?" Rocky asked as he dropped down to sit on the chair.

Twain shook his head. "They're here to do what they tried to do on the *Flower*: steal. People like them care only about themselves."

"I can't believe they threw a rock at those poor dogs," Gizmo said, her eyes wide. "That's... that's just *mean*!"

Max opened his mouth to agree with her, but as he turned back to face the docks, he saw the symbol that the woman had painted on the wall.

Three rings in a straight row, connected at the edges.

It was *the* symbol. The one on Madame's collar and tattooed into her skin. The one represented by the three suns he kept seeing in his dreams.

It was the symbol Madame had said would lead them

to the people who had started all this, just before she died. And those people, she'd said, could take them to their pack leaders.

Max didn't have the first idea why the woman with the bad people would paint the symbol, but she had. And it was a sign he couldn't ignore.

"I found them," Max whispered.

"What's that, son?" Boss asked.

Dropping from the machinery, Max landed on the wooden floor and began to turn in tight, anxious circles. His thoughts raced.

Before he could talk himself out of it, he made a decision.

Meeting Rocky's and Gizmo's eyes, he said, "We have to follow them."

"Who?" Rocky asked. "Those dogs? They're long gone, Max."

"No, not the dogs. Those people. They're here to help us."

Rocky slid off the chair and backed away from Max. "*Help* us? Are you crazy? Those people don't want to help us."

"Maybe they don't *want* to help us," Max said, "but they're going to help us anyway."

CHAPTER 8

CHASING SIGNS

"What?" Rocky asked.

Max was already pawing at the cabin door. "The symbol that woman sprayed on that wall? It's the one Madame told me to look for. It's the same one she had marked on her skin. She said following those people would lead us to our pack leaders."

Rocky and Gizmo leaped down from the captain's seat and raced to Max's side.

"She can't have meant those people!" Rocky yelped. "They threw rocks at dogs. I don't want to get hurt, big guy."

Gizmo's nub tail drooped. "Normally I'm all for exploring new places, but I agree with Rocky."

Max turned back to the other dogs—Twain and Boss stood by the big spoked steering wheel.

"Madame knew things we didn't," Max said softly. "I wish she was here to help us along, but..." His tail drooped. "She's not. All I know is that I trusted her. Still do.

"Ever since we've been on the river, I've been having dreams about what she told us back at the Corporation. The symbol painted on that boathouse was tattooed on Madame's neck and was part of her collar, and I keep seeing it when I sleep. That symbol means something. I think it will help us find our people."

"We only just found the *Flower*," Rocky said. "Can't we rest for a while, buddy?"

"This clue is all we have, Rocky," Max admitted. "We can't stay here forever, and blindly following the river to the ocean could get us hurt or worse. I just...have a feeling this is the right thing to do." He nosed the little Dachshund. "It's what Madame would have wanted us to do."

Twain said, "You got what's called a hunch, son. I get 'em, too. Never led me astray." He crumpled his big, bushy brows. "Well, except that once."

Max looked between Rocky and Gizmo. "You two don't have to come with me. If I find anything, I'll come back for you."

Gizmo leaped forward, her nub tail wagging. "Don't be silly! Of course we're coming with you! I don't trust those bad people one bit, but I do trust you, Max. You got us this far, after all."

With a groan, Rocky stood on all fours. "You two crazy mutts are determined to make my life interesting. A lot more interesting than I ever wanted, I swear."

"What happened to the dog who wasn't afraid of big old elephants?" Gizmo asked with a twinkle in her eyes.

"Hey, I'm not afraid!" Rocky said. "I just prefer a stocked pantry and a nice bed to scrounging for food on the road. Can you blame me?"

"So you'll come?" Max asked.

"Of course," Rocky said. "You think I'd ever say no to you, big guy?"

Max paced in front of the cabin's door. "Well, we'd better get going before we lose the people's trail. Thanks for showing them to us, Twain." He nodded at the mustachioed dog, then noticed Boss staring up at the wall of plaques and framed photographs opposite the cabin's windows. The big dog's eyes settled on an image of the city skyline that he'd shown Max and Rocky the night before. He seemed lost in thought. "Thank you for your hospitality, Boss."

Before Max could turn to shove through the cabin door, Boss snapped to attention and barked, "Wait!"

Max started to protest. "You can't change my mind, Boss, I—"

"No, no, nothing like that," the big dog said. "I'm coming with you."

"Oh." Max thought about what that might be like—the dog was bigger, older, and a clear alpha. During the trip so far, Max had been the leader, even when he hadn't wanted to be. The idea of having another dog along trying to take charge made him feel a little uncomfortable.

"Yeah, I figure I should," Boss said as he padded toward Max and his friends. "I wandered this area for weeks and know it better than anyone. Plus, I've seen that symbol you've been going on about. You'll need my help to get where you need to go."

Boss had a good point. Despite his misgivings, Max smiled at the older dog. "All right, Boss. Welcome aboard."

"More like welcome off board, seeing as how we're going to dry land," Boss said, then chuckled at his own joke. He looked at Twain. "You and Captain are in charge for the day. You think you can handle all those pups out there?"

"Oh, so there *is* a captain on board the ship," Rocky said. "Is he another dog? Why isn't he in charge instead of Boss?"

"Captain is indeed a dog like us," the bushy dog said with a wag of his tail. "He used to be the big dog 'round here, until Boss showed up and proved better at wrangling all the strays." To Boss, Twain said, "And sure thing, Boss, we'll look after everyone. Captain will be delighted to give orders again, I guarantee. Don't you worry none, though. I won't let him or any of the other dogs bully me into giving them more meat than you said we can have."

“Good plan.” Brushing by Max, Boss nosed open the cabin door and slipped through. “Follow me!” he barked.

Rocky and Gizmo darted past Max and raced outside. Still a bit uneasy about being led by another dog after all that had happened with Dandyclaw and the Chairman, Max told himself that Boss was different. Swallowing his pride, he followed as well.

🐾

Boss led Max, Rocky, and Gizmo back down to the main floor and through the casino. As they crossed the lush gaming room, the dogs who had been hiding began slipping out from beneath tables and behind booths to resume lounging about.

“Is it all safe?” Gloria the Golden Retriever asked as they passed the bar. Max could barely hear her puppies whimpering behind her over the sounds of the slot machines.

“It is for now,” Boss said. “Your little ones aren’t going to get hurt under my watch, no, ma’am.”

Gloria wagged her tail. “Thanks, Boss.”

Boss led Max and his friends through the shiny, silvery kitchen and then back along the plain hallway to the door that led into the bowels of the ship. They opened the door and bounded down the metal stairs to the pipe room.

Zephyr’s familiar head, with the slash of black across her snout, popped out from behind some machinery upon hearing the footsteps. Dalmatians and other dogs peered out as well.

"Are they gone?" Zephyr asked.

Boss wagged his tail. "It's safe now. You and your fire-dogs can get out of this hole."

Cosmo stepped forward as well. "Where are you going?" he asked. "You're not going out there where *they* are... are you?"

"We are," Max said, brushing past the young Dalmatian to stand next to Boss. "We have a mission we need to do, and Boss has kindly agreed to help."

A murmur of voices echoed through the red-lit metal room as the dogs talked anxiously among themselves.

"But what about us?" an unseen dog cried from behind the pipes. "What if those people come back and try to attack us again?"

One of the Dalmatians yelped and spun in a frantic circle, as though unsure whether to run. "Oh, no," he wailed. "We won't be safe without you, Boss. They'll get us!"

"Hey, now!" Boss barked. The dogs grew quiet as he looked among them with his pale, stern eyes. "I've been here for you this long, so you all better believe I'm not fixin' to abandon you now. I'll only be gone for a short time. Twain and Captain will see you through until I'm back. Just lie low and don't do anything stupid if those bad people come back. Got it?"

"Yes, Boss," Zephyr said.

The other dogs murmured their consent as well.

"All right," Boss said, then peered back at Max, Rocky, and Gizmo. "Shall we continue?"

"I'm starting to have doubts again," Rocky said, trembling with nerves.

"Don't worry," Gizmo said between reassuring licks of his face. "With Max and Boss here, we'll be just fine."

"I guess so," Rocky grumbled.

While the other dogs observed with wariness, Boss continued leading Max, Rocky, and Gizmo. Max expected Boss to take them to the back end of the boat, through the supply closet, and then out of the hole where the waterwheels were, since that was where they'd come in. But instead, the big dog took them to the opposite corner, the front of the boat, which faced toward shore. Walking around tall cabinets covered with buttons, they discovered another, smaller hole in the ship's hull. Daylight cut through the dim red lighting of the ship's underbelly.

His tiny legs a blur, Rocky darted forward and stuck his head out of the hole. "Hey, this goes right onto the sandbar!" he shouted. "Why didn't the Dalmatians tell us this instead of making us walk on trash on a rushing river?"

Boss chuckled. "That's Zephyr being overly cautious and testing your mettle. Just following my lead, really. Of course, we wouldn't make dogs like Gloria come in that way. You know, since she had a belly full of puppies and all."

"No worries!" Gizmo said, her pink tongue hanging out happily as she strode to the hole. "We like a good challenge anyway." Then, pushing past Rocky, she jumped outside.

"Wait for me!" Rocky barked after her before disappearing through the hole as well.

Max followed. The hole was smoother than the one they'd come through on the river side of the boat, but it was smaller and a bit of a squeeze. He pushed through and landed in damp, shifting sand. It oozed up between his paws.

Max took in a big, gulping breath of fresh air. It was nice to be outside again. The boat was fine, but he'd never liked walls much.

He turned in time to see Boss force himself through the hole, sprawling onto the wet sand next to a big, smooth boulder. That must have been what the riverboat had hit to make this hole. And the enormous hole by the waterwheels had been caused by the bad people ramming the *Flower of the South.*

Boss took the lead again. They left behind the sandbar; walked through shallow, cold river water; and then were on the grassy shore.

"Yay, grass!" Gizmo shouted in glee. She plopped down on her side in the damp grass, then rolled around, enjoying the feel of it on her tan-and-black fur. "We've been on boats since *forever*; it's nice to be on real live dry land again."

Rocky raced ahead of her, bounding up the steep incline that led to the road. "Yeah, and it's nice and flat up here, too," he said as he reached the asphalt. "Not all slanted like the *Flower*." Tail wagging, he added, "And not constantly rocking back and forth like that little boat."

Boss, Max, and Gizmo climbed up the incline as well and came to stand next to Rocky.

"I have to admit," Max said as he ran in a wide circle over the warm road, "this is really nice. I almost feel wobbly, though, like my legs aren't used to land anymore."

With a laugh, Boss walked past the gleeful dogs. "Sounds like you never quite got your sea legs, as Captain and Twain call them. But I don't blame you. I tend to prefer dirt and grass myself."

Gizmo and Rocky leaped at each other, nipping playfully and laughing. Max's tail wagged, and he longed to join in the fun—but then he caught sight of the three-ringed symbol painted in dripping black along the side of the red boathouse.

"Hey, guys," he said, gently nudging his small friends with his nose. "We can play later. We've got a mission to do."

"Aw," Gizmo said, though her tail still wagged.

"Oh, you still wanna chase those people?" Rocky asked. "Well, if you insist, big guy."

It was a warm, sunny day, but the cool air flowing off the water kept them from getting too hot as Boss led them down the middle of the street that would take them toward the city. The street ran parallel to the river, between the boathouses and docks, before curving around the gravel parking lot and heading straight toward the city. The tall buildings and redbrick structures could be seen on the horizon, with some sort of curving bridge swirling over and between the buildings. That was their destination.

Just past the line of trees where they had seen the starving dogs run away, there was a cross street. A small store sat on a corner, its windows plastered with colorful papers and posters showing cans of worms. The glass front door was shattered, and Max didn't need to ask if it had already been ransacked for food—torn bags and smashed glass bottles littered the store's parking lot.

They passed more side streets as they walked down the main road toward the city. Small homes lined these avenues, their windows dark and their lawns overgrown. Much like the cities and towns he'd already come through on his journey, everything was empty, quiet. Cars were parked oddly on the sidewalks, some with their doors open. Here and there windows were smashed out. Debris fluttered past them, but there were no voices, no sounds.

A gust of wind rose up, carrying stale city smells to Max's nose, as well as the recent stench of gasoline from the bad people's SUVs.

And there was something else. Something familiar.

Images from his dreams flashed in Max's mind.

A dark, feral, giant wolf with glowing red eyes, chasing him. Dolph.

"Stop!" Max hissed.

His whole body went stiff, and he spun around, sniffing madly at the air.

"What is it, big guy?" Rocky said, head darting back and forth.

"Anything wrong back there?" Boss called from the road ahead.

"It's wolf," Max said. "I could swear I smelled wolf just now."

The other three dogs raised their snouts into the air and joined Max in sniffing. One by one, they turned to him, their looks quizzical.

"Are you sure?" Gizmo asked. "I don't smell anything. And you kept saying you were seeing and smelling wolves while we were on the river, and then told us it must have been your imagination...."

"Rocky?" Max asked.

The little Dachshund averted his gaze. "Uh, sorry, big guy. I'm not smelling it, either. Not that I'm calling you a liar! It's just after all the wolves did to us, I can't blame you for being a little paranoid."

Max turned his attention to Boss. The older dog only shook his head.

Snorting again, Max smelled only grass and trees and the dusty scents of the empty city.

"I could have sworn..."

Then he saw it.

Up ahead, a dirt road veered off through trees on the left side of the main street. A battered metal mailbox sat atop a wooden pole at the road's end, and just behind it, slightly obscured by the trees, was the metal mesh of a chain-link fence surrounding someone's property.

And hiding between the trees, in front of the fence and behind the mailbox, was a wolf.

The creature was small as far as wolves went, with brown fur and eyes as pale and icy as Boss's. But seeing that Max noticed it, the wolf angled back its ears and bared its fangs.

"You, meat," the wolf snarled. "We will make you a meal!"

"Hey!" Boss barked. Hackles raised, he stalked toward the wolf. "You'd better think twice, boy. There's four of us and only one of you. And this isn't the first time any of us would have gone toe-to-toe with a wolf, no, sir. Get!"

The wolf snarled and snapped his teeth.

"I said get!" Boss bellowed and darted forward.

The wolf spun on his heels and raced off, disappearing down the dirt road and out of sight.

"Wow," Gizmo said, her nub tail wagging. "That was great. Way to go, Boss!"

"Yeah," Max said. "Thanks."

Boss ducked his head. "Not a problem, son. Don't get wolves much 'round these parts, so I figured he'd be alone. Sometimes you just gotta show 'em who's, well, boss."

"Sorry we didn't believe you, big guy," Rocky said, nudging Max's side with his head.

"It's all right," Max said. "For some reason, I thought I smelled *Dolph.* I guess I can't help but be worried he'll come for all of us, and, you know, I vowed to protect you two."

"Aw, thanks," Gizmo said. "It's always nice to have friends looking out for you."

"Especially when they're big like these two!" Rocky yipped.

With the wolf gone, the dogs continued their trek down the street. Max had to admit it didn't seem likely that Dolph and his pack would have come here, too. It was probably just as Boss said: a lone wolf, separated from his pack, no threat to them.

At least, he hoped so.

The sun was high in the sky by the time they reached the outskirts of the city. They sauntered side by side down the main street, taking in the sights. The buildings here were bigger than the ones they'd passed near the docks—redbrick buildings with giant windows, trees rising up from the sidewalks surrounded by iron fencing, wooden benches for people to sit on.

Some buildings had brightly colored awnings jutting from their fronts that covered round tables and fancy metal chairs. They smelled vaguely of people food, and Max guessed these were places where humans would go to eat out. Through other windows Max could see clothing hanging on racks, and one store had shelf after shelf of computers. Another was nothing but cases and tables overloaded with books.

The street was neat and clean, as though it had been tended to very well when the city was busy. As long as Max ignored the overgrown trees and the withered, brown flowers in vases on the outdoor restaurant tables, it almost seemed as if there might be some humans about, just minutes away from coming to shop and eat and laugh and enjoy a life where dogs were pets and not enemies.

Max noticed as they walked that every few blocks, massive concrete pillars rose from behind the stores and restaurants and coffee shops. The pillars supported train tracks that swirled overhead and disappeared between the skyscrapers farther into the city. Max and his friends walked in the shadows as they explored the shopping center lining either side of the road, but Max didn't give it much mind—until the road trembled ever so slightly and a distant rumble could be heard.

As the dogs looked up and watched, a sleek, silver train whooshed past on the tracks at speeds even faster than Max had seen cars go. The train was made up of a dozen connected boxes with windows on the side. Fluorescent light lit up the interior, but the cars were empty.

And in a flash of steel and a rush of noise, the train was gone.

"Whoa!" Rocky said, his tail wagging. "What was that? It was so shiny and fast!"

"I could never quite figure it out," Boss said, resuming their trek down the main street. "It comes and goes every ten minutes or so. I suppose the humans must have used it to travel around, but how they got inside when it's going so fast I couldn't tell you."

"Maybe we can figure out a way," Gizmo said, bouncing chipperly at Boss's side. "It would make our trip a whole lot faster."

Boss said something back to her, but Max didn't hear what. Instead, his ears perked up as much as the floppy things could.

He heard people voices. The same people voices from the docks.

"Hey!" he barked quietly. "Listen!"

Rocky looked over his shoulder at Max. "It's not wolves again, is it?"

Max shushed him. All the dogs went silent—and then their eyes widened as they heard the voices, too.

Max and his friends rushed as fast as they could—

out of the center of the road, past an abandoned car, and into the doorway of one of the storefronts. It was at the corner of an intersection, and the voices were coming from the building's side that faced the cross street. Stoplights dangled over the intersection, changing between red, green, and yellow with audible clicks, guiding no one.

With everyone huddled silently in the shadow of the doorway, Max crouched low to the ground and crept on his belly back to the sidewalk. Slowly he made it to the corner of the brick building and peered around its edge. There, in a parking lot beneath a giant glowing sign, were the two big black SUVs.

As Max watched, the four humans stepped through a broken window out of another building and back into daylight. Their boots crunched over glass as they carried big boxes and shoved them into the open trunks. The woman from earlier still hefted the duffel bag over her shoulder, only now it seemed to be partially full—with what, Max didn't know.

The woman tossed the bag into the back of one of the SUVs, then leaned in, searching for something. Producing the can of spray paint from earlier, she shook the can and sauntered to a sign on the end of the parking lot opposite from where Max watched. It had a big arrow on it pointing toward the crossroad, which left the shopping area and wound up in a distant hill, along with people words Max couldn't read.

As the dogs watched, the woman pressed the nozzle on the top of the can and swirled her arm in big circles. The familiar interconnected rings appeared, obscuring the words on the sign. Black paint dripped, making the three circles look like they were bleeding.

That done, she ran back to the cars, where the men were slamming the trunks closed and preparing to climb in.

"There's the symbol again," Max whispered. "She has to be painting it for a reason." His eyes followed the arrow to the road, then up the hill. Past the blackened husks of other stores and at the top of the hill were two large white buildings behind a high fence. On the right building, the one directly in front of the end of the road, was a darkened entrance. A neon sign the size of a billboard glowed bright white above the entrance: the three-ringed symbol, shining like a beacon.

"There," Max gasped. "That has to be it." Looking over at Boss, he dared to smile. "That must be where we're supposed to go!"

"Oh, no, son," Boss said, his eyes wide. "You definitely do not want to go there. It's dangerous there." He shook his head angrily. "I knew I recognized that symbol. I knew it!"

"But Madame told Max to go there," Gizmo said. "Why would she tell us to go somewhere dangerous?"

"Something bad happened there," Boss said, his voice deeper, gruffer than usual. "The people won't go anywhere near it—especially not your pack leaders. It's the whole reason my own pack leaders took me to this city. It's the last place they figured anyone would think to look for us."

"But what happened?" Max asked. "Does it have something to do with why all the people disappeared?"

Boss shook his head. "I don't know for certain. But I suspect some of my acquaintances may know a thing or two about it. One in particular."

Before Max could ask any more questions, someone laughed.

The noise was high-pitched, staccato, mocking.

More important, it was loud.

All four dogs turned to find a creature sitting in the middle of the road. It was smaller than Max, with matted, spotted black-and-brown fur. It looked like some weird, runty mix between dog and cat, with a tiny pointed face and big, round ears that ended in points.

"Don't you all look funny, crouching there," the thing rasped out. Then she laughed again, even louder.

"Shhh!" Gizmo said to the creature.

But it was too late. From the lot beside the building, the humans began shouting. Max looked around the corner to see all four of the bad people racing right toward them.

CHAPTER 9

THE CACKLING PEST

"Run!" Max bellowed.

All the dogs bounded away from the corner of the redbrick building, away from the people, off the sidewalk, and onto the street. Still cackling madly, the catdog spun on her heels and ran diagonally across the wide street, darted between a truck and a blue mailbox, and ducked into an alley between two clothing stores.

"You gonna chase me, huh?" the creature yipped. "Come on, come and get me!"

"You bet I'm gonna chase him," Boss growled. The big dog veered away from Max and toward the alley.

Behind them, heavy footsteps thudded from the parking lot. Human voices shouted, echoing loudly through the empty streets.

And then came a loud crack.

A brick landed on the road right next to Max, breaking in two and sending chalky red dust into the air.

A rock flew over his head, followed by the woman's can of spray paint, which clanked against the road and then exploded in a cloud of acrid black.

Max yelped, lowered his head, and ran to follow Boss and the cat-dog to the sidewalk on the other side of the main street.

"They're trying to hurt us!" Rocky howled. "I knew we shouldn't have followed! I knew it!"

"Just keep running!" Max barked.

Ahead, the cat-dog and Boss disappeared into the shadows of the alley. Parked on the street in front was a bright red truck. Max veered around the front while Gizmo and Rocky darted beneath.

The humans hollered, and there came a crash and tinkle of shattering glass as a brick hit the windshield. Max winced instinctively as little pebbles of glass rained down on his fur.

Skidding, Max darted onto the sidewalk, finally behind cover with the truck between him and the bad people on the street. Rocky and Gizmo were already ahead of him, racing into the alley. Max followed, limbs aching, heart pounding. He gasped for air but didn't dare stop. The humans could still be after them.

Instead, he focused on his companions, who galloped out of the alley into a wide concrete lot built behind the main-street buildings, open on its eastern edge to the cross street so that people could drive in and park. Cars lay abandoned here, some with flat tires, others missing windows.

In the center of the lot, one of the big concrete pillars rose into the sky to support the bridge on which they'd seen the silver train zoom by. Concrete steps climbed the pillar's side, winding their way up to a platform high above. Max could see the furry shapes of the other dogs already ascending the first flight of steps, Boss still in the lead, chasing the cat-dog.

Max took the steps two at a time, even though his lungs ached and his legs burned. He reached a landing and followed the others up the next set of stairs. Then another landing and another long climb of steps. And another. Panting, he finally reached the landing at the very top. He squeezed through a narrow metal gate and found himself on a swath of square concrete big enough to fit dozens of human cars.

Glass walls surrounded the concrete platform on three sides, with the open side connected to the big bridge that they'd observed the silver train race across. Up here, Max could see the black tracks that ran atop the bridge, and that the bridge was divided from the rest of the area by a wide strip of yellow plastic covered with rounded bumps. Several rows of brown plastic benches faced the tracks and lined the glass walls. Garbage cans and dying plants sat between the benches, and near the stairs was a tall, boxy machine with a transparent front that seemed to contain little packets of people food.

In a corner of the platform opposite the stairs, Boss towered over the cat-dog, his sharp teeth bared, his ears flattened against his skull. Any smart dog would back down in the face of aggression from such a big dog, but the spotted creature merely laughed some more.

Max looked through the glass walls down at the city street below. He could see the tops of the buildings, with their big metal exhaust vents, and the alleyways and the parking lot and the sign that the woman had painted the three rings across. The SUVs and the people were nowhere to be seen.

Max's gaze darted everywhere, but he couldn't see the people no matter where he looked. He even slinked back to the top landing of the stairs and listened, worried that they might have driven their cars into the lot beneath the platform, but he heard no voices, no footsteps.

The bad people were gone.

"You can stop growling, doggy," the cat-dog rasped. "I ain't scared."

Max turned to see the cat-dog rudely brush past Boss and leap atop one of the plastic benches. She sat back on her haunches, looking like a human waiting for a train.

Her dark brows narrowed, Gizmo marched forward.

"Well, you should be scared!" she barked up at the creature. "You could have gotten yourself hurt. Not to mention us! Why did you do that down there?"

The cat-dog shrugged her bony shoulders. "Can't help it, lady. It's in my nature." She chuckled, then raised a paw over her snout to try to muffle the noise.

"What kind of dog are you supposed to be?" Rocky asked. "I mean, aside from a kind that's very annoying and loud."

"Hey," the creature said. "That's not nice, puppy. Words hurt, you know." She giggled again.

"She's no dog," Boss growled as he approached the bench to stand snout-to-snout with the thing. "I've seen her kind before. They're called hyenas."

"Yup," the hyena said. "That's me. I live at the zoo in the city here. But woo-whee, it's been boring there. You got no idea, doggies. So I came out here to see what I could see. And all I found is you dumb puppies trying to hide in plain sight." Cackling, she leaped off the bench and strolled away from Boss.

"If you're from a zoo," Gizmo said, "then how did you get all the way out here?"

Before the hyena could answer, the platform beneath their feet vibrated, sending a shivering sensation up Max's legs. A great gust of wind rose from their left, and the tracks began to rumble.

The ground quaked, and the wind came faster and faster—and that was when Max saw the big silver train rushing toward them. It shoved the air forward, making Max's fur blow in every direction.

"Hide!" Max barked. "Don't let it hit you!"

Gizmo and Rocky leaped beneath a bench, cowering under their paws as they hid their faces. Max and Boss raced to the farthest corner from the track and huddled together. The noise of the thing was deafening, and the whole world seemed to rattle and shake around them. Max was certain the platform might crumble.

But just when he thought the train might raise up such a storm that they'd be blown through the glass walls, there came a soft hiss of brakes, and it slowed to a stop right next to the platform. Doors on the side of each car slid open to reveal the brightly lit interior. Above each door, an electronic sign showed people numbers in glowing red.

"I came on that. The monorail. How else you think?" The hyena laughed and shook her head. "Stupid, stupid doggies. Afraid of a little train."

"Hey!" Rocky protested. "Words can hurt us, too, ya know!"

"We weren't afraid anyway," Gizmo said, puffing up her chest as she emerged from beneath the bench. "We were just being cautious."

"Everyone," Max barked, trying to pull their attention away from the hyena and the train. "Hey, listen up!"

Gizmo perked up her ears, then sauntered over to where Max and Boss stood by the glass window.

"Are the people still coming?" Gizmo asked. "I don't like them."

Max shook his head. "No, but that's the problem. I wanted to follow them, but we were so busy running we didn't see which direction they went. But maybe, if we work together, we can spot them from up here. Everybody spread out and look."

From behind Max, Rocky's voice rang out, strangely muffled. "Hey, maybe this was where we meant to end up, big guy. This train is nice and posh! Very cozy."

Max ignored him. He paced back and forth in front of the glass walls, combing the streets below for any sign of the people.

"What are we supposed to do? Madame was very clear that the people with that symbol were going to lead us to our pack leaders."

"What about the building with the three-ringed symbol?" Gizmo asked. "Maybe they went there?"

"I sincerely doubt that," Boss drawled, his eyes apologetic. "No people are going to want to go there."

"Why not?" Max asked, suddenly curious. "What's so bad about it?"

Boss backed away, his tail tucked. "Not really my place to say, as I wouldn't know what I was talking about. But I reckon there are some who might have a better idea."

Gizmo dropped from the glass. Tail wagging furiously, she said, "Then what are we waiting for? Who do we need to talk to?"

Boss jerked his head over his shoulder. "Unfortunately, we've got to go where that hyena came from: the zoo."

"Unfortunately?" Max asked.

"There are some nice animals there," the old dog grunted. "But there's a whole lot more like the hyena. They're not from around here, and they're all kept locked up in cages. Can drive any friendliness out of an animal. They can be more than a little mean, pups."

"I don't care," Max said, turning and walking back toward the benches. "We've dealt with a world of mean on our way here. We can handle it. We'll just ask—"

He stopped in his tracks, realizing quite suddenly that the hyena was nowhere in sight.

And neither was Rocky.

"Rocky! Hyena!" Max called out. "Where did you go?"

A human voice answered.

Startled, Max spun in a circle, certain the woman with the spray paint had somehow sneaked up after them. But his ears led him instead to speakers embedded on the walls beneath the glass windows. It was some sort of recording, like the movie on the riverboat, with just sounds, no pictures.

Max couldn't understand what the woman's voice was saying, and he had only the vague sense that she was repeating the same phrase over and over again. Then the recorded voice stopped and a chime sounded.

Mocking laughter echoed across the platform.

Max turned his attention back to the train and saw the hyena sitting in one of the open doorways. Above the door, the glowing numbers flashed once, twice—and then the signs went black.

"Dumb, dumb doggies!" the hyena yipped. "Don't know how to ride a monorail!"

Before anyone could respond, the doors on all the cars shut with a quiet hiss. The platform vibrated underneath them once more as the cars began to rumble out of the station.

And Rocky's muffled voice cried out, "Hey, who was that lady talking? And why did the doors shut? Let me off this thing!"

Too late, Max realized that Rocky had gotten on the train when they weren't paying attention. Rocky stood on the other side of the windows, his paws atop the back of the seats, his nose pressed against the glass. His big, watery eyes were wide with fear.

Then the train whooshed away, zipping down the track like a silver blur, disappearing into the city—and taking Rocky with it.

CHAPTER 10

THE ZOO

"Oh, no, Rocky!" Gizmo cried. "He's going to be so lost without me." She glanced at Max. "I mean, us."

Max ran to the edge of the platform and waited, straining to see into the distance, hoping that the flash of silver would reappear and the train would come back with Rocky.

Rocky wasn't safe. That hyena was with him—and though Boss and Max were much bigger than the hyena, Rocky was a fraction of the creature's size.

"We have to go after them," Max said, pacing back and forth atop the bumpy yellow plastic that divided the platform and the tracks. "We can follow these tracks. I can't let anything happen to Rocky!"

"Hold on there," Boss said. "Those tracks aren't safe.

Not with these trains whizzing back and forth. Likely to kill a dog before he could get to the next station."

Gizmo looked down the track herself. "Then how will we know where to go? Rocky might panic and get off the train anywhere! He doesn't always think before he acts, you know." She trembled, and her eyes watered. "Oh, he always gets so scared even though he pretends not to be."

Max turned away from the tracks and ran back across the platform to the glass wall. He looked down on the city, studying the streets. "Maybe we can follow the tracks from below. We can call Rocky's name and hope he hears us."

Boss padded forward and sat next to Max. "Actually, I bet I know where they'll be getting off."

"You do?" Gizmo asked, her ears perking up. "So what are we waiting for? We should go there right now!"

The big Shepherd smiled. "That hyena's a sneak and a prankster and a boaster, just like most lonely pups. She's probably going to try to impress Rocky and make friends with him."

Max said, "Why would anyone want to impress Rocky?"

Gizmo shook her head so that her ears flopped. "Rocky doesn't impress easily."

"Nonetheless, that's how creatures like that hyena think. So chances are she'll take Rocky home with her, trying to look like the big alpha of the place."

Max thought for a moment. "Her home... is that the zoo you mentioned?"

"One and the same. I think if we find the zoo, we'll find Rocky." Boss gestured at the tracks with his snout. "If memory serves, this train runs in a big circle 'round the city, so it may take a while to reach the zoo. We can take the main road and go in a straight line, and maybe we'll arrive there not too long after your friend."

"Then let's go," Max said.

The three dogs bounded down the flights of stairs, their nails clacking against the hard concrete steps.

"This way!" Boss said as he veered left down the sidewalk.

With Gizmo at his side, Max ran as fast as he could to keep up with Boss. The sun was already nearing the eastern edge of the sky and disappearing behind the big buildings of downtown farther ahead, and Max's stomach dropped. Soon it would be night, and Rocky would be all alone in a zoo full of wild animals, his only companion a crazy hyena.

The road they followed grew wider—six lanes instead of two, divided by yellow lines dotted with yellow concrete bumps. Beneath the stoplights that swayed in the late-afternoon breeze, a red fire truck sat empty, a gray hose snaking off its side and onto the road.

Instinctively, Max stopped at the sidewalk's end, beneath a utility pole stapled with weathered paper pamphlets, and looked both ways. Of course no cars were coming, though, and he shook his head—his worry for Rocky was so rampant that he wasn't thinking straight.

"Why are we stopping?" Gizmo asked, looking up anxiously at Max.

"You kids coming?" Boss asked at the same time, already rounding past the fire truck.

"Yeah," Max said as he stepped off the smooth concrete and onto the asphalt road. "Right behind you!"

Boss headed down the center of the wide, six-lane road in the direction of the setting sun. It wasn't long before they were in the middle of the city itself, with its larger buildings and stadiums all lit up with lights.

And a short while later, as daylight faded and the streetlamps clicked on to illuminate the sidewalks in puddles of orange light, the buildings gave way to slowly rising hills and tall, brushy trees that acted as a natural wall between the road and the fancy redbrick homes behind them.

The sun was merging with the distant horizon, casting long shadows that fell over Max and Gizmo as they panted and chased after Boss, who seemed to know where he was going. The great concrete track on which the train ran had curled its way through the city and again hovered high above them.

Max strained his ears, hoping to hear the terrifying rumble of the sleek silver train bringing Rocky back, so they could run to each other and Max could growl at the hyena and Rocky could be saved.

But no rumbling came. Either the train hadn't arrived yet—or it had come and gone long ago, leaving Rocky lost in the impending darkness with only the hyena as his guide.

They heard and smelled the zoo before they saw it. Distant yowls, like cats but much deeper, echoed over the darkening streets. Unfamiliar shrieks and cries pierced Max's ears. There were even, strangely enough, bird calls, though none that Max recognized.

And the smells! Some were familiar after life on the farm—the dusty smell of matted hay and the acrid stench of untended manure and the thick must of damp moss. But these were mingled in with the musks and tangs of fur and feathers that felt vaguely similar to other things Max had smelled, but were still wildly, dangerously new.

New creatures that could decide Rocky would be their next meal.

"Are we close?" Max panted as he strained himself to run faster. "We're close, aren't we?"

"We're fixin' to come right on it, son," Boss said between his own pants as he galloped off the road and onto the sidewalk on the right side of the street. "It's just up ahead!"

Max and Gizmo followed Boss, the pads of their paws leaving behind the smooth asphalt and meeting the evening-cooled concrete as well as slick leaves that had fallen from the trees. Up ahead Max could see that the trees that lined the street had thinned, opening up onto a parking lot.

The flat lot was dotted with bright streetlights and had enough space for hundreds of cars. It was separated from the smelly, noisy zoo by a tall and wide tan wall that ran the length of the lot. Evenly spaced on the wall were posters showing strange animals Max had never seen before; in the center were three large green gates. All the gates were wide open. The entrance to the place, Max guessed.

Boss raced alongside Max and Gizmo right up to the middle gate, then sat down. His tongue hung out as he panted.

"We have arrived at last," Boss said. "You two better take a second to catch your breaths. It can get a bit wild in there."

A glint of silver caught Max's eye, and he glanced up. Only then did he see the supporting pillars of the monorail track rising from the cover of trees next to the parking lot. A flight of stairs led from a sidewalk between the grass and the lot to another platform—where the monorail train sat silently. Distantly, Max could see the glowing, blinking symbols above the open doors.

The train was here. Which meant Rocky could be, too. They could have found him just in time!

"Hey!" Max barked, running toward the stairs despite his tired limbs. "Rocky! Are you up there? We're here! We've come to save you!"

The same human voice from the speakers at the other platform sounded from above.

"Wait!" Max barked. "Don't leave yet! Rocky!"

But it was too late. He'd barely reached the bottom of the concrete steps before he heard the train doors hiss shut, felt the ground vibrate, and saw the monorail whoosh away.

Hanging his head, Max plopped down in front of the concrete stairs. What if they were wrong? What if Rocky had gotten off somewhere else, or found a way back to where they were? What if the hyena had hurt him?

Boss and Gizmo padded up to stand next to Max. "He would have barked back if he was up there," Boss said. "Any dog would when hearing their name. You didn't lose him."

"But we *did* lose him," Max said. "If only I hadn't been so worried about that stupid symbol and had been paying attention, we could have gotten Rocky off that train in time. He was my responsibility, and I failed him."

A small nose nuzzled Max's side. Gizmo.

"You didn't let him down," she said. "This isn't your fault. And anyway, we're going to find him."

Max didn't feel so sure. In fact, he was so terrified of all the ways Rocky could be hurt and alone that his heart wouldn't stop pounding and he couldn't stop thinking about how he was a failure. But he couldn't tell the chipper terrier that. She looked up to him.

"Well, there's no use sitting here," Boss grumbled. "Come on, son. Let's go see if Rocky made it into the zoo."

Together the three dogs walked back to the dark entrance. Sunlight was fading rapidly now, though the lights in the parking lot grew brighter as it did, bathing everything with a hazy yellow glow. Passing through the gates, the pads of their paws walked over cold tile in a big, dark, empty room. There were more animal posters in here, backlit and casting a soft blue glow, the only light in the place. Set in the walls on either side of the gates were glass booths. Green racks stood nearby, filled with pamphlets and magazines.

Then they went through another gate and were outside once more. As soon as they stepped foot on the wide gravel path beyond the gate, Max's eyes went wide.

The zoo was like no place he'd ever seen.

The gravel path went straight down a hill until it stopped at the edge of a wide field surrounded by a mesh fence. The field was sparsely dotted with tall, dark trees, between which Max could make out animals around his size.

From there, the gravel path split in two. To Max's right was a shimmering waterfall that fell from rocks that seemed to be connected to the building they'd just exited. It splashed into a pool surrounded by metal chairs bolted to concrete. Next to the waterfall, atop a polished log set on its end, was a wooden figurine carved with a pattern of feathers.

To his left, behind another tall fence, were tiered levels of land portioned off by jagged tan rocks that acted like natural dividers between the sections. Lithe, shadowy figures that smelled strangely like house cats moved between sparse trees and spiky bushes.

"This isn't what I expected when you said there were animals in cages," Max said. "This reminds me of the farm I used to live on, with lots of room for the animals to run around."

"Yeah," Gizmo agreed. "This is the biggest park I've ever seen! Oh, there's so much to explore." Tongue lolling out happily, Gizmo looked up at Max. "After we find Rocky, you think we can explore?"

Boss grunted. "Trust me, just because there aren't any metal bars doesn't mean these animals aren't caged."

"That's the truth," a deep voice said.

Max darted his head back and forth but didn't see anyone.

Then he noticed the feathered figurine on the log start to move.

Wide yellow eyes appeared on an oval face, which twisted around to look at the dogs. The bird's small, sharp beak opened, and he let out a "*hoo hoo hooHOO*."

"Watch your step around here or you just might get yourself eaten," the bird hooted. "I've seen it happen more times than I can count." He fluttered his wing toward the shadowy creatures to Max's left. "Especially in cat country over there."

"Cats?" Gizmo asked. "Oh, but cats just *love* me. They'd never try to eat me."

The bird looked down his beak at her. "Yeah, well, these cats are ten times the size of your friends. And they're pretty grumpy about being trapped here, especially since some of the other big animals got taken away or let loose before all the people left. You'd be nothing but an appetizer to one of them." Stretching his neck, the bird made his eyes open even wider. "A tasty, fluffy appetizer!"

Boss chuckled. "Hey, now, Oliver," he said. "Don't go scaring the girl."

"I'm not scared," Gizmo said. "In fact, now I'd like to meet these giant cats even more, just to see for myself whether you're telling the truth!"

"A bird!" Max said. "You're the first one we've seen in a long time. We thought all the birds flew away."

The owl fluttered his wings and peered down at Max with his big eyes. "The local birds did fly away, same time the humans left. Us zoo birds would have, too, but they had us all in cages. By the time we managed to get out, the instinct to fly away had passed." He nipped at his feathers. "Though that's partly because we didn't know exactly where to go. So we just stayed put."

"Meet my owl friend, Oliver," Boss said, his tail thumping on the ground. "Oliver, this is Max and Gizmo. We're looking for a friend of theirs."

"Let me guess," Oliver hooted. "Small dog who looks suspiciously like a black-and-brown sausage on legs? Accompanied by one of those insufferable hyenas?"

Max's tail wagged. He turned in a tight circle. "Yes!"

he barked excitedly. "That's him! Did you see where he went?"

Oliver ruffled the feathers around his neck, then twisted his head to pick at them with his beak. "Yeah, they wandered off down the path. It wasn't too long ago. You mutts with your keen noses can probably track the scent if you can pick it out from all the other smells around this place."

"Of course we can!" Gizmo said. "Thanks, Oliver. You're the best owl I ever met!"

Oliver glanced at her out of the corner of his eyes. "You know a lot of owls?"

Gizmo shook her head. "No. You're the first I've seen. But that doesn't mean you're not the best."

Oliver hooted. "You're funny." To Boss, he said, "She's funny, this one. Keep an eye on her. Be a real shame if she got eaten." Then the brown owl began preening his feathers again.

"I'll do that," Boss grunted.

Max didn't join in the conversation. He was too busy huffing at the air. He smelled grass and trees and the same murk of musky, unfamiliar animal smells that he'd noticed from the road. The mixture of new scents threatened to overwhelm his senses, but Max focused. Finally, there, woven faintly in the riot of other odors, was a trace of dog. The hint wisped through his nostrils and was gone, just long enough to evoke Rocky's personal scent. Not the strongest trail, but strong enough.

"Come on!" Max barked back at Boss and Gizmo. "I got him!"

Leaving Oliver behind, the three dogs raced down the gravel path. Max sniffed the ground and the air, following the scent trail that belonged to Rocky.

The smell only grew stronger and stronger as Max reached the fork in the path and skidded left.

They passed an enclosure surrounding an area of flat desert land full of creatures that looked like large, skinny rats with their ears cut off. They stood on their hind legs, watching the dogs race past and shouting out.

"What are they?" one of the creatures asked in a high voice.

"More of them?" another added.

Gizmo looked to Boss. "What are those things?" she asked. "They're so cute!"

"Those are meerkats," Boss said. "Just rodents, if you ask me."

"Where are they going?" one of the meerkats shouted.

"Should we go, too?"

"Oh, let's go talk to them!" Gizmo said, jumping in circles in delight as more of the meerkats popped up from behind rocks and scrubby bushes to watch them. "Maybe they can help us find Rocky."

Max hefted his snout up so he could peer back at her, momentarily losing the scent trail. "There's no time, Gizmo. Just follow me. I can find him!"

The gravel path angled downhill, and the enclosed

desert gave way to new scenery, which Max had seen from the zoo entrance: swampy, musty land overflowing with water behind a fence on their right. Bumpy-skinned reptiles sat still, silently watching the dogs, while snakes slithered through the grass. Very close to the edge, just beyond another mesh fence, long, triangular, fanged jaws opened wide, and a creature Boss said was a crocodile called out to them. Its voice was low, deadly.

"Come visit me," it said. "Come explore here."

"Can we?" Gizmo asked.

"No!" Boss and Max barked at the same time.

The path soon led them in front of the glimmering pool dotted with white-painted rocks. Up close, now Max could see that the enclosure was filled with big black-and-white birds that waddled around and flapped their smooth wings. Penguins, Boss told Gizmo before she could even ask. The big, sleek birds ignored the dogs, choosing instead to slide on their bellies into the water, splashing around under the evening sky.

Across from the penguins, on the other side of the path, was a stretch of concrete, on top of which were several round buildings with open walls and circular roofs. Inside were leafless trees on which all sorts of brightly plumed birds perched, many sleeping. The mesh that had covered the walls was torn open in places, and small yellow birds darted out upon seeing the dogs, chirping, "Get away!"

Along with the owl, they were the first birds Max had

seen since escaping Vet's office so long ago, and they must have been the birds he'd heard from the main street outside the zoo. He didn't have time to appreciate the discovery. Rocky's scent had grown even stronger.

And just as strong was that of the hyena.

Beyond the birdhouses on the left side of the path was another flat concrete area. Long plastic benches in front of weathered tables filled the center of the space, with covered metal trash cans between them that stank of mold and rotting meat.

Brightly colored booths acted as a perimeter around the eating area, arranged in a half circle. Each building had a window on its front, above which was a striped awning. Pictures of people food—hot dogs and hamburgers and cotton candy and ice cream—were plastered onto the peeling red and blue paint. The whole place smelled of stale grease and sticky sweetness.

And Rocky.

"Here!" Max barked, veering off the path and toward the food booths. Behind the centermost booth were two squat, plain white buildings. A door was ajar on one, letting light spill out.

This was the place.

Head low, Max forced himself to run as fast as he possibly could. He could hear sounds from behind the door. A low, ominous chuckle—the hyena. And then the sound of teeth wrenching into meat and jaws snapping as it swallowed down its meal.

His friend was being hurt. He'd failed him. Just like he'd failed Madame.

"Rocky!" Max bellowed. "No!"

He leaped against the door, shoving it open. He barreled into the room, teeth bared, prepared to fight off the laughing hyena.

There, sitting in the middle of the floor, next to an open refrigerator, was Rocky. He looked up at Max, startled, a hot dog hanging from his jaws. Next to him, the hyena, unfazed by Max's entrance, shoved her head into an open bag of hot dogs and took a big mouthful.

Max gulped in a breath and blinked rapidly. "Rocky?"

The little Dachshund swallowed down his hot dog, then grinned up at Max. "Hey, there, big guy! Barbs and I were just having some dinner. Want some?"

CHAPTER 11

WILLA AND THE TWINS

Max blinked, catching his bearings. The lights in the storeroom were so bright, especially since every surface was gleaming white, and here was the friend he'd run halfway across a city for, who he was certain was in mortal danger, hanging out with a hyena and happily eating hot dogs.

"Rocky! Yay!"

Gizmo darted past Max and leaped on Rocky. He rolled to the side and squirmed as she began licking him in glee.

"Hey, now," Rocky sputtered. "Watch the fur. I have it the way I like it."

Gizmo ignored him and kept licking his face.

"Well, all right," the Dachshund said. "If you insist."

Barbs the hyena cackled. Spittle and little bits of hot dog flew from her mouth.

Boss nudged Max with his snout. "What did I tell you, son? Your friend was right here, safe and sound."

Max ignored Boss. Eyes narrowed, he stomped forward, then swatted the bag of hot dogs across the floor with his front paw.

"Hey!" Barbs rasped as she leaped to her feet. "Why did you do that, dumb doggy? Those are mine."

But Max's eyes were on Rocky.

"We've been chasing after you all day," Max said. "We could have gotten hurt or lost, all because we thought you were in danger. But here you are, eating and playing like nothing happened!"

Rocky's tail drooped, and he ducked his head. "Hey, uh, sorry, buddy. I was real scared at first, I promise, but—"

"Did you even try to stay in a place where we could find you?" Max barked. "Do you even realize how dumb it was to go running off like that?"

"Hey!" Rocky protested. "It was an accident!"

"Did you even think about how the bad people are still out there, and that this zoo is full of big animals that want to eat you? Or did Barbs just tell you there was food and you forgot all about your friends?"

Rocky's jaws opened and closed, but he wasn't able to say anything. Panting, Max towered above him, more angry at the little dog than he'd ever been before.

Giggling, Barbs crept over to the bag of hot dogs and stuck her head back inside.

"Hey," Gizmo said softly, coming to stand in front of Rocky and look up at Max. "You don't need to yell at him. He was just making the best of a bad situation."

Max met Rocky's wide, watering eyes. The little dog scrunched in on himself, looking smaller and more afraid than Max had ever seen him. Taking a deep breath, he let his hackles down and took a step back.

"Sorry," he said to his two friends. "I'm really sorry. I didn't mean to yell at you, Rocky; it's just I was so scared we'd lost you forever. And that it was all my fault. Seeing you disappear on the train just made me think I'd failed at everything."

Relaxing, Rocky waddled across the tiled floor toward Max. "I'm sorry, too, big guy," he said. "You're right, I should have been more careful. The last thing I want is to be separated from you and Gizmo ever again. Still friends?"

Max wagged his tail. "Always."

Behind Max, Boss grunted. Max looked over his shoulder to see the old Australian Shepherd walk between the rows of cabinets to Barbs the hyena and the bag of hot dogs.

"It's good you pups made up," he said as he sniffed the meat. "We've got to stick together out here. If there's anything I learned when the people left, it's that I wish I'd made them take Belle with us, too." He turned away from the food and looked at Max, Rocky, and Gizmo with sorrowful eyes. "Trust me—hold on to the ones you care about for as long as you can."

Max nodded solemnly. "We will, Boss. Thanks."

Gnawing on another mouthful of hot dogs, Barbs wrapped her spotted paws around the bag and hugged it against her. She looked among the four dogs.

"You doggies keep sniffing and throwing around my food," she said. "If you're not going to treat food right, you stupid puppies can leave."

Rocky said, "Hey, Barbs, don't be like that. You're my friend now, right?"

Barbs swallowed and eyed Rocky. "Guess so."

"Then my friends are your friends, too!" Rocky said gleefully. "There's more than enough to share. I bet they're really hungry. Aren't you, guys?"

Now that Rocky had been found, Max realized his stomach was aching with hunger.

"Fine, fine," Barbs said. "Gobble up some goodies, doggies." She let go of the bag.

Max, Gizmo, and Boss all rushed the open bag of meat and buried their snouts in the hole. Cool water stuck to Max's fur as he pulled out two of the glistening hot dogs. He gobbled them so quickly that he barely chewed, just savored the meaty flavor as they went down. Granola was fine for the crunch, but there was nothing like a mouthful of meaty goodness, as far as Max was concerned.

The dogs were so preoccupied with eating their dinner that Max almost didn't notice Barbs's eyes go wide, or sense the shadow that fell over them from the storeroom door.

He did notice, however, when someone behind them screamed.

It was deafening—a piercing roar that echoed off the metal cabinets and walls and seemed to come from everywhere at once.

Almost choking on his last bite, Max spun around and stiffened, prepared to fight.

In the doorway was a tall, wide, humanoid figure bigger than any person Max had ever seen. Its legs were thick and squat, its arms just as muscled as its legs and long enough so that it could press its closed fists against the dirty floor. Its face and body were covered with black fur, and it had tiny eyes and a flat, wide nose. Its big mouth was wide open, revealing its sharp white teeth.

The creature stepped through the door and stood up to its full height. Screaming again, it slammed its big fists against its broad, muscular chest.

"Barbs!" he hollered. "This is the last time!"

The hyena cackled, then slapped her paws over her snout. "No!" she cried. "I'm not laughing at you, Willa! Please don't hurt me!"

Max didn't know what to do. The big creature's

attention was fully on the hyena—but Max and his three companions stood directly between the two animals. If this big hairy thing tried to attack...

Tittering laughter came from behind the big beast. Two small creatures slipped between his legs and into the storeroom. They looked sort of like the raccoons Max always chased away from the trash cans on the farm. They had red-brown fur, round faces with white splotches, rounded ears, and bushy tails with white stripes.

The two little raccoon things sprang atop the counters, running along the length and sending cooking utensils clattering to the floor. They put their paws in front of their snouts and giggled to each other.

"What do you have to say for yourself, Barbs?" the towering black-furred beast roared.

"Ooh, girl, he's gonna kill you this time!" one of the little red creatures called in a high-pitched voice.

"Definitely gonna kill you!" the other chimed in.

"You really messed up!" they said at the same time. Giggling once more, they leaped atop the refrigerator to get a better view. Both of them crouched down, hanging their heads over the top to watch the scene below.

"I'm sorry, Willa!" the hyena howled in her rasping voice. "I had to! Dumb doggies followed me, and they needed food! I had no choice! I—ow!"

A little packet Max had seen people squeeze sauce out of smacked the hyena on her forehead. From atop the refrigerator, the two raccoon things dug into boxes and tossed more of the packets down at Barbs.

"Ooh, you gonna take that, Willa?" one chirped.

"She's lying right to your face!" the other added.

And at the same time, they cried, "She's a liar, Willa, a big, fat, laughing liar!" They fell onto their backs, dizzy with laughter as they rolled around.

Willa's tiny eyes opened wide with rage. His nostrils flared. "You're *lying* to me?" he bellowed. One of his massive fists flew out to the side, smacking a hole into the wall. Max winced. Beside him, he heard Rocky whimper.

"Okay, okay, I was telling half a truth," Barbs said. "I was being greedy, greedy, greedy. But never again! I promise, never again!"

One of the red creatures leaped above Max's head to the shelves opposite the refrigerator. "Just kill her, already!" she said as she flew through the air.

The other red creature darted back down to the counter next to Willa. She examined the hole his fist had made. "Yeah, punch her like that!"

Growling, Gizmo swatted at the ringed tail of the creature. "Hey!" she barked up at it. "Stop being so mean! Barbs was just being nice and giving us some dinner."

The creature gasped and looked down at the Yorkie's angry tan face. "The ball of fluff talks!"

Her sister swung down the shelves like a monkey on a ladder. "The ball of fluff has a mind of its own!"

"What are you supposed to be?" they asked in unison.

Brows scrunched in confusion, the big furry animal called Willa squinted down at Gizmo, too, as if noticing the dogs for the first time. He seemed to be at a loss for words.

"As for *you*," Gizmo barked up at Willa, "you're just a big bully. What do you think coming in here yelling at us is going to accomplish?"

Willa pointed a thick black finger at the hyena. "This hyena is always in here," he grunted. "Always stealing my food. She has plenty of food back with her pack, but she keeps taking mine. It makes me so *angry*!" He huffed through his nose, his nostrils flaring once more.

Gizmo's tufted ears perked up. "Well, have you ever actually told Barbs that? Or do you just yell at her? 'Cause she seems like the type who does things she's told not to, but she'll help you if you ask nicely. And then you can be friends."

"Who wants to be friends with a hyena?" one of the red sisters crowed, sticking her tongue out in disgust.

"I'd rather let those wild-eyed meerkats ask me questions till I go crazy!"

"Well, I'd rather dive into the swamp and get chased by crocodiles!"

"I'd rather eat nothing but people garbage forever and ever!"

"Even getting pecked by the birds would be more fun!"

Willa huffed as the creatures went on and on about

all the stuff they'd rather do than be friends with the hyena. He still glared at Barbs, but he wasn't shouting anymore. Max heard a gulp and dared a glance over his shoulder: The hyena was sneaking another hot dog.

The sister on the ladder dangled her head upside down. "I bet it would be more fun to go swimming in the farm-animal poo than be friends with that hyena!"

The other red creature screeched with laughter, clutching her furry stomach. "Gross! But not as gross as Barbs!"

Sauntering forward, Gizmo rubbed her head against Willa's ankle. "Don't listen to them," she said. "Barbs isn't that bad. Just relax and talk normal. Okay?"

Willa sighed. "Fine," he grunted. "Barbs, stop coming in here and stealing from me. I need food, too. You don't want me to starve, do you?"

"What about me?" Barbs whined. "I'm hungry!"

Flinging his fat hand back to gesture toward the door, Willa said, "You have a whole enclosure full of hyenas who found where their food is locked up."

"Yeah," Barbs said, "but I don't like them. They laugh too much."

Willa's small eyes narrowed. Then he clutched his gut with one hand and bellowed a laugh. "'They laugh too much'! I never thought I'd hear such a thing." With a shake of his head, he asked, "It's a small trouble to deal with to eat, isn't it? You don't hate me so much that you have to keep stealing my food, do you?"

The hyena flicked her round ears, considering. "I suppose not, Willa. And I don't hate you. I wouldn't keep coming back here if I thought you were a bad gorilla." She backed away from the bag of hot dogs. "I'll leave your food alone from now on."

"Good," Willa said. "Or I'll kill you."

The red creatures giggled, and Willa joined in with his own friendly laughter.

Gizmo sighed. "I suppose that will do for a start," she said. Turning to Barbs, she barked, "And try not to push Willa's buttons again, Barbs! You should know better."

"Yeah, yeah, doggy," said the hyena. Then she cackled her high-pitched, staccato laugh.

Eyes scrunching into confusion once more, Willa looked down at Gizmo and the three other dogs. Only when his eyes came to rest on Boss did his features relax.

"Boss!" the gorilla bellowed, his tone surprisingly happy. "I didn't even notice you there! Why didn't you say something?"

Now it was Max's turn to be confused. Still tensed, ready to flee or fight if needed, he watched as Boss sauntered casually past him to sit at Willa's feet. The big creature bent over and gently patted Boss's head with one of his huge hands.

"I know better than to interfere when you're having a fit, Willa," Boss said with a chuckle. "Unlike some of my companions, anyway." He nodded to Gizmo.

Willa patted Gizmo on the head, too. She licked his palm playfully.

"I like this little fluffball," Willa said. "She's bold."

"So are we!" Rocky yipped, daring to show his head from behind Max. "We were just, uh, waiting to be introduced. Right, Max?"

Max blinked, then looked between Rocky and Boss. "Yeah," he said. "So you know these, um, animals, Boss?"

Boss sniffed. "Willa here is a gorilla. And his loud-mouthed friends are red panda sisters—Scarlett and Rose. Say hi, ladies."

"Nah," one said with a flick of her paw.

"No way," the other said, turning back to sniff at the hole in the wall.

"Bored now!" they chirped as one.

"So is this the friend you were taking us to meet?" Max asked Boss, walking up to the old dog.

"Me?" Willa grunted. "Nah, he wouldn't take you to meet me first. You're probably looking for the Mountain."

The two red pandas snapped to attention. "The Mountain?" they asked as one.

One paw outstretched dramatically, one of the red pandas sang, "Climb the Mountain to touch the sky!"

The other clutched her paws together and fluttered her eyes. "See the Mountain and you will cry!" she sang.

"Atop the Mountain are words so wise!" the first trilled.

In a deep voice, the second sang, "Up on the Mountain is your demise!"

Their song finished, they both bowed to no one in particular.

"We made that up ourselves."

"We're quite talented. Unlike Barbs."

Boss looked warily between the two strange red pandas and Willa. "What's this mountain? Is it an exhibit? I'm looking for an old friend. Is he there?"

Willa grinned, showing off his gleaming fangs. "Oh, yes, the Mountain is where you need to go." Meeting Max's eyes, he added, "That's where you'll find the answers you're looking for."

CHAPTER 12

THE LIVING MOUNTAIN

The big gorilla stepped carefully over Gizmo and opened the top door of the refrigerator. Cold air rushed out as Willa stuck his face inside to examine the contents.

"So where is this Mountain?" Boss asked.

Willa reached inside the freezer and produced a brown-specked banana glazed with ice crystals. "Oh, not far," the gorilla said, sniffing at the frozen banana with his big nostrils. "Scarlett and Rose can take you there. Right, girls?"

One of the red pandas leaped down from the counter, landing between Gizmo and Boss. "Oh, sure," she said.

Her sister jumped down as well, nearly landing on Max. She rose up on her hind legs and sniffed Max's face. Scrunching his nose, Max took a step back.

"Nothing interesting happening in here anyway," she said, turning and falling to all fours, then sauntering away toward the exit.

"If you're not going to smash Barbs—" the first one chirped.

"—then we'll go visit the Mountain and sing more songs!" the other finished.

"Wait," Rocky said, eyeing Boss nervously. "How big is this Mountain? We're not going to have to go on a long hike, are we? My paws are already dead tired."

"I've got no idea, son," Boss said. "I didn't even know there were any mountains around these parts. This is all new to me."

Cackling echoed from behind Max. He turned just in time to see the hyena clamp her jaws shut and try to stifle her laughter.

"Oh, silly doggies," Barbs said. "Everyone knows the Mountain. There you go being all stupid again."

Willa looked down at Barbs. "Are you still here?" he asked before turning his attention back to the contents of the freezer. "Ugh, frozen as solid as a rock. I can't eat this." He tossed the frozen banana over his shoulder. It landed on the counter behind him with a sharp thunk.

"Sorry, Willa!" Barbs rasped. Gobbling up another mouthful of hot dogs, she slipped past Max and Rocky and out the door. "See ya around, doggies! Have fun at the Mountain!" Her laughter echoed through the park as she disappeared into the dark zoo.

"You two going to lead the way?" Boss asked as he shoved himself between the two red pandas. .

"If we have to!" said one.

"You have to," Willa said, his head again in the freezer.

"Then follow us!" said the other.

The two red pandas pranced out the door. Gizmo didn't hesitate even a moment before racing after them, followed by Boss's slow amble.

"Uh, I'm not sure this is the best idea," Rocky said, looking up at Max nervously. "No one ever said anything about mountains, big guy. They're steep and covered with rocks and get supercold. I don't think it's worth it!"

"You're not afraid, are you? You've braved things far worse than a little old mountain. You just spent a day zipping through a strange city on a monorail! You just made friends with a hyena and survived a run-in with a gorilla!" Glancing up at Willa, who was now bent over and smacking around boxes in a cupboard, Max added, "Uh, no offense. You were kind of scary."

"None taken," Willa said, still focused on finding a meal.

"You know, I *have* been pretty brave lately," Rocky said, sauntering toward the door with his head held high. "That train ride was frightening, let me tell you."

"I bet it was," Max said.

Rocky wagged his tail. "I suppose my help is necessary to conquer this mountain. If nothing else, I can inspire you all to be your best."

"Exactly," Max said. "So let's go before we completely lose track of Boss and the girls."

Max galloped out of the bright storeroom, Rocky at his side. Darkness washed over them as they took a quick sampling of the air with their noses, and then swerved left in the direction the others had gone.

Max and Rocky ran behind the food court booths, their paws pounding on asphalt littered with torn tickets and crushed popcorn kernels. The air smelled of sweet human candy and the scents of dogs and red pandas. The braying of a donkey echoed over the empty park, followed by a chicken clucking and scolding the creature to keep quiet. Max figured another animal exhibit must be nearby.

Rounding a trash can, Max finally caught sight of Boss, Gizmo, and the red panda sisters far ahead. They were running through a sort of ghostly playland—there were small, toylike versions of cars on a stage, and in a pool were boats made of pink and blue plastic. Everywhere around them were booths from which brightly colored triangular flags hung, and beyond them were people games, with plush animals dangling from the walls.

Beyond the booths, in front of the wall that surrounded the entire zoo, was a large wooden structure that looked a lot like the monorail track, only it rose in hills and valleys that looped around in a big circle. A series of connected cars were parked on the tracks just beyond a maze of metal poles. Max guessed that maybe people got into the little cars and let themselves get flung all through the tracks, but that seemed awfully scary.

Max rounded another game booth and found Boss, Gizmo, and the two red pandas sitting in front of a sandy enclosure near a building covered with sinister-looking clowns.

And in the middle of the enclosure sat a big, gray boulder.

"They're stopping at that rock," Rocky panted beside Max. "That's not much of a mountain. More like an anthill!"

"Yeah," Max said, "that's not really a mountain, is it? Maybe they were just making fun of us?"

Rocky bristled, his black-and-brown fur standing on end. "Hey, I bet those mean red pandas were trying to say that boulder might as well be a mountain, since me and Gizmo are so small. Ooh, big guy, I'm gonna tell them what's what."

Max and Rocky slowed their pace as they neared the others. Both Boss and Gizmo sat patiently next to the boulder while the two red pandas poked at it and slapped it with their paws.

"Hey!" Rose—or was it Scarlett?—shouted.

"Wake up!" the other trilled.

"You got visitors!" they said together.

For a moment, nothing seemed to happen. The little red pandas continued pounding on the rock.

"What are these two crazy girls up to now?" Rocky asked.

Gizmo leaned down, her hindquarters still high in the air, as she tried to peer beneath the massive boulder. "Maybe Boss's friend lives inside or under this thing."

Boss laughed. "Actually, I think I'm finally understanding why Willa sent us here."

Max crept forward and sniffed the boulder. It didn't smell like a rock, as much as rocks smelled like anything—it smelled vaguely of hay and mud. Its surface was gray dusted with a coating of brown dirt, and it seemed to have a wrinkled, textured pattern running along its length.

In fact, this boulder was starting to not seem like a rock at all. As Max watched, it expanded ever so slightly, like it was breathing.

The Mountain was *alive.*

More movement caught Max's eye. Paws kicking up sand, he backed wildly away from the living boulder to rejoin his friends. As he watched in surprise, something flat and wing-shaped lifted off the wrinkled side and flapped at the air. It was the same gray as the rest of the rock, with its lower, ragged edge tinged a pale pink. Was the Mountain some sort of strange bird?

Then, as Max watched, the entire boulder began to move.

What had once looked like a tall and wide rock shuddered and started to revolve away from the dogs. A cascade of dirt fell off the creature's back as it rolled onto its expansive, round belly, falling like dark rain to the sand below.

What Max guessed was the front of the creature rose up to reveal a thick, tree-trunk-sized leg that had been curled up and hidden beneath its body. It placed one giant, flat foot on the ground, then another. As muscles strained beneath its leathery gray skin, its hindquarters shuddered, and it climbed to its back feet as well.

Max, Rocky, and Gizmo watched in awe as the Mountain rose on its four thick, tree trunk legs, higher and higher until it seemed even bigger than a house. It flicked at the flies buzzing around its backside with a long, skinny tail that ended in a tuft of black fur.

The Mountain turned its massive body to face them, unfurling its floppy, winglike ears and revealing a head unlike any Max had ever seen. Two weary, small, dark eyes peered down at them from behind wrinkled eyelids. But it wasn't the ears or eyes that Max was focused on—it was the long appendage that looked like a pig's snout stretched out to the length of a giant snake that Max assumed was a nose. To top the whole thing off, yellow tusks curved out from either side of the creature's mouth, which was otherwise hidden beneath its great long nose.

It was the biggest, most amazing animal Max had ever seen.

"Oh, wow," Rocky whispered. "It's an ellie—ellefff—one of those big things! Get a load of its nose!"

"This is an African elephant," Boss said. "And that *nose* is called a *trunk*."

The trunk moved around in the air like a snake, rising up and bending this way and that, tasting the air. The elephant blinked the sleep out of its eyes as it took in the motley crew crowded at its feet.

"You're finally up!" one of the red pandas chirped, waving her paws in the air.

"About time!" the other said, circling one of the elephant's wide, flat feet.

"Are you going to stomp things?" the first asked.

"Ew, I hope not. I don't want to get squished—then I'd have a snout as ugly as Barbs'!"

The two red pandas laughed.

The great big elephant groaned. "I'm afraid there won't be any stomping today, Scarlett and Rose. You'll have to get your entertainment elsewhere."

"Aw!" they cried in unison.

One red panda turned to the other. "Wanna go throw nuts at the zebras?"

"Sure!" her sister replied. "Maybe they'll stampede again."

In a flash of red fur and giggles, the two red pandas scooted around the elephant and vanished into the dark outside the enclosure.

"Good-bye!" Gizmo yipped. "Those two aren't very nice, are they?"

The elephant groaned, a deep, throaty sound. "They're

too energetic for their own good," he said with a shake of his head and a flap of his giant ears. "I could do without them always trying to wake me up."

"Don't blame them," Max said, bowing his head as he walked forward. "We were looking for a friend of Boss here. The gorilla Willa said we could find answers at the Mountain. So, I guess...you're the Mountain?"

The elephant trumpeted a laugh through his trunk, his eyes disappearing behind a cascade of eyelid folds. "That's what they call me these days, little Labrador."

"And no wonder I didn't know what they were going on about," Boss barked up at the big elephant. "Here I thought I was looking for my old friend Mortimer, and they kept chirping about mountains."

"Could that be...?" the Mountain asked, his tail flicking in surprise. His trunk curled downward, the slitted nostrils at its end huffing as it smelled each of the dogs in turn. "Boss!" the Mountain exclaimed. "As I live and breathe, I never thought I'd see you again. The zoo is hardly the most hospitable place these days."

"I wasn't planning to come back here, old friend," Boss said. "But I got these pups here who are trying to find their people. I thought you might be able to help."

"I see," the Mountain said, looking down on Max, Rocky, and Gizmo each in turn. As he did, his trunk reached down and gripped a handful of sand. As Max watched in amazement, the elephant raised his trunk high over his head and let the sand cascade over his back and sides.

"Mmm," the Mountain said, closing his eyes once more in bliss. "Nice and cool."

"You might could do for a bath, old friend," Boss said, scrunching his nose.

The Mountain flapped his ears, sending the sand that had gotten trapped in their nooks falling down. "Maybe," he grumbled. "I just haven't felt like it lately, is all."

Wagging his tail, Max bowed his head before the great beast. "It's nice to meet you," he said. "Sorry we woke you up."

"Sleep is easy enough to find," the Mountain said, his eyes still flicking over the three dogs. "Friends, less so."

"You looked bigger on the TV," Rocky said, shaking his head.

Gizmo nipped the Dachshund's side. "Rocky!" she scolded. Then, wagging her nub of a tail, she barked, "You're plenty big! You're the most impressive animal I've ever seen! And I bet you're supersmart and never forget *anything*. That's what they say about elephants, anyway."

"It's true, I am intelligent," the Mountain said. "More intelligent than any other animal in this park, in fact." He snorted through his long trunk, the sound trilling like a horn. "All thanks to Praxis."

"Praxis?" Max asked. "What's that?"

"It's a long, complicated story, little Labrador," the Mountain said. "The sort of story that an elephant can't tell when thirsty." He turned slowly, gracefully, and walked off toward a trough set to one side of the enclosure. His trunk dunked into the water there, and he slurped it up.

"He *drinks* through his *nose*," Rocky whispered. "Gross!"

Hearing him, the Mountain cast a glance back, then raised his trunk out of the trough and shot a jet of water at the little Dachshund. It caught Rocky smack in the center of his chest and blasted him back a half-dozen feet.

"I don't drink through my nose, silly pup," the Mountain said before going back to drinking his fill. "But I can shoot water from it just fine."

Max couldn't help but laugh at Rocky standing there, soaking wet and shivering with wide, startled eyes. Gizmo giggled, then ran to help lick the water off his mussed black-and-brown fur.

Rocky spat out water that had gotten into his mouth, then sneezed. "Sorry," Rocky said. "Didn't mean to insult you, big guy."

The Mountain flicked his tail. "No worries." Dunking his trunk in the trough again, he slurped up more water, then curled the end of his trunk so that it was aimed toward his mouth. He shot another stream of water into his mouth, smacking his gray lips as he slaked his thirst.

"Now, where were we?" the Mountain asked as he turned his attention back to Max and his friends.

"I believe you were fixin' to tell the young ones here your story," Boss said.

"Ah, yes," the Mountain said. "As you can imagine, I didn't always sleep alone in an abandoned amusement park in the middle of a zoo. Or not this zoo, anyway. I was born long ago in a zoo far away from here, somewhere to the north, where the climate is colder. When I was still very young, several humans came to visit me. They stopped by every day over the course of two weeks, peering into my ears and sticking me with needles and sometimes just watching me play in my enclosure."

"They sound like Vet!" Rocky barked.

The Mountain took another noseful of sand and let it rain over his head. "Not quite. They were scientists, and they wanted to make sure I was healthy before they purchased me. I was soon separated from my mother and the other elephants of the zoo and transported to this city in the back of a truck. It was a long, lonely, bumpy ride, but when the back doors of the truck opened, they herded me into a big field next to white buildings. I was still inside a fence, but I was no longer in a zoo—I no longer had human children throwing peanuts at me while laughing."

"But you were the only elephant there?" Gizmo asked as she curled up in the sand beneath the Mountain. "That sounds lonely."

"I suppose," the Mountain said. "I think about that a lot now, but at the time the scientists kept me so busy that I never did much more than play with the trainers, eat, and sleep. They'd bring me into one of the big white buildings and have me walk through a maze until I found a big silver bowl of food, and the next day into a different maze with a different path to follow. They would show me images on cards, and I would have to pick up the matching item off the floor with my trunk. It all seemed like games at the time, but of course they were nothing but tests. And I wasn't the only one—there were eighteen of us test subjects in all, all of us different animals. We bonded as much as our various species could while we rested in our enclosures."

His dark eyes crinkled shut as he remembered more, and his deep voice grew quiet. "Then, I was... changed."

"How?" Max asked softly.

"I was taken to a big room filled with metal cages. High above my head were strange metal bars with claws at the end. The scientists left me there and watched me from the other side of a glass window. Then, as they watched, large noises filled the room. I was scared, I remember. I leaped up onto my hind legs and slammed my front feet down. I stomped in a circle and flapped my ears. But they just watched me as the noises became too much to bear. I even slammed against the doors and the glass, trying to escape—but there was no way out.

"Then, in a flash of light from the claws on the ceiling, I felt electricity and warmth run all throughout my body."

The big elephant's entire body shuddered at the memory, the sides of his chest heaving as he took in heavy breaths. "Over the next few weeks, I started to change. They took me to the mazes, but instead of futilely following them, I just smashed through the walls, taking the quickest route to my prize of food—it seemed the most logical thing to do. They tried to flash their cards at me, but I could remember the notches on each card's side so well that I was able to select their object of choice even before they showed me the picture. They tried hiding behind a screen so I couldn't see the back of the cards before they showed me the images, but even then I could hear them saying the names of the objects aloud to one another as they recorded the data. I was still a step ahead of them."

Max gaped. "Are you saying... that you understood people speech?"

"What?" Rocky yipped. "No way, big guy. That's not possible!"

"It's certainly possible," the Mountain said. "And that's not all I learned. I can even observe small details and discover someone's secrets."

Eyes focused, the Mountain shook his great head, flapped his ears, and looked down at Rocky. "You're a Dachshund, and judging from the sag of your skin, until recently you never knew anything but the luxury of a home. You were well fed and well loved and had attentive, healthy people to take care of you."

"Wow, that's right!" Rocky said, peering at his friends in amazement. "And yes, I loved my people. I still miss them." His tail drooped, and he lowered his head.

The Mountain poked Rocky's belly with the tip of his trunk. "It also appears that you were once quite portly for an animal of your size and breed, but you've lost a lot of weight recently. Probably because you've had to travel so far from home."

"Hey!" Rocky barked. "I don't know what *portly* means, but I'm pretty sure I was never it."

The Mountain turned his gaze to Gizmo. "You, too, have come a long way, little Yorkshire Terrier. If I'm not mistaken—and I rarely am since undergoing the Praxis procedure—you prefer the outdoors. Your fur is healthy but hasn't been groomed in a long while. From your sunny general demeanor, I expect you ran away from your people in a fit of excitement, and have been looking for them ever since—longer, even, than your companions have been searching for their people."

"Wow!" Gizmo said. "That's really impressive. Did this Praxis thing make you magic?" She went wide-eyed. "Can you read our thoughts?"

The Mountain chuckled, the sound like distant thunder. "Not magic. Just too smart for my own good." Staring at Max, he went on. "And you, young Labrador Retriever, must be the leader of these two. I might have thought Boss was the alpha in this group, him being a natural leader and all, but the two small dogs' body language toward you suggests a familiarity with you that they lack with our Australian Shepherd friend, not to mention a clear deference on your opinion." His trunk rose and thoughtfully curled up beneath his mouth. "You also have an air of single-mindedness about you, the kind of mental state that would be absolutely necessary to inspire a dog to travel across the country—braving all sorts of dangers—in search of his owners. Looking at all the scratches and bite marks on you, at how thin you've become recently, it is painfully clear that no one and nothing will stop you until you find your people."

Max bowed his head. "It's true. It's all true. I owe it to my people to find them. They must be so lonely without me. I know I miss them very much."

All the dogs fell silent. Images of Charlie and Emma flashed in Max's mind, memories of them playing fetch with the ragged, old tennis ball in the fields behind their farmhouse, or leaping into the nearby pond on hot summer days.

Max shook his head clear of the distant memories. "But how did you know all that?" he asked. "If it's not some sort of magic trick."

The Mountain flapped his ears. "Observing and deducing. It's just logic. Simple, really. Or simple if you've been mentally enhanced by Praxis."

Rocky peered back and forth conspiratorially. "So,

uh, let us know, big guy—where can we get some of this Praxis stuff?"

"Trust me," the Mountain said, "you do not want it."

"All right, all right," Boss grunted. He dropped to his belly and rested his head on his front paws. "Enough with the theatrics, Mortimer—I mean, Mountain. The pups here need help."

The Mountain opened his mouth wide in a yawn. "It will have to wait," he said, starting to swing his massive body away from them. "My drink of water has awakened my hunger. I must seek out some vegetation to eat. A pleasure to meet the three of you. Thank you for the mild diversion; it was fun to tell my story to newcomers. For a brief while, at least."

Max opened his jaws to ask the big elephant to stay, but he found he didn't know what he might say to make the creature listen. If his friend Boss couldn't get him to help...

Moonlight shone down on the Mountain's broad back, and that was when something caught Max's eye—a tattoo half-hidden in the folds of his neck. And not just any tattoo, but the same three-ringed symbol that Max kept seeing everywhere.

The same symbol that had also been tattooed on Madame Curie.

"That symbol! The three rings!" Max barked, jumping toward the Mountain. "I've seen it before."

The elephant stopped moving, one of his great feet held up in the air as he looked back at Max. "In the city, you mean?" he asked.

"The three rings," Max said quickly. "They were on the neck of my friend Madame Curie. She was the one who told me to follow the symbol, which is what led us here."

Dropping his foot, the Mountain swung back around. His entire demeanor had changed—his ears perked up as much as they could, his eyes opened wide.

"Madame?" the Mountain asked softly. "A black Labrador?"

"Yes, that's her!" Max barked.

"You knew her?" Rocky asked.

"'Knew'?" the Mountain repeated. His eyes wrinkled and his trunk drooped. "Knew. As in past tense. You mean to tell me she's passed on."

"Yes," Max said softly, his own tail lowering sadly. "We went looking for her, but before we found her, another dog had hurt her badly." He remembered her lying on the floor of a dark, abandoned conference room, nothing but skin and bones. He shuddered at the memory. "She died."

"I see," the Mountain said. "I did indeed know her. She was one of us—one of the eighteen. She was a very good dog. She was a very good . . . friend."

Before Max could speak to tell the Mountain how sorry he was, the elephant's entire body began to tremble. Stomping his front feet, he raised his trunk high and let out a loud, piercing shriek that echoed through the park. Distantly, Max could hear other animals hollering and yowling and screeching in response.

Body stiff, Boss backed away. "Get back," he warned Max, Rocky, and Gizmo in a low voice. "He's having a fit."

Rocky and Gizmo took a few steps backward, but Max stood his ground. He understood being upset about Madame, and even though he didn't fully understand the elephant's reaction, he shared his grief about their lost friend.

"Alone!" the Mountain bellowed into the night sky. "I'm so terribly alone!"

"But that's not true!" Gizmo barked. "There are animals all around you."

The elephant's massive sides heaved as he took in deep, gulping breaths. "You don't understand," he cried. "You'll never understand. No one can, except those of us who were at the lab. And now another one of us is gone forever." Shaking his head, he moaned, "I came to this zoo to be with other African elephants—my kind, who are like me—but I was too much smarter than them, too different. They shunned me. They may have looked like me on the outside, but they weren't like me where it counts, deep inside. So I left them and wandered the zoo until I found this empty enclosure."

The Mountain used his trunk to wrench a trash can

up from the ground, then flung it into the night. The metal can clattered against the dark struts that held up the twisting steel tracks nearby. "Do you think I want to sleep alone in the shadow of a roller coaster with no one to talk to who understands me? Do you think I enjoy this life?"

Max sat and watched the elephant as he calmed down and walked back toward the group. "You feel sorry for yourself," Max said.

The elephant huffed. "I do. I do feel sorry for myself. Is that so bad?"

"Yes, it is." Max began cleaning his front right paw.

Beside him, Rocky said, "Hey, pal, no reason to upset our friend here. Have you seen how big his feet are?"

But Max ignored him and addressed only the Mountain. "Madame never felt sorry for herself. She fought until the end. The only thing that stopped her was her death. Otherwise she'd be fighting still."

The Mountain stared down at the Labrador silently for a moment and then broke into bitter laughter. "Clever of you, little Lab. Trying to manipulate my emotions to get what you want."

"That wasn't what I was—" Max began to protest.

A short, sharp burst of noise from the elephant's trunk cut him off. "Oh, don't bother denying it. It was a smart move, to try to appeal to my pride. But you see, I no longer have any pride. I gave that up long ago. Now I just eat and drink and wait to go to that place where

Madame has already gone. I don't even bother to bathe anymore. What's the point?"

"For someone so smart, you sure are acting dumb!" Gizmo barked, prancing forward to stand beside Max. "Madame died wanting to help other animals. And you just sit here feeling sorry for yourself."

Max stood again. "It's not too late. Maybe there are still others. If we go back to the lab, perhaps we can find some of the other test subjects and you can be with them again."

"Nice try," the Mountain said, pacing back and forth in front of the group, "but no. The labs are dangerous. There isn't any reason to go back, and the smartest of us know that. Only a fool would go there."

"Then we are foolish dogs," Max said, "because that's where we're heading next."

The Mountain stopped his pacing. "You likely saw the laboratory building on your way here. You can't read the humans' writing, but I'm sure you can recognize a symbol if you've seen it often enough. Apparently you already knew where it is you must go. You came here to ask me questions just to torture me."

Max stretched. "Not at all, Mountain. We just needed to know how safe it would be. Now that we know, we'd best be going. We've wasted enough time here."

The great elephant stomped forward, much quicker than Max thought a creature so big could move. Eyes wide and ears unfurled, the Mountain lowered his head as close as he could to stare directly into Max's eyes. "Give up your plans of ever finding your humans, dog," he trumpeted. "Unless the mutated virus that escaped the lab is mutated further, into a safe form, the humans can't risk going near you. If you carry the virus, it could hurt them. And these days, most of us animals *do* have the virus!"

Rocky's head popped up from behind Boss's back. "A *mew*-what?" he asked. "And a virus? I don't feel sick. What are you going on about, big guy?"

The Mountain let out an exasperated sigh and raised his head again. "How can I put this in terms you dogs can understand? You three have all visited veterinarians, yes?"

"Oh, sure!" Rocky said. "That was Vet's name. My family's pack leader, I mean. He was called that."

The elephant said, "Exactly. Vet. That name means he is an animal doctor. When you were there, did he sometimes poke you with needles?"

"Oh, yeah," Gizmo said, scrunching up her snout. "I hated when my people took me to that place. The woman there seemed so nice, but then she always jabbed me with something sharp."

"Of course, little terrier. No one likes being stabbed with sharp things." The elephant was beginning to sound less agitated. "But those needles were used to give you medicine to make you healthy. Not so at the lab where I used to live."

“What do you mean?” Gizmo asked.

“Praxis was a two-step process. First we were infected with a form of a virus that is harmless to animals. It basically sleeps inside you until activated. That virus is then exposed to an electrical process, and the virus awakens and changes our brains. It was the, uh, *medicine* that made us smarter. It worked wonders on all eighteen of us. You’ve seen what I can do—that was only the tip of the intellectual iceberg.” The Mountain’s eyes slowly looked among the four dogs. “But something changed in the virus serum—in the medicine. An airborne form of it was accidentally released from the labs and spread for hundreds and hundreds of miles and infected all sorts of animals. Soon, the virus mutated into a new form that could spread to humans. And though the virus doesn’t harm us animals, a few people started to get sick.”

Trembling again, the elephant took in great, heaving gasps.

“Hey, there, Mountain,” Boss said, his gravelly voice soothing. “Calm down, my friend.”

“Why bother? Don’t you get it?” the Mountain asked. “All my friends are gone. I can never be like the other elephants. And because of this Praxis process—this supposed medicine—the people who could have fixed me had to flee. Now they can never come back!”

A desperate determination filled the Mountain’s oncekind eyes. Trunk snaking high into the air, the Mountain let out another deafening trumpet of noise. Then, as the four dogs watched, stunned, the great big elephant turned and began running. The Mountain charged right through a flimsy wooden ticket booth, utterly razing it as he thundered past and into the inky darkness behind the roller coaster.

"I'm going to destroy those forsaken labs!" the Mountain's voice echoed into the night. "I'm going to make sure no one ever gets hurt again!"

CHAPTER 13

AN UNEXPECTED ALLY

"Wait!" Max barked. Shaking off his shock, he raced after the rampaging elephant. "Please come back! We didn't mean to upset you!"

He didn't get more than a few steps before Boss barked at him, "Let the elephant go!"

Max skidded to a halt near the wreck of the ticket booth, listening as the Mountain's thunderous footsteps faded away. The shaking of the ground gradually lessened.

"Oh!" Gizmo cried, racing over to Max. "What are we going to do? You said we need to go to the lab to find our people, but he's going to destroy it." She looked at the mess of broken boards that had been the ticket booth. "Just like he destroyed *that*."

"I don't know," Max admitted. "But we have to get to the labs before the Mountain does. That place holds the key to finding out why the people left. That's why Madame sent us here."

"Are you kidding?" Rocky yelped, waddling up behind them. "You heard the elephant—that place is dangerous and full of viruses and mutations! Boss said the same thing." He peered back over his shoulder. "Didn't you, Boss?"

The old Shepherd nodded as he trotted up. "I never knew the whole story until this evening, but I sure remember the Mountain going on and on about why we all needed to stay far away from those three rings. My pack leaders seemed scared of them, too, even though they drove right toward where everything began."

"That's why we have to go there," Max said. "It all began there. So whatever it will take to end it must be there, too. At least, that's what Madame must have thought."

Max's mind raced. Maybe the long run to the laboratory would calm the elephant. Maybe the Mountain wouldn't even be able to get in to destroy anything—a wooden booth was a lot more fragile than a building made of stone. Or maybe—

"Hey!" a distant voice called.

Max almost didn't pay attention. In the wake of the Mountain's tantrum, other animals throughout the park had all started making noise. Not too far away he could hear the deep, throaty yowls of some very large cats and the trills of exotic birds, mixed with distant braying and manic screeching.

Then the voice called out again.

"Hey, you dogs! Aren't you supposed to have good hearing? Get your furry butts over here!"

Max's floppy ears perked up. "Shh," he whispered to Rocky and Gizmo. "Someone is calling us." The voice was coming from his right, past the game booths and from the direction where he'd smelled farm animals earlier.

At Max's side, Boss growled. "I hear her, too. It's coming from the petting zoo. That's where little ones went to touch friendly animals. That area is just past the carnival rides."

"Maybe it's Barbs?" Rocky asked. "I could go for some more hot dogs right about now."

"I hope it's not those red pandas again," Gizmo said. "I really didn't like them. And I like *everybody*."

"Stop your yapping and get over here, already!" It was a deep voice, but it definitely belonged to a girl.

Max padded forward, leading the way with Boss at his side and the small dogs trailing just behind. They slipped between two of the game booths and walked beneath what looked like a great big umbrella. Dozens of swings hung down on long chains, gently creaking in the wind.

Up ahead, his nose told him, was a farm.

It wasn't much compared to the farm Max had grown up on. There was no rolling pasture, no field after field of planted crops. Instead, a big red barn sat open in the back, in front of which were dozens of pens surrounded by small white fences. In one, several goats lay sleeping. Sheep nuzzled against one another, while nearby chickens crept around a coop, pecking at feed. From the dark depths of the barn came the sound of animal snores.

The whole place was earthy and musty. It didn't look much like Max's old farm home, but it sure smelled like it—the air was thick with hay and animals and even the aroma of all the animal manure that had gone uncleaned without the people around.

As the four dogs neared the pens, a few of the chickens squawked, flapped their wings, and stumbled toward their coop.

"Predators!"

"Run for your lives!"

"Flee! Flee in *terror*!"

"Wait!" Gizmo called out to them. "We're not here to hurt you!"

But the birds didn't listen. In a flash, they were all huddled together inside their little house.

"Forget them," the voice called out. "Ever since a couple of the big cats came by and ate a few chickens and one of the goats, they've been paranoid."

Next to the chicken coop ran an old wooden fence. Max peered through the slats and saw a mostly empty pen. On one side was a long, low trough half filled with water, next to which was another trough with a few traces of animal feed. Opposite the troughs was a small wood enclosure that reminded Max of a doghouse, only the entire front wall was missing. Hay covered the floor and was mounded up inside the small home.

And lying on the mound of hay beneath the roof of the little house was a fat pink pig.

"Are you the one who's been calling us?" Max asked.

The pig snorted. "Yes. It's about time you listened and came over. I've been calling for ages and ages."

Rocky nosed Max's side. "Don't mean to interrupt you, buddy, but did the pig here just say some big cats came and ate the smaller animals?"

Grunting a laugh, the pig shook her head. "Should have seen it. Feathers flying everywhere while a lady lion pounced from the darkness. The chickens were so scared. Ha!" She grunted again. "All I can say is, better them than me. Of course, I'm smart enough to stay in the shadows."

"Poor chickens," Gizmo said.

"Poor us!" Rocky cried. "I think we should leave for the labs right away!"

Getting to her feet, the big pig waddled over to the fence. "That's why I've been calling you. I couldn't help hearing the commotion going on over there with the Mountain—'I'm all alone! Boo-hoo!' "

"It's sad!" Gizmo said from beside Rocky.

"Sad is having to listen to that elephant whine day in and day out."

"We'd best be going," Max said, turning. "I don't think we can help you."

"No, it is *I* who can help *you.* If you lot are going to the laboratories, you're going to need more information. You're going to need help getting in and navigating the hallways." She flicked one of her trotters at herself. "And here I am."

"You?" Boss asked.

"You?" Rocky said. "Look at you! You're a pig!"

"Be nice, Rocky!" Gizmo said.

"Yes, I am a pig. Is that so bad?"

Boss rose up and hooked his front paws over the top of the fence. "I ain't seen you around before. What would a pig know about the labs?"

With a sigh, the pig turned to the side and lowered her head. "I'm not just any pig. I'm Gertrude. And take a look."

Standing over Rocky, Max peered down at the pig's back. At first he didn't notice anything—her pink skin was mottled with spots of thick brown dirt—but then he saw it.

The three rings tattooed on her neck.

"You were one of the test subjects," Max said.

"Your powers of deduction amaze me," Gertrude drawled. "Yes, I, too, was one of the animals from the laboratories. Despite what the Mountain implied, he's not the only smart animal here at the zoo. He's just the biggest, loudest, and whiniest. In fact, I'd wager I'm

smarter than even him, what with that brute always moping around making a spectacle of himself when he should be doing his best to not draw attention."

"You don't *smell* smart," Rocky said, sniffing loudly. "Just dirty."

Gizmo tilted her head. "Why did the Mountain say he was alone if another of his friends was so close by?"

"Friends?" Gertrude snorted. "Oh, trust me, dog, I *tried* to make nice with that creature. Were we not alike? Were we not both born into our new states of elevated intelligence together? As he told you, no one here—especially not mere dogs—can understand what it's like to be as keenly perceptive as we are!"

"Maybe Praxis just makes you say too many big words?" Rocky asked, but Gizmo shushed him.

"I tried to reason with him, tried to persuade him to go back to the laboratories with me, but he always refused. Not for looking back, that one—oh, no. Finally he told me he no longer desired my company, and he refused to talk to me ever again. Refused me! The smartest pig who has ever walked the earth!" She snorted. "The arrogance of that one pachyderm cannot be overstated."

"If it was such a big deal, why didn't you just go by yourself?" Rocky asked.

The pig grunted another laugh. "Silly, stupid dog. Your sort can go running through the streets because you've got sharp teeth and claws and can defend yourselves. If a predator sees you, it has to decide whether a fight is worthwhile. But if a predator sees *me,* it just sees a ham lunch." She shook her head. "With all the hungry animals filling the streets these days...No, I am going nowhere without an escort."

Max wasn't sure what to think of the pig. She wasn't exactly friendly, and she seemed like she thought the dogs were too dumb to speak to with respect. He was rapidly growing tired of other animals treating him like he was stupid. Still, if she knew about Praxis, the symbol, and the labs...

"What if we escorted you?" he asked. "With the four of us, no one would dare bother you."

Gertrude sniffed, then turned away, leaving Max face-to-face with her broad backside. "No, I don't think so," she said as she slogged back toward her little house. "I considered sharing my knowledge with you, but I can already tell that you four are unworthy of the...of the gifts of Praxis. Taking mutts like you there would be downright absurd." She climbed up onto her pile of hay, walked in a tight circle, then plopped her considerable bulk down. "In a word, you lot are too, well, *dumb.*"

Gizmo growled. "Add pigs to the list of zoo animals I don't like," she whispered. "Why do so many of them have such bad attitudes?"

"Could be that the cages make them irritable," Boss grunted, his teeth bared. "But I don't think that's the case with this one. I think this is a case of bad manners, plain and simple. Maybe all this Gertrude is good for *is* a ham dinner."

"I agree," Max muttered, "but we need her help. There's got to be a way to convince her we're not...too dumb."

"Of *course* we aren't dumb, Max!" Rocky said. "She just got the wrong impression, is all. Watch me turn this around."

The little Dachshund crawled underneath the fence, belly to dirt, then waddled to the center of the pen. He cleared his throat.

Gertrude ignored him, choosing instead to nibble at her flank.

"Ah-HEM!" Rocky tried again.

The big pig sighed and looked at him. "You're still here? Did I not dismiss the four of you?"

"I don't think you've given us a fair shake, big gal," Rocky said. "We're a lot smarter than you suspect. Just watch."

"Roll over!" he barked. With a flourish of his head, Rocky rolled over dramatically, then jumped up onto his feet. Without waiting a beat, he yelled, "Beg!" then jumped up onto his hind legs and held his front paws in the air. Then, without dropping to all fours, he jumped into the air, spun around, and howled, "Hiiiiii-*yah*!"

"Woo-hoo!" Gizmo called. With her front paws propped on the bottom slat of the fence, she had a perfect view.

"Thank you, thank you," Rocky said, bowing his head toward Gertrude and the dogs. "Any requests from the audience?"

"Play dead!" Boss barked.

"My specialty!" Rocky closed his eyes and took in a deep breath. Then, after a pause, he opened his eyes wide, gasped, then yipped as though he'd been hurt. Stumbling forward, his head lolled back and forth as he let out a long, low howl.

Finally, he collapsed onto his side and lay there, eyes closed and tongue hanging out.

Max, Gizmo, and Boss barked their approval.

"That..." Gertrude drawled.

Rocky opened one eye and peered at her.

"...was a complete waste of time," the pig finished. "All dogs can do tricks. Now, how about you do *this* trick: *Leave me alone*." The pig snuffled and rested her massive head on the ground. "I'm finalizing my plans for a mud bath addition to my pen. If I tear down the fence and take over the goats' pen...but that requires moving them in with the sheep."

Tail drooping, Rocky crawled back under the fence. "Sorry, buddy," he said to Max. "I really thought that would work."

Glaring at Gertrude, Max barked, "You know what? That's fine. We'll just go by ourselves. We can follow the signs we saw in the city. We don't need some pig slowing us down, anyway."

At that, Gertrude's eyes went wide. She labored to her feet and over to the fence. "No!" she squealed. "You're not worthy! You will *not* go there!"

"And who's going to stop us?" Boss growled. "You?"

Gertrude blinked her beady eyes. "What I *mean* to say is that you cannot go there without an escort."

"Why?" Max said. "Let's go, Boss. This is a waste of time."

"Because the elephant was right! It's dangerous! And as you four are too simpleminded to listen to warnings of danger, then you need someone in the know. You need *moi.*" The pig grimaced in a way that Max thought was supposed to be friendly. "I am feeling suddenly charitable, so I will chaperone your group and make sure nothing horrific happens."

"Just a minute ago you said you'd never help us," Max said. "Why change your mind?"

"I bet it was my 'play dead,' " Rocky said. "It always wins 'em over."

"I thought it was great!" Gizmo said.

"Let's just say that your desperate attempt to impress me has made me take pity on you." The pig jutted her snout into the air. "However, if I provide you with this huge, enormous, grand favor, then I will need a favor in return."

Boss sighed. "Favor, huh? You need us to get you to the lab more than we need you, piggy."

Breathing noisily, Gertrude glared at the old dog.

"Ah, so you know your way around the place and how to get through the doors, do you?"

Boss glared back.

"Exactly," Gertrude said. "So how about it. A favor for you, then a favor for me?"

"Oh, whatever," Rocky said. "Sure, we'll do you a favor."

"No, the word of the little ones isn't worth anything," the pig sniffed. "I want *his.*" She pointed her trotter at Max. "The alpha makes me this promise and you get what you want."

Max bowed his head. "All right, Gertrude. You have my promise. You do us this favor, and when you need a favor from us, we'll help."

Gertrude laughed. "Excellent! Then there's no time to waste. If we're going to beat that rampaging elephant there, we'll need to leave right away."

"But how will we possibly get there before him?" Gizmo asked.

Rocky's spiky tail wagged. "Easy!" he said. "I think it's time the rest of you learned to love riding the monorail!"

CHAPTER 14

RETURN TO THE CITY

Gertrude sauntered over to a gate on the front of her pen, which she unlatched with her snout. It swung open with a creak of old hinges, and the pig joined the four dogs outside the petting zoo.

"All right, dogs," she said, trotting purposefully toward the amusement park. "Take me to the monorail. I suggest the golden Lab and the old Shepherd walk on either side of me—the broadest parts of my body would make for the easiest targets—while the little fluffy one walks in front and the waddly one with the tricks can take up the rear."

Rocky scrunched his snout up in disgust. "Uh, no offense, big gal, but I don't really want to spend the whole trip staring at your backside."

The pig sniffed as she walked past the group and onto the asphalt. "Fine, then both you little dogs can walk in front. It's not as though you could protect me from a rear attack, anyway."

Max and Boss bounded forward to either side of Gertrude, then matched her purposeful stride. Rocky and Gizmo galloped to get in front of her. For such an enormous pig, she could move at a fast trot if she wanted to.

"We have names, you know," Gizmo said, looking back. "I'm Gizmo, this is Rocky—"

"And the old one is Boss, and the leader is Max—yes, yes, I know. I heard you all talking to one another." They passed under the shadows of the giant umbrella and its swings. "Let's keep our voices down until we've left the premises, shall we? There are night predators afoot."

"Good idea," Max said, grateful not to have to listen to the pig talk anymore.

Everyone fell silent.

🐾

"Oh, wow," Gizmo said, stopping in her tracks. "The Mountain must be really strong."

They had reached the gravel pathway in front of the zoo's entrance without much incident, but it was no longer how they'd left it. The pebbles on the path were scattered over the grass now, and a big crack ran up the wall next to the walkway between the zoo and the parking lot.

"*Hoo!* Who's there?"

Max recognized the voice as Oliver's, but at first when he peered at the log on which the owl had perched earlier, he couldn't make out the creature atop it.

"It's just us, Oliver!" Gizmo said. She left Gertrude's side to trot forward, then jumped up to press her front legs against the smooth log. "Did you happen to see an upset elephant run by?"

Two wide yellow eyes opened, reflecting the lights of the park. The bundle of brown atop the log shifted, and Oliver flapped his wings, revealing himself.

"Oh, good, Boss and friends have returned," Oliver said as he nipped at his feathers. "Yes, the Mountain tore past here, all right. I thought he was going to bring the place down the way he barreled through the exits! He's long gone, though. He can move pretty fast for something that big."

Gertrude snorted. "What a horribly childish display," she said. "How unbecoming."

"*Hoo!*" Oliver screeched. In a flash his brown wings unfurled, and he lifted off from the log and swirled above the dogs' heads before landing atop the wall. "What are you doing with the pig?"

"Not that it's your concern, Oliver," Boss grumbled, "but we're fixin' to take her to her old home so she can help my friends here."

Oliver blinked his big eyes. "You can't trust that pig!" he said. "Everyone here knows that. She's a sneak. Plus, she thinks she's better than everyone 'cause she can understand people talk."

Huffing, Gertrude shoved past Boss and Max and trotted toward the partially destroyed exit from the zoo. "Ignore him," she said. "He's just mad because I told the rodents in the farm area how to hide when the predators are about."

"That was nice of you, big gal," Rocky said. "Which doesn't seem like you."

Gertrude peered back at them. "Mostly I just wanted the rats to stop digging through my pen, which they agreed to in exchange for my knowledge. But I guess helping them was nice, yes. Now, can you four hurry up and resume your protective positions?"

As Max, Boss, Rocky, and Gizmo darted forward to circle Gertrude, Oliver hooted at them from above. Then he unfurled his wide wings once more and flung himself forward to soar on the breeze. "Don't say I didn't warn you!" he called back as he disappeared into the night sky.

The dogs and Gertrude padded as quietly as they could over the cool tile floor in the building that led back outside. Some of the glass displays that once held animal posters now lay shattered on the floor, and the racks had been tipped over, their pamphlets and magazines strewn everywhere.

Only then did Max realize that where once had stood three gated entryways was now one big gaping hole. The Mountain had stormed right through the two middle pillars, exploding them into pieces of jagged plaster. The three green metal gates lay twisted and broken beneath the streetlights out in the parking lot.

"We really need to get to the labs fast," Max said, bounding forward and leaping over the destruction. "If the Mountain can do this here, he can do it there, too!"

"Hey!" Gertrude complained. "No running ahead! I told you to flank me, remember?" She shook her head in disgust. "Dumb dogs."

Boss bared his teeth at her. "How about you pick up your pace if you're that worried, piggy?"

The big pig grunted. "I can only trot so fast. Don't rush me."

It was a short jaunt across the dark parking lot to the concrete staircase in the trees, and then up the stairs they went. Gertrude was gasping for breath by the time they reached the platform at the top. "What a barbaric torture, to make people scale these small mountains before letting them go anywhere!"

The waiting platform was much the same as the one they'd explored back in the city: plastic benches in rows beneath glass enclosures, with a glass wall surrounding the edges and a bumpy plastic divider at the track's edge. Gertrude plopped herself down alongside one of the benches, and Max, Rocky, and Gizmo walked over to the edge of the platform. Boss stayed near the pig, watching over her.

"It's even bigger than it looks from inside," Gizmo said, looking down over the zoo.

Max could only make out the shadows of buildings and moonlight glittering against the water in the pools and swimming holes. Even from up on the platform he still heard the night calls of prowling predators, the screeching of monkeys, and the hooting of more owls like Oliver. The musks and odors of the place wafted up on the breeze, filling Max's nostrils and overloading his senses.

Rocky waddled back toward Gertrude and Boss. "The zoo was interesting for a while, but I gotta say I'm tired of dealing with wild animals. I'm not gonna miss that place."

"Maybe we can come back and visit during the day, when it's not so dangerous?" Gizmo asked Max.

"Maybe," Max said. "But first we find our people. That's still the most important thing."

Gertrude grunted from where she lay. "And don't forget my favor. It's important, too, remember."

"Don't worry," Max said. "We won't forget."

They all had to wait only a few moments more before the floor beneath them began to vibrate and a rush of wind came to tangle their fur. Bright white headlights glared blindingly strong. Max backed away from the bumpy yellow edge, his body trembling with instinctual fear even though he knew what was coming. Rocky and Gizmo trembled at his side.

Then, with a hiss of brakes, the silver train pulled to a stop in front of them. All the doors opened, and the lighted symbols above each one began to blink.

"All aboard!" Rocky yipped. He ran through the nearest doorway, Gizmo racing after him. With a groan, Gertrude got to her feet and, with Max and Boss back at her sides, she held her head high and promenaded toward the entry.

The pig made a dainty leap and landed inside just as the human voice started to echo out of the unseen speakers.

Rocky jutted his snout toward Gertrude. "So you can understand people speak?" the Dachshund asked. "If that's true, what's that lady saying?"

Gertrude pricked up her ears, listened to the voice, and chewed her lip thoughtfully. "Oh, nothing too interesting. She's just going on about how the monorail is about to leave and if you don't want to get run over you either need to be through the doors or take a step back." She waved a trotter. "Or something like that."

The speakers crackled, and the voice fell silent. Immediately the doors to their train car whooshed shut, the entire car rumbled ever so gently—and they were off.

All five animals walked down the center aisle of the monorail car to the front. Rocky had been right—it was really nice inside. Max leaped atop the nearest two seats, and they were plush and velvety, and he realized just how much he longed to sleep. They had been walking and running and fleeing from enemies all day, and now that night had fallen, exhaustion washed over him. The lights above were dimmed and pleasant.

But no, he had to stay focused. They had to get through the towering buildings of the city and back to the brick shopping center. Beyond that, he'd seen the bright neon sign atop a hill that showed the three-ringed symbol. Now that Rocky was saved, Max could think only of his main goal: following the symbol to find the people who would take him back to his human family. His young pack leaders, Charlie and Emma, were out there somewhere, waiting for him.

Max blinked his tired eyes wide open and looked out the window. He knew that the train was what moved—he could feel it surging beneath him, vibrating up through his paws and in his bones. But as he watched the scenery fly by, it was strange that he couldn't really feel himself moving at all. This wasn't like running. Not even like riding in a car with the window open.

The monorail zipped high above the big brick houses and trees they'd walked past, everything shadowy and dark and empty. The lights of downtown glittered in the distance, rapidly drawing closer and closer. Max angled his head to look at their destination—and found Gertrude sitting in the seats behind him, staring in awe out the window, her snout pressed against the glass.

"Is this new to you, too?" Max asked her.

The pig blinked her eyes and raised her snout in the air. "Yes. Seeing the city from up here is... interesting."

"So, big gal," Rocky barked from across the aisle. "You never really said—why do you want to go back to the lab so bad?"

"I have my reasons," Gertrude said, her attention fixed on the world rushing by outside.

"So what are they?" Gizmo asked from her seat next to Rocky. "You know our reasons; it's only fair."

The big pig sighed. "I suppose it can't hurt to say that I have work there that remains unfinished."

"Work?" Rocky asked. "What kind of work can a pig possibly have?"

Gertrude shifted awkwardly on the seats so that she could face the two little dogs.

"Inquisitive ones, aren't you?" She snorted. "Fine. Remember how I said I was, in fact, the smartest animal in that entire zoo, including the Mountain? I was not exaggerating. I'm not just smart—I'm as smart as a human. I understood the words the scientists at the laboratories spoke, and I understood the words they wrote down. Now that they're gone and can't come back, the only one who knows how to create a cure for the mutated Praxis virus is *me.*"

Max, Rocky, Gizmo, and Boss all gaped at the pig. Was she really trying to say she wasn't just some farm animal... but some sort of *scientist*?

"You're saying you know how to save us all?" Boss asked. "You're saying you can use all the people equipment with those trotters of yours?"

"Yes," Gertrude spat at him. "That's exactly what I'm saying. The Praxis process didn't go far enough, and that's why the virus in its current form is dangerous." She pressed her nose against the window again. "But if I can finish the work my people began, I can render the virus harmless. Once done, I can develop a serum based on the new, safe version of the virus that will allow people and animals to coexist once again." She turned and raised her snout up proudly. "*I* can do this! I *will* do this!"

Glancing at the dogs once more, she added, "What that all means, since I suspect you find it confusing, is that some brave animal must go to the laboratories, get to the test chambers, and go through a second procedure. That animal will become immune to the bad version of the virus. And from that brave animal will come the medicine that will cure the rest of the animals—and the world!"

Max didn't quite understand all the words the pig was saying, but he more than got the idea—Praxis made the people unable to touch animals. And being immune meant that animals would again be safe to humans. The rest of what she said, he didn't comprehend, but it didn't matter. The pig had an idea about how to fix things so that if Max and Rocky and Gizmo found their people again, they could all be a family once more without anyone getting hurt.

Of course, that was only if the pig's plan worked.

"So who's going to be getting tested on?" Rocky asked, wide-eyed. "Us?"

Gertrude snorted. "Oh, don't be ridiculous," she said, peering back over her expansive body. "*I* will be the noble test subject, of course."

"Whew," Rocky said, settling down onto his belly. "I'm not really in the mood to be stuck with more needles."

Beneath Max's paws, he felt a vibrating sensation as the monorail began to slow. They could see out the window that they were now surrounded by the taller buildings of downtown, curving among the glass structures as they angled back toward the stop near the brick stores. Light glowed from windows all around, casting deep shadows in the streets and alleys. But even with all the darkness pooled down below, Max saw something: an animal or a few animals running around the corner of a building. He couldn't be sure what he saw—maybe more lost dogs or other animals from the zoo out exploring, like Barbs.

"We're here," Boss barked, interrupting Max's thoughts. The dogs and Gertrude bounded down from their seats and then walked to stand in front of the exit. The train eased to a stop, and the doors opened wide.

Cool night air met them.

"Right back where we started," Gizmo said, looking around.

"Which means we know exactly where we need to go," Max said. Beyond the glass wall on the platform opposite the monorail, he could clearly see the blue glow of the billboard-sized three rings attached to a boxy white building atop a hill.

They walked down the flights of stairs as quickly as Gertrude would allow, and soon enough were back in the mostly empty lot behind the shops. They headed through the alley where earlier they'd made their desperate escape from the bad people, toward the street they'd followed up from the docks. Max was careful to guide his friends around the side of the truck parked in front of the alley entrance—there were still glass shards on the ground from when the bad people had thrown bricks through the truck's windows.

Across the street, the parking lot where the bad people had parked was dimly lit by a nearby streetlamp. The store they'd been looting was dark, its windows shattered, but at least the people were nowhere around. Max focused on the sign at the end of the parking lot with an arrow painted over with the three-ringed symbol.

Gertrude shook her head at the spray-painted symbol. "That paint smells fresh. Are people still doing that? How ridiculous."

"What?" Max asked. "Why were they painting that symbol?"

"Oh, just humans being humans," she said. "I remember watching it on the television. Some officials started spraying the Praxis symbol on buildings with infected animals, as a warning for people to stay away. They made the Praxis logo mean something bad! But it's not! Praxis was only ever supposed to better animals!"

Rocky huffed. "And you're what one of those better animals looks like?"

But Gertrude wasn't listening. She flicked a trotter at the dripping symbol. "Other humans took to spraying versions of the Praxis logo as fake warnings, to scare other people away from areas that were perfectly safe. I'm guessing the bad people you mentioned were doing the same just in case any other humans came about and tried to steal their things."

"But there are no other humans here," Rocky said.

"Then whoever sprayed this was being paranoid, weren't they?" Gertrude snorted. "No matter. Just around this fence we'll be on the sidewalk of the street that leads up the hill, where we shall find the Praxis facility."

The dogs and Gertrude padded past the sign and onto the smooth concrete parking lot of a gas station next to the looted building. And there, just as Gertrude had said, beyond the road that ran in front of the gas station and at the top of the hill, sat the dark laboratory. From this distance it appeared to be two tall, featureless white buildings standing beyond a parking lot enclosed by a barbed-wire fence. The billboard sign above the entrance doors with the people words and the three-ringed symbol was a glowing blue beacon, pointing them to their destination.

Max's nostrils were quickly overwhelmed by the foul odor of gasoline as they entered the concrete lot of the gas station. The stench was so strong that it made his eyes water.

There were two rows of gas pumps beneath a ridged metal awning, under which flickered and buzzed fading yellow lights. Farther back from the road was a small, dark convenience store. An alleyway ran between the convenience store's brick wall and the gas station's slatted fence.

"It appears that we beat the rampaging elephant to our destination," Gertrude grunted as Max led them into the light beneath the awning, past the stinking gas pumps. "We'd certainly hear the beast's tantrum if he was nearby. Of course, with my help I knew we would get here first."

Max looked over at the pig, about to remind her that it was in fact *Rocky* who had come up with the idea of riding the monorail, when a grumbling of engines met his ears.

Max stopped in his tracks and spun around just as the glare of bright white headlights engulfed the four dogs and the pig.

It was the bad people.

CHAPTER 15

DANGEROUS PLANS

Max froze. For a moment, all he could see was white, and his panicked brain went blank.

Then the lights veered away as the two cars angled toward the gas pumps, and Max hissed the first word that popped into his head: "Hide!"

None of the dogs nor Gertrude questioned him. Heads low, they galloped as quickly and quietly as they could into the shadows of the alley beside the gas station. Huffing for breath, they hugged the brick wall and hid between two garbage bins they found there, then turned back to see if they had been spotted.

The black SUVs pulled to a stop next to a pump, and a moment later the engines grumbled and fell silent.

Doors opened with creaks and slammed shut as the bad people jumped out of their vehicles.

Max watched the woman and the skinny man walk around one of the SUVs and open up the back. He tensed as they reached into the dark trunks, expecting them to pull out something heavy and dangerous they could throw at the dogs.

But when the two people leaned out of the trunks, they carried only the boxy red-and-black jugs Max had seen them load onto the cars back at the docks. They spoke in quiet, casual tones, and though they moved quickly from the trunks to the gas pumps, there was no urgency to their steps. The woman and the man chatted with each other as they produced more and more of the jugs, lining them up next to each of the six gas pumps.

Max let out a long, shaky breath.

"It's all right," he whispered to the others. "They didn't see us."

"What's going on, then?" Gertrude asked. She shouldered forward, bumping Boss and pushing him out into view. He scrambled back into the alleyway. "Let me see."

Rocky shushed her. "Keep it down, big gal! They somehow missed us; we don't want to go calling them over here now."

Gertrude raised her snout in the air. "I *know* how to hide from predators, thank you very much. I just want to hear what they're saying, and you mutts are in my way."

"Oh, right!" Gizmo whispered. "You can understand

them! These were the people we were following; maybe you can tell us where they're going."

"So we can go the opposite direction," Rocky grumbled.

Pivoting her ears so that they were aimed at the gas pumps, the pig muttered, "Hmm, yes, yes, I guessed as much."

A heavy, hollow thump sounded near the cars, and Max snapped back to attention. The two burly men—the one with no hair and the one with the cap—tossed larger red-and-black jugs out of the second trunk, not caring that they got dented as they landed against the concrete.

Max had sat in the car while his pack leaders' parents had filled up their cars with gas, so he knew that it was like food for cars—it kept them going. It made sense to him that two of the gas pump nozzles were connected to the sides of the SUVs.

Strangely, though, the humans also filled up the red-and-black cans, two at each pump. Maybe they needed extra gas for the road, he guessed. But there were usually stations like this all over—how weird that they'd need so much extra.

While the bad people set about their mundane task of tapping codes into the pumps' screens and switching out cans as they got full, they talked to one another in low voices, occasionally laughing but mostly serious. Gertrude nodded slightly as she listened.

"So?" Boss grunted. "What are they saying?"

Gertrude snorted. "I'm listening; don't rush me. They keep mentioning something about a fire. They want to burn something and 'get rid of the vermin once and for all.' "

"What's vermin?" Rocky asked.

"Rats and mice and bugs, usually," Gertrude said, distracted. "The big man with the bald head is worried this fire is going to be dangerous." She went silent again as the people resumed speaking.

Max watched the woman raise a small device, then flick the top with her thumb. A small flame appeared.

One of the big men shouted and then slapped her hand. The flame went out and the little device fell to the ground. The woman smirked as the skinny man laughed.

"The bald guy got angry and smacked away her lighter, asking if she's trying to kill them all," Gertrude whispered. "I doubt you're aware, but the clear, foul-smelling liquid they're pouring into the barrels is called gasoline. It's highly flammable. That means that when touched with a match or the fire from a lighter, it would go up in a ball of flame."

"No wonder the man was angry!" Gizmo said.

With a groan, the pig lay on her belly atop the grimy alley floor, then tilted her head so that her other ear was aimed toward the humans.

"Mostly they're talking about money," she said, then laughed. "Money! Humans are obsessed with the stuff, and as far as I can tell it's just slips of paper and small metal disks. I tried to eat one of the paper ones once and it was completely unappealing!" She shook her head. "Anyway, these people are talking about some safe they saw that would be full of the stuff."

"Like a safe place?" Max asked.

"Perhaps," Gertrude said. She raised a trotter before anyone could ask any more questions. "Hold on, they're speaking again. They're going to stop by the banks in the city before... they go to the docks."

"What are banks?" Gizmo asked. "Like riverbanks?"

"No," Gertrude said, still listening. "They're buildings where humans store their money. The humans want to steal all the money that was left behind."

Max watched the people. The gas pump nozzles now lay haphazardly against the ground, liquid oozing from their ends. The humans' faces turned red, and their biceps bulged as they carried two full jugs at a time back to the trucks. Liquid sloshed inside each container, some splashing out of the few jugs they'd neglected to screw closed.

In the back of the second SUV were two wooden crates, stacked one atop another. People words were painted in red on the side.

"What's it say on those wooden boxes?" Boss asked.

Gertrude squinted her eyes. "They say *Caution: Dynamite.*" Her eyes went wide again. "They sure are serious about blowing up that boat."

"Boat?" Max darted his head to meet Gertrude's small eyes, unsure he'd just heard what he thought he heard. "What boat?"

Gertrude waved a dismissive trotter. "I don't know—a boat! Big floating things! There are tons of them!" She snorted. "All I know is they keep talking about some boat with a safe they want, but the boat is overrun with dogs. So they're going to set the thing ablaze until all that's left is the safe. Apparently it's immune to fire."

"A boat full of dogs?" Gizmo yelped, then raced anxiously in a wide circle between the grimy brick wall of the convenience store and the slatted fence. "That's the *Flower of the South*! They're going to burn our friends' home!"

"Quiet!" Rocky hissed, swatting her gently with his paw. "They'll hear!"

The four dogs and Gertrude all held their breath and turned back to the bad people. The three men were struggling to load the bigger jugs into the back of the car, but the woman had stepped away. Her expression was strange as she took a dozen slow, careful steps away from the cars, out from under the awning, and into the shadows near the fence that ran alongside the convenience store.

Directly toward where the dogs and pig were hiding.

Max tensed, ready to make a run for it if absolutely necessary. But first he had to be sure Gertrude had heard what she thought she heard.

The woman called out, her voice soft and appealing in the dark night. Max recognized a word: "Doggy."

"She said, 'Did anyone hear that?'" Gertrude whispered. "Then she called out, 'Here, doggy. Sheila won't hurt you.'" The pig grimaced at Max. "'Much.'"

The woman took another step, and then another. She was only fifteen feet away now, and crouching down. Her arm was cocked at the elbow, her hand at her waist. Max could barely make out some sort of weapon held there by her belt.

A hunting dagger.

Rocky's tail wagged against his leg. "Maybe she's friendly?"

"I don't think so, Rocky," Max whispered.

The woman fingered the dagger's hilt, her eyes darting as she tried to peer into the shadows. She kept blinking, over and over, and Max guessed she was trying to gain her nighttime vision. Unlike animals, humans had a tough time going from bright lights into the darkness and being able to see.

But soon she'd be able to make out the shadows of the dogs. And Max had a sinking feeling she didn't have anything nice planned if she caught them.

She whispered again, "*Something something,* doggy," and Max took a quiet step back. If she attacked, maybe he could leap and distract her while his friends made it to safety.... Maybe he could get away, too, before her friends came to help or, worse, she freed her knife....

The woman gripped the knife handle and took another step forward, still crouching.

A man's voice called out, and the woman stopped. They shouted back and forth at each other, then the woman relaxed, stood up, and strode back to the SUVs.

The dogs let out shallow, shaky breaths.

All except Boss.

"You sure they were talking about a boat?" Boss growled at Gertrude, his eyes narrowed. "You'd best not be lying, piggy."

"Why would I lie?" Gertrude asked. "They want some money that's in a safe on a boat overrun with dogs. And to get rid of the dogs, they're going to burn the thing down. Which means they're going down to the docks and will be far away from here. Now we can safely go to the laboratory without worrying about them. How convenient!"

"No. We need to go warn everyone. Now!" Boss growled. "I made a vow to lead those dogs on the *Flower*, and I won't let them down, not like I let down Belle."

Groaning, Gertrude laboriously raised herself up, then shuffled around to face Boss snout-to-snout. "You *can't*," she said. "You *promised* to help *me*. We are to go to the labs before that crazed elephant gets there, and I am to complete my work. We had a deal."

Confused, Max glanced back and forth between Boss and Gertrude in the alleyway, and the people loading gasoline into their cars. At the top of the hill beyond the gas station, he could see the labs and the three-ringed symbol blazing bright white against a field of glowing blue.

He had to follow the symbol to find his people—that was what Madame had said. And they were so close.

But images of Zephyr and the other Dalmatians came to mind, of the spotted dogs racing through a field, dreaming of becoming dogs at a firehouse. Not to mention the burly dogs trying to figure out the people games, and the Golden Retriever surrounded by her newborn puppies. And there were all the dogs lounging around the pool, watching a people movie on a loop and reminiscing about the families who had abandoned them.

"I'm sorry, Gertrude," Max said. "Our friends are in danger. We'll come back to help you, but—"

Rounding on Max, Gertrude jabbed a trotter into his side and squealed. "You promised! I risked my life coming out here to get you into those labs, and you agreed to help me in exchange. Do not go back on your word, dog! You'll regret it!"

Boss bared his teeth and snarled. "I'm not a part of your agreement, piggy. I'm leaving. Now." To Max, he said, "Come and help me or don't, it's up to you. We got along fine without you three before yesterday, we'll get along now. You know the way."

Before Max or anyone else could respond, the old Australian Shepherd turned on his heels and ran away into the deeper darkness at the back of the alley. They saw his silhouette as he reached the fence, but then he slipped through a hole in the slats and was gone.

Gizmo took a few steps in the direction Boss had run, then looked back over her shoulder. "What are we waiting for?" she whispered. "Let's go before he gets too far ahead!"

"Wait!" Gertrude hissed. Heaving for breath, the pig offered a porcine smile. "Just listen a minute. I am not without empathy—"

"What's empathy?" Rocky asked.

"Of *course* I don't want your dog friends to die at the hands of these money-crazy humans."

"Could have fooled me," Rocky said.

The pig kept talking as though she hadn't heard. "Look, if those trucks head straight to the riverfront, there's no way you or your old friend will be able to make it to the docks first. Cars are faster than dogs. It's a plain fact."

Max growled, and Rocky joined him.

Backing up a few steps, the pig said, "But I know a faster way to the docks. A way that will get you there even before the trucks. As I'm feeling generous today, I'll do you a favor and tell you the shortcut without asking another favor in return—but *only* if we stick to our original plan and go to the laboratories first."

Max's front leg shook anxiously. He looked back at the humans to find them loading the last of the gas-filled jugs into the back of the trucks next to the dynamite crates. They'd be leaving at any moment.

"Max?" Gizmo asked, stepping back toward the group. "We need to go!"

"What do you want to do, big guy?" Rocky asked, peering up at him. "If it's true that Boss can't get there in time..."

Gertrude's eyes never left Max's. "You need to decide now, Max. The Mountain is still on his way, remember. And those people aren't going straight to burn the boat. First they want to stop and rob some banks. They aren't heading to the docks until it's near daylight, and dawn won't be for hours yet."

"So there's enough time for Boss to get back to the docks," Rocky said.

"Not necessarily," Gertrude said, still looking at Max. "The important thing is, this means they'll be busy for a little while, but not for long. If we go to the labs now, we'll have time for me to continue my work, for you to discover what the symbol means, and for me to show you how to get to the docks quickly—in time to save your friends."

There was something in Gertrude's eyes that made Max uneasy. A knowing glimmer as they reflected the lights of the cars.

But he had to admit, when she put it that way—that everyone could get what they wanted—he had no reason to say no.

The truck doors slammed shut, and Max looked back just in time to see the two SUVs rev their engines, turn in a half circle, and zoom down the road in the opposite direction of the labs. He watched the red lights on the back of each car disappear.

"All right," Max said, turning back to Gertrude. "Fine. You had better not be lying about getting us to the docks quickly."

"I give you my word," the pig said.

Max tried to look reassuring as he gazed into the worried eyes of first Rocky and then Gizmo. Finally he looked back up at Gertrude. "We'll hurry to the labs, do whatever it is you need to do, and then you show us the shortcut. Deal?"

Gertrude's fleshy lips parted in a sly grin, and she let out a delighted squeal. Max shuddered at the sound.

"Deal."

CHAPTER 16

THE LABORATORY

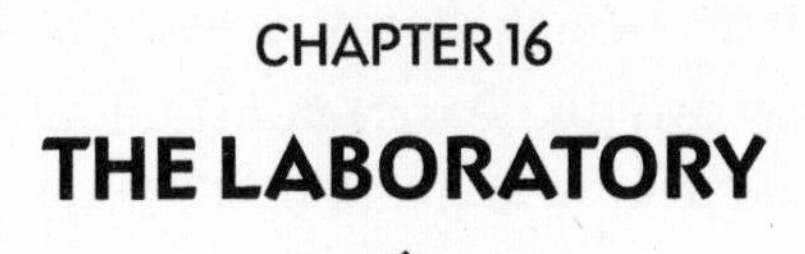

The walk up the dark road to the labs was spooky and quiet. They stuck to the center of the winding street, climbing the hill in silence to the laboratories at the summit. With Boss gone, Gertrude demanded that Max walk to her immediate left, while Rocky and Gizmo both guarded her right side.

Though the blazing windows of downtown were only a few blocks behind them, the street was shrouded in blackness. The storefronts on either side were completely dark, shadowy ruins. Max peered at them as they passed and saw shattered windows, blackened walls, and caved-in roofs, as though the buildings had all been set ablaze. Why? What happened here that an entire block went up in flames?

As the hill steepened, Max noticed even more destruction. A car lay upside down against a half-fallen utility pole, its windshield a spiderweb of cracks. A big truck with official-looking symbols painted on the doors lay half in and half out of a storefront, having crashed through the walls. Rubble and glass shards littered the parking lots and gutters.

The air smelled of smoke and melted plastic, but it was an old smell, one that only a dog would be able to sniff. Gertrude's trotter steps were loud against the asphalt, echoing up and down the barren street.

Near the top of the hill, the buildings gave way to trees and dirt. The road ended in a chain-link fence topped with spiraling sharp wire. The fence disappeared into the trees on either side of the road, but Max was certain it surrounded the entire facility.

"We're here!" Gertrude squealed softly, delight obvious in her voice. The glow of the laboratory's sign cast a blue light over her face and into her determined eyes.

The fence was gated across the road, with a separate section on wheels that could move back and forth. Luckily, at some point a human must have rammed a big vehicle through the gate. The chain link where the gate met the fence was bent inward, the barbed wire dangling off the top. Four dark tracks in the parking lot just past the busted gate led to a van that lay overturned, one of its wheels deflated.

The pig and her dog escorts carefully made their way

past the bent gate and barbed wire, and around the overturned car. Ahead were two big white buildings. They were both several stories tall, boxy and featureless. Max heard a rush of water and a whirring of gears, partially muffled by the dense rows of trees on either side of the facility. Between the two buildings was a small, dark road.

And, of course, there was the big blue three-ringed symbol glowing atop the main building, reminding Max of the three blazing rings he saw in his dreams.

He was close to finding what Madame had told him to find. He could sense it. And whatever he found out, he was sure it would lead him back to his people. He could almost feel the hands of Charlie and Emma running through his fur, scratching behind his ears, massaging his belly until his hind leg kicked uncontrollably.

A brief, intense feeling of longing washed over him then, and he almost whimpered. He was so tired, physically and mentally, after the long day and now night running all through this city. He wanted nothing more than to curl up in his pack leaders' laps and let them pet him until he slept, surrounded by their warmth.

But they were still so terribly far away. And there was much more to do before this night was done.

Max heard Rocky let out a low growl. He peered over the broad back of the pig and saw the little Dachshund recoiling, his hackles raised.

"I don't like this place," Rocky said. "It doesn't *smell* good." Looking up at Max, he added, "Maybe Boss and the Mountain were right, big guy. We should turn back."

Max sniffed the air. It tingled with electricity and sizzled with chemicals, and just the faintest stench of fading but recent fear. Only then, as they neared the main building, did Max see that the glass doorway was cracked, that the upper windows were shattered open by rocks or bricks thrown through them. Pale curtains that had once decorated someone's office floated in and out of one dark window, partially shredded by shards of glass still in the windowpane.

Spray paint was all over the white bricks of the lower walls, too. Circle after connecting circle in dark black and bloodred, the drawings erratic and oblong and always dripping down to make it look like the hastily scrawled Praxis symbols were melting. Max could almost feel the anger radiating off the wall.

Rocky was correct. This place didn't seem right at all.

"Something bad happened here," Max said softly. "That's true. But it's abandoned now, and Boss and the Mountain said the humans are too scared to come here. So we should be safe."

"I don't know...." Rocky said. He backed up a few steps.

Gertrude sighed, exasperated. "We don't have time for you two to be fraidy cats."

Gizmo turned to Rocky with a smile and a wag of her

tail. "We've come this far," she said. "And we've faced things a lot more dangerous than an empty building! You made buddies with wild animals today—you're super-brave, Rocky!"

Puffing out his chest, Rocky relaxed and stepped forward. "Yeah," he barked. "That's right! I *am* brave! I'm no cat! I'm braver than all of you combined!"

Max raised his brows.

Rocky lowered his head sheepishly. "Uh, I mean, at least as brave as the rest of you."

Gertrude trotted forward. "You mutts done?" she grunted. "If so, follow me. We're on a tight schedule!"

Max expected her to take them to the shattered doors beneath the glowing sign, but instead she led them to the small, dark road between the two white buildings. They trotted down the road until they emerged on a square swath of concrete.

Floodlights atop tall black poles lit up the square. In the center, surrounded by benches, sat a fountain still trickling with water. On the right was another white building, this one with dark windows through which Max could barely make out desks and chairs and computers. To their left was a great big field surrounded by more chain-link fencing and bordered by trees. The grass was trampled, and the field seemed divided into sections. Each had a trough that could be filled with animal food, and some sort of housing for animals of various sizes to hide beneath when it rained. Max guessed that was where the Mountain and the other animal test subjects were kept when they weren't being tested.

And directly ahead, on the other side of the fountain, rose a square building that was taller than the rest. Twin steel doors sat in the center of the front wall, on either side of which were small metal pads.

Apparently no longer caring about protection, Gertrude laughed and ran away from the dogs, winding around the fountain and heading straight toward the shiny steel doors.

"Hurry, hurry!" she called. "This is the laboratory!"

Max, Rocky, and Gizmo raced after her. They stopped outside the locked door, completely befuddled. Max studied the thing, unsure how to get past it. The doors had no handles that he could see.

Gertrude stood beneath the metal pad on the left of the doors. Unlike the pad on the right of the door, this one had a keypad next to it with people symbols on it and a little glowing screen. With a groan and a grunt, Gertrude leaped up with her front trotters and pressed them against the smooth wall. Stretching her neck, she aimed her snout toward the pad.

And missed as her trotters slipped on the wall.

Gasping for breath, the pig dropped down to all fours.

Gizmo's tail wagged, slow and wary. "What are you doing?"

Gertrude looked sideways at the fluffy tan-and-black dog. "After I type in an access code, we need to hit this pad and the other simultaneously—that means at the same time—in order to open these doors. I bet Max can hit the one on the other side of the doors just fine, but I'm going to need you two little ones to heft me up so I can enter the code and press this pad."

Rocky scrunched his snout. "You want us to shove you up under your belly? Are you kidding?"

"Well, it's not ideal!" the pig snorted. "But it's necessary. Now, get over here! And you, Max, get ready to press the other button."

Max stood beneath the metal pad on the right side of the door. He watched, amused, as Rocky and Gizmo crawled beneath Gertrude's expansive belly and shoved up with their heads.

"Careful!" Gertrude squealed as she rose. "My skin is sensitive!"

Rocky groaned. "Just hurry and press the buttons, already. You're heavy!"

Gertrude sniffed but crawled up the wall with her front trotters as Rocky and Gizmo pushed her from beneath her belly. The pig rose higher and higher, her snout drawing ever closer to the pad.

"You ready, Max?" Gertrude called.

"Yup!" Max called back.

Rocky and Gizmo shoved upward, and with the extra support Gertrude managed to reach above with her left trotter to delicately tap the keypad. There came a beep, and the pad glowed green—and Gertrude used the last of her strength to smack her snout against the metal pad. Max leaped up at the same time, slamming his paw atop the smooth metal panel on the opposite side of the doors.

Max dropped to all fours while Gertrude, Rocky, and Gizmo fell into a heap atop the concrete.

"Get off me!" Rocky yowled, shoving Gertrude's fat belly with his black paws.

"I can't breathe very well!" Gizmo panted as she attempted to escape the pig's bulk.

"Oh, lay off it," Gertrude grunted as she struggled to get to her feet. "I'm not *that* heavy."

Both of the pads, having been hit at the same time, glowed yellow. And with a creak of gears, the steel doors split apart.

Gertrude, Rocky, and Gizmo collected themselves and joined Max to stand in front of the doorway as it slowly slid open. Pure white light blazed from within, and Max had to look away—it was almost like staring into the sun. Cold, sterile air whooshed out as the doors parted, rustling Max's golden fur and meeting his nose. The chill and the chemical scent were so unnatural that he couldn't help but take a step back.

Max blinked until his eyes got used to the brightness of the labs. In front of them was a wide white hallway that seemed to go on forever, though Max knew it had to be some kind of illusion. The tile floors were polished, the walls and the chairs lining them spotless, with none of the mess and anger displayed in front. The air was stale—no one had been here in a long, long time.

"Oh," Gertrude gasped, trotting ahead onto the cold tile. "It's just as I remembered it. Pristine and wonderful. Home sweet home!"

"This isn't like any kind of home *I'd* ever want to live in," Rocky whispered. "This place smells weird."

"It feels like a tomb," Gizmo yipped, wrinkling her snout.

Max touched noses to theirs. "It'll be okay," he said, following Gertrude inside. "The humans just sealed it off to protect the other humans. Right, Gertrude?"

The pig didn't look at him. Her fat head darted back and forth, taking in their surroundings. "Yes, yes, yes," she said. "Come, we need to walk in farther."

Gertrude pranced ahead, her trotters echoing against the tile, the dogs following behind, their tails tucked.

A turn took them down a left hallway. It was lined with closed gray doors. Hanging from the wall beside each door was a strange, full-body white suit, like a deflated person. Max remembered dogs telling him of humans walking around in suits like this.

He shivered once more.

"This is the place!" Gertrude squealed, standing in one of the bright doorways. "My work is through here. Hurry, dogs!"

Max galloped down the hallway to where Gertrude had disappeared, Rocky and Gizmo at his heels. They turned and padded into a brightly lit office. On the wall to the left of the door was a shelf that held several computers. Behind the computers was a broad glass window looking out onto a dark room. Next to the window was a wide steel door not dissimilar to the ones they'd opened to enter the facility. To the right were cabinets with binders stacked atop them; a clean whiteboard hung behind them.

Hanging opposite the hallway door, above a potted fern that had browned and shriveled, was a framed picture. Max shook his head upon seeing it, certain it couldn't be what he thought. But the image didn't change when he looked at it again.

The picture was of an old human woman with white hair pulled back in a ponytail. She smiled warmly as she wrapped her arms around a black Labrador.

A Labrador Max knew: Madame Curie.

Max rose on his haunches and scrabbled up the wall with his front paws, then pressed his nose against the glass covering the photo.

"Madame!" he gasped. "That's my friend Madame. And she's with her human."

Gertrude trotted up beside Max. "Ah, the old woman?" she asked. "That's Madame Curie's pack leader. You knew Madame?"

Max barked, "Yes!"

"I thought so," Gertrude said. "I heard you say as much when talking to the Mountain. I suppose you should know that Madame was the old woman's first test subject. She was the one who devised Praxis, and all the scientists and animals looked up to her." The pig sighed. "Even me."

Max did not drop down. He studied the old woman's face. The curve of her nose, the wrinkles at the sides of her eyes, the paleness of her skin.

This was the person who had turned Madame into such a wise, dedicated dog. Who had intended to make countless numbers of animals smart like Gertrude and the Mountain.

Her eyes were kind, welcoming. Looking into them, Max decided: This was who the symbol was supposed to lead them to.

Madame's pack leader would be the one to take Max, Gizmo, and Rocky back to their people.

Max dropped down to all fours and rounded on Gertrude. "That woman!" he barked. "Do you know where she is? Do you know where we can find her?"

Gertrude trotted to the metal door next to the desks and observational window. "I might know, and I might not," she said coolly. "But my work isn't in this room. What I want is through this door. We still have to finish my work."

Rocky and Gizmo walked up on either side of Max.

"Is that really who we're looking for, big guy?" Rocky asked.

"She looks so nice," Gizmo said with a sigh.

"I don't know," Max said. "But it's like Twain said, I have a hunch. *She* feels right."

To Max's surprise, Gertrude bellied up from the tile floor onto one of the swivel chairs, then clambered noisily atop the counter. She tapped at one of the computer keyboards with her trotter.

"Whoa!" Gizmo yipped. "What are you doing up there?"

The pig didn't answer. Both of her beady eyes stared down at the keyboard and computer monitor as she carefully typed in commands.

And then, with a whoosh, the big metal door on the wall slid open.

"There!" Gertrude grunted, peering down at the three dogs. "We're finally here. Go on, make sure it's safe. It's going to take me a moment to get down from here, and I'm feeling rather modest."

"Strange time to be shy!" Rocky said, rolling his eyes.

Max raised his head high and led the way through the door, Rocky and Gizmo behind him. As they padded slowly into the center of the room, the ceiling lights buzzed and turned on, one by one.

The lights revealed a white, sterile room like the room where Vet would sometimes examine Max, but larger and with more metal surfaces. The entire space smelled of chemicals that made his nostrils tingle and his eyes water. Gleaming metallic equipment dangled from the ceiling and the walls, and there were open cages in the corners. A small bed atop four shiny silver poles rested near one of the cages.

Max turned in a circle in the center of the room, pacing over the polished floor. The only ways in were through the door they'd just come from and a giant pair of steel doors opposite the observation window. These looked exactly like the enormous sealed doors they'd opened with Gertrude's help earlier. He guessed that these big doors were for big test subjects—animals such as the Mountain.

Max didn't like the room much—it felt like a place where animals had been afraid; there were no warm corners or soft things, only the glint of cold steel and tile—but there were no dangers that he could see. Certainly nothing that could harm a full-of-herself pig.

He turned toward the windows. "It's safe!" he barked back at Gertrude. "There's no one here, just a lot of old junk."

The pig stood on the countertop next to the computers just behind the glass. "Oh, good!" she shouted, her voice carrying in through the open door. But she didn't appear to be making an attempt to follow.

Before Max could ask her what was next, she smirked at them and pressed a button on the keyboard in front of her.

And the steel door that led back into the office slammed shut.

CHAPTER 17

PRAXIS UNLEASHED

"Hey!" Rocky barked.

He skittered away from Max and Gizmo and clawed at the door. His angry voice echoed through the room. "She locked us in!"

"She's a liar!" Gizmo shouted.

Still standing on the counter behind the window, Gertrude bent over and flicked a switch with her snout. A buzz and a crackle sounded from above their heads, and Gertrude's voice filled the room.

"My friends," she drawled, "I *was* telling the truth when I said I intended to subject myself to further procedures, but... I have to admit, Rocky's idea of using you three as test subjects proved more appealing to me than

I first thought. You see, there was always one snag in my plans: me."

"You tricked us!" Max barked. But it was possible she couldn't hear him—or she chose not to listen. She kept speaking as though he hadn't said a word.

"I fear I have been far too exposed to the Praxis process to develop the necessary antibodies to stop the mutated virus. But *you three* have only gone through the first step. You've been infected by the virus, just like all the animals in the evacuated areas, but it hasn't been activated. With my adjustments to the second step, you could be cured of the mutation." She smiled at them through the window. "You're perfect!"

Max leaped at the window, slamming his paws against it. Snarling at the pig, he scrabbled at the glass, but his claws didn't even scratch the surface. He slid to the floor and bounced back onto his feet.

Gertrude watched Max curiously. "You don't seriously think you can break through this glass, do you?" her voice said through the speakers. "You're hardly the biggest animal that's been in that room. It's strong enough to withstand the Mountain. One little dog can't hope to do anything."

Panting, Max spun away to face the room. There were grunts and the slapping of paws against tile from where Gizmo and Rocky were jumping in the air, each one trying to get high enough to hit a pad on either side of the metal door—pressure pads just like those by the main entrance.

"Let us out!" Rocky howled.

"We were doing you a favor!" Gizmo barked.

Gertrude's voice boomed out, "I thought this was what you wanted—to help come up with a cure so that you can see your people again!" She sighed. "Stupid, shortsighted dogs. No, I'm not letting you out. At least not until I've subjected you to the second step of the process."

Gertrude turned so that her fat bottom and curly tail were all they could see through the window, and then she leaped off the counter. She left the intercom on, however, so the sounds of her huffing and trotting echoed through the white testing room.

"What do we do?" Rocky asked. "There's no way Gizmo and I can reach those pads, and they need to be hit at the same time."

Max paced back and forth in the big room, his eyes scanning the walls. The great big door opposite the window had pressure pads to open it, too, so that wouldn't help—and they didn't even know what was beyond that door, anyway. It could be something dangerous.

His eyes turned to the cages and the machinery hanging from the ceiling—long poles and weird claw-like devices all connected with black wire.

"Maybe we can try to use some of these machine things to smash the window," he said. "I'll jump up and shove it toward the window to break it, and then you two can leap off my back into the office and open the door."

"I don't think that will work," Gizmo said. "Gertrude said even the Mountain couldn't break that glass—nothing in here is as strong as an elephant!"

Max whimpered. She was right. "Maybe we can move one of the cages to the door, then you guys can climb up on top of it to reach the pad."

He went around the back of one of the cages and shoved his shoulder against it. Metal screeched against the tile, but it barely moved. Shoulder throbbing, Max took a step back. "It's heavy," he said, "but maybe if we all push it together—"

A high-pitched whine pierced the air, and Max stopped speaking. Crying out, he dropped to his belly and placed his paws over his floppy ears. He caught sight of Rocky and Gizmo writhing in agony as they did the same thing.

The whine gave way to a low hum and a rhythmic, thumping churn, like the sound of the machine his family used to dry their clothing. The noise grew louder and louder, and as it did the air around Max crackled with electricity. All of his fur stood on end.

He looked over at his two friends. Gizmo was now a round puff of tan-and-black fur, and Rocky seemed to have doubled in size with all his hair rising away from his body.

"She turned the machinery on!" Max barked over the thumping and humming noises.

Rocky ran in a panicked circle, almost as if chasing his tail. "Oh, no, oh, no, oh, no!" he yipped. "She's going to fry us with Praxis!"

Heavy breathing filled the room, drowning out the sound of the unseen machinery. Gertrude was again standing on the countertop in the window, watching them.

"There's no escape, my friends." Her low voice rumbled like thunder. "I know the sensations might be alarming, but just ride it out. Soon the virus will be transformed into something harmless, and you'll be able to be with the people you love again. But you'll have something more, too—the gift of Praxis! You'll be like me!"

"Like you?" Rocky barked. "What a nightmare!"

"Never mind her!" Max turned his attention back to the metal cage. "Come help me move this!"

Rocky and Gizmo stood next to him, all three bending their heads and putting the front of their bodies against the cold metal grid of the cage wire. At once, they all shoved. Max gritted his teeth and forced every muscle to its limit, but even with his friends' help, the cage scraped only a few inches.

Gertrude's voice boomed around them. "You'll just get one tiny dose of radioactivity and it will be all over. The four of us will be the smartest animals in a world overrun by dumber beasts—animals who live only by their instincts. Just imagine it!" Her squeals of delight were as painful to listen to as the whining of the machines themselves.

"This is what I wanted all along, the favor that you promised me," Gertrude announced. "I want only one thing in life: to once again be surrounded by animals as smart as me. Animals with more on their minds than eating and sleeping. The people are gone, and so that means it's up to me to create more smart animals like myself. That elephant had promise, but he's so glum! He never saw the possibilities. He never saw how we could rule this new, animal-run world!"

Growling, Gizmo ran into the center of the room and glared up at Gertrude. "We don't *want* to rule the world," she barked. "Especially not with someone like you!"

Snout trembling, Gertrude stared down at the little Yorkie. "I'm giving you a gift you don't deserve," the pig said. "In mere moments, the machinery will be at full power and you'll be transformed! You'll thank me once it's over. You'll *all* thank me!"

Recoiling, Gertrude slammed a trotter down, and the speaker turned off with a crackle. Then the pig leaped down from the counter, disappearing from view.

With a frustrated whine, Rocky said, "There's no time! You heard the pig: We're gonna get zapped any second, big guy!"

Max gave up on moving the metal cage. His back hurt, and the sizzling, electric sensation in the air of the room seemed to dig deeper into his skin, making his muscles vibrate uncontrollably. The room had been cold when they first entered it, but it was growing warmer and warmer by the minute. Max's throat ached for water, and his eyes felt itchy, dry.

Was this how he'd fail to keep Rocky and Gizmo safe? Where his journey to find his family would end? Was this where Madame had led him? It didn't seem possible.

"What do we do?" Rocky asked, looking up at Max with big, frightened eyes.

The whirring of the machinery grew even louder. It sounded as though giants were standing outside, pounding at the walls with angry fists.

Max didn't know what to say. He didn't know what to do.

"Hey!" Gizmo shouted. "What about this?"

The little Yorkie was standing beneath the bed Max had seen when they first entered the room. It was really a thin mattress atop four poles. Metal bars connected the poles at the front and back, stabilizing them.

But what Gizmo was pointing at with her nose was something Max had missed in all the panic: Each of the poles ended in a small black wheel.

"Yes!" Max barked. "A bed on wheels! That will work!"

"That's brilliant, Gizmo," Rocky said. "You saved us!"

Gizmo let her tongue loll out in a smile. "Aw, it was nothing. I was just being observant!"

"We're not saved yet," Max barked over the heavy, thumping noises. "Both of you should climb up top and I'll push it over by the door."

"Then we'll both press the pads and we'll be free!" Gizmo said. "Let's go!"

Max sat next to the cage beside the wheeled bed and rested his chin on its flat metal top. First Gizmo and then Rocky galloped awkwardly up his back, their tiny paws digging into his skin. "Sorry, big guy!" Rocky said, stepping on Max's head before jumping next to Gizmo on the roof of the cage.

From there it was a short leap through the air to the soft surface of the thin blue mattress. The bed squeaked as they thudded atop it, but it didn't move.

"We're ready!" Rocky called down.

Max ran around the front end of the wheeled bed, the edge facing the hallway. He grabbed the connecting bar between the two front poles in his jaws and pulled back, expecting the entire thing to easily roll over the tile.

It didn't budge.

Max let go and smacked his jaws. Maybe it needed more effort than he thought. Grasping the bar again, he pulled once more.

The bed jerked but stayed in place.

"Everything okay down there?" Gizmo asked, peering over the edge of the mattress.

"Why aren't we moving, buddy?" Rocky asked.

The lights above their heads dimmed and flickered,

and Max looked up. The tips of two of the claw-ended poles that hung from the ceiling flared as bright as the sun. A great flash of white seared his eyes as a bolt of electricity arced through the air between the two claws.

"Whoa!" Rocky and Gizmo barked at the same time.

Panic flooded Max's body. The noise from the machinery was growing louder and the air felt more thick, like a staticky blanket. They were going to be blasted any second.

Max sniffed at the two wheels in front of him. They were both normal, and nothing was blocking them.

"Max!" Rocky yelped. "We've got to hurry!"

"I know!" Max shouted back. "I just need to—"

His eyes fell onto one of the wheels in the back. Unlike the others, it had a little metal switch connected to it. A switch that was flipped down.

"Found it," he said.

Ducking his head, he scrabbled his paw against the switch. It clicked up and immediately the bed started to roll.

"Get ready to press that pad!" Max barked.

This time when Max wrapped his jaws around the connecting bar and pulled, the entire thing wheeled easily.

Wheels squeaked over the tile as Max ran backward, dragging the bed. He rolled it against the wall below the door pad just as the booming of the machinery reached its loudest. The lights flickered overhead, and the clawed poles behind them crackled with electricity.

Max shoved the broad side of the wheeled bed up against the door. As soon as the bed hit the wall, he heard Rocky and Gizmo slam their snouts against the pad. He scrambled to the side and raised himself up and smacked his paws against the other pad.

The metal door slid open with a whoosh, letting cool air wash over Max's tender skin and singed fur.

"Hiiii-*yah*!" Rocky's voice rang out.

And then the white room exploded into light.

CHAPTER 18

CORNERED

The noise was deafening.

Max sprang through the door. Electricity tingled his hind paws as he dove beneath the countertop where Gertrude had been perched. He skidded to a stop in the corner by the wall.

Rocky and Gizmo came flying in right after him, and not a moment too soon: Behind them, the steel door whooshed again and slammed closed.

The two smaller dogs landed against Max's side, and they all fell into a furry pile.

A harsh blinding light filled the room, shining through the observation window. Max could only imagine what it would have felt like to still be inside that room, in the heart of that light!

"Are you okay, Max?" Gizmo asked as she crawled off him.

"Is *he* okay?" Rocky rolled off Max's belly and onto the tile. "What about me? I almost got fried!"

"We didn't land on top of *you*, Rocky."

Max got to his feet. His skin still felt warm, his eyes and tongue were dry, and his back ached. But otherwise he was no worse for the wear. He looked down at his two friends—and almost burst out laughing.

It hadn't been so funny when they were in imminent danger, but Gizmo puffed out like a cotton ball and Rocky's body seemingly plumped up by his on-end fur was suddenly the most hilarious thing he had ever seen.

"Hey," Rocky said, batting at Max's front leg. "What's so funny, big guy? We almost got microwaved!"

"I know!" Max said. "But we weren't. We're safe. And we look ridiculous."

Gizmo giggled. "He's right. You two *do* look really crazy with your fur puffed out like that!"

Rocky chuckled nervously. "All right, sure, we look funny. But that was a superclose call!" He shivered. "We need to stop listening to the wannabe world leaders. They're always trying to get us hurt!"

"Oh!" Gizmo said, her ears perking up. "Where is Gertrude, anyway? I want to have a word with that pig!"

Max spun in a circle, looking in all the corners of the room. The room beyond the window no longer

glowed white but now flickered with bursts of brightness, and the shifting shadows made it hard to see. But Max was fairly certain there was nowhere behind the cabinets or under the desks that the pig could be hiding.

Which meant she had fled out the wide-open door into the main hallway.

"She's running away," Max said. "She must have seen us escaping."

"She's not *that* fast," Gizmo said. "Let's go get her. She still needs to show us how to get to the docks."

"You don't have to tell me twice!" Rocky said.

Rocky took off running after their fuzzy friend, but Max halted for a moment to look again at the picture of Madame Curie's pack leader that hung above the dead plant. He needed to memorize her face—the fullness of her cheeks, the wrinkles around her eyes, the length of her gray hair.

The symbols had led him to the image of this woman. Now he just needed to find her in person.

Lightning was still crackling throughout the white room, arcing among the machinery and crawling atop the metal cages. Whatever Gertrude had tried to do, it didn't seem possible that the humans would put any animal in a room and then expose them to *that.* Certainly not Madame's kind-faced pack leader. Which meant that pig wasn't nearly as smart as she thought she was—she could have gotten them killed!

In the hallway Max caught sight of his friends' tails

disappearing around the right corner at the end of the hall. He raced after them, past the closed doors and the white suits hanging from hooks. He caught up with Rocky and Gizmo just as they ran through the big metal doorway and into the floodlight-lit square. Gertrude's trotting steps echoed between the dark buildings. She wasn't far ahead.

"There you are, buddy," Rocky said as Max took his place between the Yorkie and the Dachshund. "We thought we lost you."

"You couldn't lose me if you tried," Max said. "Come on: We've got a pig to catch!"

They circled around the fountain and down the dark road between the two front buildings that led to the parking lot. The sound of the pig's trotters stopped abruptly, as though she was waiting for them, but Max didn't slow his gait. He wasn't afraid of that pig. There was nothing she could do to the three of them.

It was only after he, Rocky, and Gizmo ran out of the shadows and into the empty parking lot that he caught a whiff of the familiar scent.

Max skidded to a stop. Gizmo and Rocky piled against him.

Gertrude stood ahead, frozen in the otherworldly glow of the blue sign. Her eyes were open wide—in fear.

Max sniffed the air again and knew why. The wild, musky stench of wolves.

Six of them stood in a half circle in front of the pig,

between her and the open fence that led to freedom. Their gray heads were slung low, and their pointed ears lay flat back against their skulls. They watched her with narrowed yellow eyes, growling deep in their throats and snapping their jaws. They were better fed than the starving wolves of Dolph's old pack, their brown-and-gray fur not as scarred or mangled, but that didn't stop them from leering hungrily at their prey.

Fangs bared, they took a step closer to the pig, closing the circle and hemming her in.

Max remembered the wolves following their boat alongside the river. The small brown wolf on the road up from the docks, the animals he saw from the monorail darting through the streets...These wolves had been following Max and his friends. And it turned out Gertrude had been right: She did need protecting from wild animals, after all.

Gertrude caught sight of the three dogs hanging back near the entrance to the small road between the buildings.

"Oh, my friends!" she squealed. "My protectors! There you are!" Trembling, she took a step away from the wolves, trying to escape their circle before the beasts completely surrounded her.

"We're not your friends," Rocky said, then growled. "You almost fried us."

The pig grunted. "Oh, my experiment! Yes, it got a little out of my control, but I promise you would have been perfectly safe. I'm sorry for my subterfuge, but can't we let bygones be bygones? I could use some help."

"Shut up, meat," one of the wolves snarled.

"Help yourself, Gertrude," Gizmo yipped. "You're the smart one who knows everything, remember? We're just dumb dogs."

A deep, throaty laugh came from Max's right. He looked over to see three more wolves stalk out from among the trunks of the dark trees that lined the edge of the parking lot just past the second building.

Max gasped in surprise.

The wolf who clearly led the other two was huge and gray. Three jagged scars ran across his snout, an old wound that stood out pale and white against his dark fur. It was a terrifying, feral face Max knew all too well.

This wasn't just any pack of wolves. This pack of new, well-fed wolves belonged to Max's old enemy, Dolph.

And now the wolf leader he thought he'd left behind for good in the Chairman's city stood only a few feet away.

"Hello, Max," Dolph spat.

The wolf's gray eyes were narrowed and burned cold.

"We were being followed," Gizmo whispered.

"I can't believe it," Rocky said, backing away from the approaching wolves. "Who would come all this distance on foot?"

Max didn't care that his fears had been proven right,

that Dolph's thirst for vengeance had carried him this far south to find the three dogs. In fact, he wished he'd been wrong all along. His eyes darted back and forth, looking for the quickest path away. The only escape seemed back through the access road to the fountain square.

But more wolves appeared from the darkness. Two stalked out of the street between the two main buildings, coming up behind the three dogs. Another pair came from their left, popping out from behind the fallen van and racing forward to join the circle.

The dogs were surrounded.

Max, Rocky, and Gizmo turned to face the wolves who had come up from the side street, then slowly padded backward toward Gertrude in the center of the parking lot. Their bodies were tensed, their tails raised.

Behind them, Gertrude laughed bitterly. "Like it or not," she said, "it looks like we're in this together. *Friends.*"

Max sensed the pig behind him and knew he could walk no farther. He, Rocky, Gizmo, and Gertrude stood back-to-back in the glow of the lab's signs as Dolph and his wolves made a circle around them.

Max recognized the smells of a few of the wolves, but many were new to the pack, and others he'd known—such as the white-furred brute named Wretch—were nowhere in sight.

Dolph slowly left the circle and came to stand snout-to-snout with Max. His breath huffed against the fur of Max's snout, but Max did not back down, did not lower his head or tail in submission. He looked the wolf straight in his dark eyes.

"You've been hard to find, mutt," Dolph said. "But you must have known you could never get away from me. You made an enemy out of the wrong alpha."

Max swallowed down his fear and made himself speak calmly. "The last I saw of you, the Chairman and his dogs were fighting your pack."

Dolph paced in front of Max, restless. "Ah, yes. Nice trick getting those dogs to fight your battle. Some of my pack actually did fall to those mutts. But not me. I will never be taken down by a dog." He howled into the night sky, and the rest of his new pack joined in. "Never!"

"So you came all this way?" Gizmo asked with a tilted head. "Just for us?"

Dolph stopped pacing. Snarling, he looked past Max at the little dog.

"That's right, Bite Size," he said. "Just for you. I got the upper hand on that Doberman who called himself the Chairman, and he ran off with his tail between his legs. I would have followed and finished him off, but I saw you three floating away on the river, thinking you'd escaped my wrath." He laughed, a sharp, angry sound. "You were the real prey. So I rounded up the remains of my pack and followed, gathering more members as we traveled, ones you wouldn't recognize who I could use as scouts. I knew sooner or later we'd find you."

Signaled by some silent cue, the circle of wolves

crouched down and began to pad forward. They growled and snapped their jaws, their fangs glistening blue in the sign's light.

"The time for my vengeance is now!" Dolph howled.

"All right, dogs," Gertrude said, her voice trembling. "This is why I asked you to escort me here. Go get them. Fight them off!"

Rocky moaned. "There's too many. There's no way we can beat them all."

"Don't say that!" Gizmo barked. "We have to try!"

Max glanced down at his two friends. Rocky didn't take his eyes off the approaching wolves, and he shivered as though cold. Gizmo glared at the pack, certain that she was ten times bigger than she actually was.

He loved these dogs. These funny, brave little dogs who'd stuck by him for so long. It wasn't fair that they'd survived so much and come so far only to end up a meal to a bunch of wolves. Especially not after they'd narrowly escaped the white room in the lab.

But Rocky was right.

"There are too many," Max said softly so that only his friends and Gertrude could hear. "There's only four of us and over a dozen of them. And the pig can't fight."

Gertrude snorted, offended, but did not disagree.

"Dolph really only wants me," Max said, smiling down at his friends. "So I'll fight back as hard as I can. But while I distract him, you three need to run as fast and as far away as possible."

"No!" Rocky barked. "I'm not going to leave you, buddy."

Gizmo bared her teeth at the wolves closing in on her. "There's no way we're letting you do this alone."

"I'm fine with this plan," Gertrude said. "You distract them by being eaten and then I'll run, I promise."

Max sighed. "Do you remember the old woman in the picture? Madame's pack leader?"

"We're not—" Rocky started to say.

"Do you?" Max interrupted, his voice raised.

The two little dogs quietly barked, "Yes."

"Find her. Find our people. I'll try to get away, but if I don't..."

He turned from his friends and met Dolph's eyes. Any second now, he and his wolves would attack. They were so close that their rancid breath fouled the air.

They were just waiting for their moment.

"If I don't," Max finished, "then try to find my people, too. And let them hug you for me."

Dolph's lips curled back. The wolf leader snarled, then barked a command.

And the wolves prepared to attack.

CHAPTER 19

THE RAMPAGING BEAST

Max braced for claws and teeth, ready to fight for as long as necessary so that his friends could escape.

And then a loud, trilling trumpet of noise echoed through the night.

It was so unexpected a sound that the wolves were too shocked to attack as commanded. Startled and fearful and confused, their vicious expressions disappeared as they turned their attention to the laboratory road.

"What was that?" one of the wolves asked, crouching low, its hackles rising.

"Is it humans?" another rasped, slinking backward.

"Never mind!" said Dolph, but he was drowned out by a second trumpet blast, one that sounded full of anger.

A booming shook the ground and seemed to fill the air, a rhythmic pounding that grew louder and louder as a massive shadow rose up at the laboratory gates.

"What comes?" asked a skinny dark brown wolf, creeping behind Dolph.

"The thunder that destroys!" barked a fourth wolf. "Run!" He turned tail and ran down the alleyway between the buildings.

"Get back here!" Dolph ordered, but the wolf had already disappeared.

The shadow raised a long, snakelike trunk and blasted another burst of deafening noise.

"The Mountain," Gizmo whispered.

Max was happier than he'd ever thought possible to see a rampaging giant barreling down on their group. He had almost forgotten that the Mountain was heading here.

Max let out a shaky breath and slowly backed away from Dolph's pack. Silently, Rocky, Gizmo, and Gertrude did the same.

The Mountain emerged into the bright blue light of the illuminated sign. He burst through the half-destroyed gate, sending poles and chain link and barbed wire flying with a cacophonous clang.

"I'm all alone!" the Mountain trumpeted into the night sky.

The giant African elephant didn't slow down. Lowering his great head, the Mountain butted the fallen van.

It tumbled over and over and crashed into the gate operator's booth in an explosion of sparks and flying shards of wood.

"What is this thing?" a wolf howled.

"Is it meat?" another asked.

"It is coming to attack us!" another shouted. "We must attack it first!"

The Mountain zigzagged through the parking lot, wobbly and off kilter, barely looking where he was going. Each stamp of his giant flat feet shook the asphalt so deeply that the vibrations seemed to travel up Max's very bones.

The crazed elephant was coming right toward them.

And it looked like he didn't even realize any of the wolves or dogs were in his path.

"Move!" Max barked to his friends.

They turned and ran back to the darkened street that cut between the two white buildings.

Dolph caught sight of their escape and howled to his pack, "Ignore that creature! Get the dogs!"

But it was too late for the alpha to rein in his wolves.

Five had already gone to attack the elephant. At the last minute, two veered around the Mountain's left side, the other three to his right. Snarling, they leaped up at the Mountain's massive belly, trying to bite him with their sharp teeth and ripping at his tough hide with their front claws.

The Mountain stopped running. "You brutes think you can hurt me?" he trumpeted.

Twisting to one side, he hooked his tusks underneath a wolf and then snapped his head up, launching the wolf into the sky. It howled as it flew through the air, then landed awkwardly with a snapping of branches in the trees around the lab. Yipping in pain, it limped off into the darkness.

The Mountain wrapped his trunk around another wolf and flung it to the ground. It bounced once and ran away.

The elephant shook his entire body, stamping from side to side and casting off the three wolves who had latched their teeth and claws into him. They fell to the asphalt and lay stunned.

Eyes flaring in rage, the Mountain raised up his giant front feet to stomp the wolves flat. But before he could bring them down, the wolves scrabbled onto all four paws and, tails between their legs, fled through the open gate.

The Mountain shook his head at the remaining wolves huddled together near the main lab building. His ears flapped violently as he blew another challenge through his trunk. "Who will be next?" he bellowed.

Then, lowering his head, the giant elephant charged.

But by the time he reached them, all the wolves were gone. They'd run after the rest of their pack, vanishing in the thick darkness around the lab.

All except Dolph.

"Wait!" Gertrude said, huffing for breath. "I'm a pig, not a long-distance runner."

The three dogs stopped in the shadows of the road between the buildings and looked back. The vast parking lot was entirely empty except for the big gray wolf and the bigger gray elephant facing off.

"You do not frighten me, strange creature," Dolph growled. Ears flattened, front crouched down low, and lips raised in a snarl, he snapped his jaws at the Mountain. "You are not a predator. I can smell the leaves and grass on your breath. You do not eat meat; you *are* meat. Your carcass could feed my pack for a month."

The Mountain laughed. "Scrappy, foolish wolf," he said, his eyes examining Dolph. "You are clearly one of the biggest wolves, but you've never been the smartest. You wear your scars on your face like a badge of honor, but all they show is that you lead solely by fear. The only way you could win the leadership of a pack was by being the most savage among your fellows. Even as alpha, you are so insecure that you must challenge me—a beast a hundred times your size—just to save face in front of your pack."

The fur on Dolph's back bristled. "Why do you say these words? You do not know Dolph!"

"I don't have to know you to know you, little wolf," the Mountain thundered. "Your history is written all over your snout. Now get out of my way so I can destroy this building. Or I'll just walk over you to get to it. Your choice."

"Never!" Dolph howled. "Prepare to die, meat!"

Claws extended, the wolf threw himself toward the big elephant's underbelly.

With a sigh, the Mountain kicked out with one of his tree trunk–sized front legs.

The Mountain's massive foot caught Dolph's side and sent the wolf spinning through the air. He smacked against the side of the building with a thud and collapsed to the ground, unconscious.

Raising his trunk high, the Mountain sent forth a triumphant blast. And then he stopped abruptly and lowered his head. "I am more than this!" he shouted. "I am an intellectual, not some beast that hurts other animals. And I know this only because of this wretched laboratory." He stomped his feet. "It must be destroyed!"

Focusing on the cracked glass entrance doors, the Mountain charged.

Suddenly Gertrude shoved Max aside and strode forward. "Mortimer!" she shouted, her gaze never leaving the Mountain. When the elephant stopped charging, midstep, the mottled pig trotted up to him. "You psychotic pachyderm, quit your whining and *stop*!"

The Mountain, one of his front legs still raised, angled his massive head to look down at her. "You?" he asked. Blinking, he took in the dogs as well. "And the canines? What are you all doing here?"

"Why do you think I'm here?" Gertrude asked as she reached him. "We discussed this endlessly. I'm here to save the laboratory."

"Why would you want to save this place?" the Mountain asked, gesturing with his trunk at the building and the grounds. "After all they did to us?"

The pig plopped down on her wide bottom and waved a dismissive trotter. "Destroying it will not change the past, Mortimer. You know this."

The Mountain lowered his foot gently to the ground. "But it's a bad place!" he bleated.

"Yes, well, so is the zoo!" Gertrude said. "That place is filled with animals who want to eat me, and unlike you, I don't have size on my side. If not for the wily smarts this laboratory gave me, I probably wouldn't have survived the first week." She snorted. "I can sincerely say I'm glad I was made as smart as people."

The Mountain's trunk coiled in agitation. "We," he said, enunciating each word slowly. "Are. Not. People!"

"Blah, blah, blah, so much arguing," Rocky grumbled beside Max. Snout raised high, the Dachshund trotted forward.

"What are you doing, Rocky?" Gizmo asked.

He looked back and winked at her. "Just something I learned from a friend of mine."

Gertrude and the Mountain didn't notice Rocky sit down next to the pig. They were talking over each other now.

"I just wanted to be normal!"

"And you think destroying everything will help?"

"This place has to go!"

"We need this lab!"

"Ahem," Rocky said. *"Ahem!"*

Snorting, Gertrude glanced over at the little dog. "What do you want, Dachshund?"

The Mountain sniffed and peered down at Rocky as well, listening.

"For two animals who claim you're so much smarter and better than the rest of us, you sure are acting dumb," Rocky said.

The Mountain chuckled.

"Excuse me?" Gertrude asked.

Rocky jabbed a paw into Gertrude's massive side. "You heard me! And I heard you. And it seems to me that you two need to do some compromising."

"Compromise? Ha. Either he destroys it or not, little dog," the pig sniffed. "He can't compromise and destroy only *part* of it."

"There can be no compromise when something is evil!" the elephant said.

Rocky barked loudly. "Stop it, both of you! All Mortimer here wants is to be normal again. And, Gertrude, either you only want to zap up some dogs to make more smart animal friends, or you were telling the truth and want to do that *and* reverse the bad virus that made the humans go away. Am I right?"

Gertrude raised her snout in the air. "More or less."

"You are correct, little dog," the Mountain said, his voice calm.

"Maybe he's right." The pig cleared her throat. "Perhaps if we worked together, we might be able to turn you back into a normal elephant. And I can continue my work with your protection and added insight." She looked pointedly away. "That is, if you don't still consider me so awful that you'll refuse to be around me."

The Mountain looked up at the glowing laboratory sign. The light cast blue halos on his eyes. "Me," he said simply. "Normal again. I would no longer be shunned by my people."

"Then that settles it!" Rocky barked with a wag of his spiky tail. "You two can help each other out, and nothing gets destroyed! Besides, you're both always going on about how no one understands you. Maybe until you're normal again, Morty, and until you solve the Praxis problem, Gertrude, you two can be friends."

The pig stared up into her fellow test subject's eyes. "I suppose that would be an agreeable plan."

The Mountain flapped his ears. "It sounds fine to me, as well. And if you ever call me Morty again, little dog, I'll stomp *you*." He chuckled.

Beside Max, Gizmo bounced into the air and shouted, "Woo-hoo! Yay, Rocky!"

Max and Gizmo sidled up between the Dachshund and the pig.

"When you know how to speak to someone, you really know how to speak to them, huh?" Max asked his short friend.

Rocky smiled. "I learned some tricks from Gizmo back at the zoo. Talking down a gorilla and talking down an elephant aren't all that different."

The Mountain cleared his throat. "I'm still standing here," he said. Blinking his eyes, he took in the destroyed van and Dolph, who still lay unconscious against the wall. "Oh, where did all those wolves go? I hope they weren't friends of yours."

"We're not even a little bit friends," Max said.

"Which is a shame," Gizmo said, "since usually I can make friends with *everybody*. We just keep meeting bad animals and people lately, and—oh!" Ears perked up, she looked at Max with frantic eyes. "We almost forgot! The bad people! The riverboat!"

Max snapped to attention. The images of the trucks filled with gasoline and explosives came back to him. The bad people were going to try to burn up the riverboat dogs' home.

"You promised to show us a shortcut to the river," Max said, turning to Gertrude. "You weren't lying to us again, were you?"

She snorted. "No, I was not. And I wish you three would stop trying to make me out to be some sort of bad pig. I was trying to *help* you... in my own way."

"Sure thing, big gal," Rocky said. "But never mind that. Are you gonna take us to this shortcut or what?"

With a groan, Gertrude rose to all fours. "It's close by. But I should tell you something first."

Gizmo's tufted ears drooped. "Aw, what now?"

The pig ignored her. Instead, as the dogs and the Mountain watched, she trotted to the edge of the lot, scooped up a trotterful of mud, and then walked purposefully to the graffiti-covered wall nearest Max.

As she swooped her trotter over the white bricks to paint an image, she spoke. "The old woman you're looking for—the one in the photograph? She'll be downriver. And if I know her, she'll be looking for dogs like you just as much as you're looking for her."

"That's great," Rocky said as he waddled forward and sniffed the wall warily. "But what are you doing?"

With a grunt, Gertrude nudged the small Dachshund away with her snout, then stepped back. "Take a look."

Max padded forward to look past the pig's bulk. He discovered that she'd scrawled a crude drawing on the wall with the mud—a circle with an *X* in its middle.

"The beacon," Max heard the Mountain mumble behind him.

"What's the beacon?" Max asked.

Gertrude looked up at him. "The lab has protocol in case of emergencies. And I'm sure they probably consider this the biggest emergency of all." Not taking her eyes off Max, she pointed at the circle drawing with her trotter. "The old woman you're looking for is going to be leaving beacons behind her as she travels, two each on top of a small orange-and-white barrier. The beacons will be plastic and glow orange. You know what the color orange is, right?"

"Of course!" Rocky said. "It's the color of that round fruit people eat. I think it's called a... uh... rrrr... No, a guh... It's on the tip of my tongue...."

Giggling, Gizmo nudged his side. "It's called an orange!"

Rocky held his snout high. "I knew that."

Gertrude sighed and shook her bulbous head. "Fine, good, you know what the color orange looks like. These beacons send out a signal, but you won't be able to hear it. So just keep your eyes open as you travel—the beacons will lead you to Madame Curie's old lady."

"Thanks for telling us," Max said. "That will be a big help. Despite trying to fry us, you're not so bad."

"You'll thank me for that later." The pig sniffed as she trotted away. "Now follow me, and I'll take you to the shortcut."

The pig led them in front of the spray-painted wall of the main lab building, past the shattered doors beneath the glowing blue sign, to where the edge of the parking lot met earth and trees.

Asphalt gave way to grass and rocks, smooth and slick beneath Max's pads after walking so long on rough road. The sounds of rushing water and whirring machinery met his ears once more, the same sounds he'd heard when they first entered the lot, only louder.

In the shadows behind the building, half hidden in

the trees, was a concrete block the size of a school bus. The metal machine noises sounded from inside, and frothing white water gushed out. It formed a torrential waterfall that cascaded down into a concrete ditch as wide as the city's main street, with sides that appeared tall, though Max wasn't sure how deep it was. The dark water filled the ditch almost to the top and gushed down at an angle that led down toward the great river. Chilly drops of water splattered into the air, meeting the dogs' fur and making them shiver.

"You take this!" Gertrude shouted. The splashing and roaring of the water was so loud they almost couldn't hear her. "It'll get you where you need to go."

"Take what?" Gizmo asked.

"Yeah—what are we supposed to ride?" Rocky asked. "I don't see any boats!"

"There aren't any boats!" Gertrude answered. "You're going to have to swim for it. You know how to dog-paddle, right?"

Rocky backed away from the rampaging, man-made river's edge. "I don't like to get wet. And I don't know if I can swim that long!"

The pig seemed to shrug. "I can't make you take this waterway, but like I said—it'll get you there fast."

That was all Max needed to hear. "Come on, guys." He walked through the grass to the moss-covered concrete lip of the waterway. He looked down into the dark water, the cool mist of droplets like an icy cloud. The waves reflected the moonlight and the lights of the parking lot, but Max still couldn't tell how deep the water was.

"All right, dogs," Gertrude said as she waddled away. "Have fun!"

Max peered down at the rushing water. Rocky and Gizmo stood on either side of him.

"Oh, this is a bad idea," Rocky said, and groaned.

"It's our only choice," Max said. He nuzzled his friend's side. "Sorry, buddy. But it'll be over soon."

Gizmo jumped in a circle, her nub of a tail wagging. "Maybe it'll be fun! We won't know until we try."

Max chuckled. "All right, guys. We can't waste any more time. It will probably be daylight soon. You ready?"

"Of course!" Gizmo said.

"Why's it always got to be water?" Rocky whined.

Max didn't respond. Taking in a deep breath, he bunched his hind legs and jumped. He soared through the night air, his floppy ears flailing above as he arced down. Then he splashed belly-first against cold water—and the impact against his belly knocked the wind out of him, it was so hard.

Just before the water overtook him and carried him away, Max heard Rocky distantly yell out a long, fearsome "Hiii-*yah*!"

CHAPTER 20

RIVER RACE

The ditch didn't just look like a man-made river. It raged like one, too.

The water was ice cold, numbing Max's still-singed skin. Stunned from the chill, he tumbled into the murky, surging depths, scraping along the walls of the culvert and turning head over heels, no idea which way was up and which way down. He was swept along faster and faster and could see nothing but blackness, hear nothing but the muffled rush of the water. He gasped for air, but his open jaws only swallowed water. Hacking, a cloud of bubbles exploded from his mouth and nostrils, rising above his head.

Rising. To the surface.

Heart thudding and eyes wide, Max paddled at the

water with his webbed paws in the direction the bubbles had gone.

With a splash, his head burst from the surging waves. Warm night air rushed over his wet fur, and he coughed up the liquid he'd swallowed while paddling frantically to keep his head above the surface.

The world rushed by in a blur as he bobbed up and down on the water. He tried to aim himself in the direction of the current, but the buffeting waves turned him this way and that. He caught sight of the laboratory up the hill behind him growing smaller by the second, and the glimmers of the river ahead. The concrete sides of the ditch rose like fortress walls on either side of him, above which shadowy trees towered.

"Rocky!" Max shouted over the rush of the water. "Gizmo!"

A yip sounded from downriver, and Max twisted his neck and saw Gizmo ahead of him, her head barely above the waterline. As she spun toward him, splashing with her front paws, he saw the determination to keep afloat in her eyes.

Rocky's head bobbed up from the dark waters to the left and just behind Max.

"Max!" he gasped. Then, gulping for air, the Dachshund went back under.

"Rocky!" Max barked.

Rocky's head popped up again, his eyes wide with fear.

"Keep paddling!" Max shouted to him over the noise. "Don't try to say anything!"

Rocky's head bobbed up again, and Max called out, "You're fine! Just hold on!"

Max had no idea how long they were trapped in the waves, swirling down toward the water's end. But he caught glimpses of the blue light from the labs growing to a pinpoint faster than he could imagine, and when he managed to peer ahead, he could see a darkened street and the distant glimmer of the real river coming close in a rush.

"Whoooooa!" Gizmo yelped.

The Yorkie's tan head disappeared. For a second Max feared she'd been pulled under the water, but then he realized: The ditch was coming to an end.

"Hold on, Rocky!" he barked as the edge drew closer. "Hold—"

And then Max went over.

He shot from the end of the ditch in a blast like water from a hose. He twisted through the air, falling forever and ever through the warm night. It was a waterfall. He saw the gentle, lapping waves of the river glimmering with reflected lights of the city, and he saw the explosion of white that was the waterfall off the lip of the ditch, and far down below, a band of rippling blackness that was a larger lake. For a brief, terrifying moment, Max thought that this was Gertrude's last, vicious trick, and that her shortcut was meant to be their doom.

And then he splashed down in cold water once again.

Max was used to the chill by now, but his lungs were empty, his belly sore. Frantic, he paddled up after the air bubbles and toward the surface.

His head popped free and back into delicious, precious air once more. The waterfall thundered beside him, churning up the lake he'd fallen into and sending a cloud of cold droplets spraying in every direction.

Gasping, Max swam in a circle where he'd landed, desperate to find his friends and see they were safe. He caught sight of Gizmo already at the lake's shore, crawling out onto dry land. Then, a moment later, a black-and-brown head burst up next to Max's.

"Never again!" Rocky coughed, shooting a stream of water from his puckered lips. He paddled away from the waterfall toward Gizmo. "I'm through with this wet stuff, Max! Water and me are officially over!"

Max almost laughed with relief at the sight of his friend, surly and bedraggled. He swam alongside Rocky, saying, "You got it, Rocky! I'll never make you do something like that again."

Gertrude had been telling the truth—the waterway had certainly been fast, faster than Max had liked, in fact. It had spilled them into a pear-shaped lake. Its wide end was beneath the waterfall, and its narrow end ran up against a road.

Rocky and Gizmo attempted to shake themselves dry.

"First we're turned into puffballs by that zapper thing," Rocky complained, "and now we're like dirty, wet rags. Oh, the indignity!"

Max pulled himself ashore and shook as well. His fur was still wet, but it was a warm night, and they'd dry off fast.

"That sure was some ride," Gizmo said.

"That was not a ride," Rocky grumbled. "That was a horrifying nightmare. I feel like I got put in a human's washing machine!"

Gizmo wagged her tail. "It wasn't *that* bad."

"Sorry, Gizmo," Max said. "I'm with Rocky on this one. But at least we made it here in one piece. Let's get to the *Flower*."

Leading his friends, Max walked quickly along the shore to the road. It appeared to run parallel to the wide river that was just beyond a swath of tall trees with narrow trunks. If they turned right and followed the road, it would lead them to the main street that had led up from the docks into the shopping centers—which meant heading in that direction would also take them to the *Flower*.

The air smelled of must and plants, and frogs croaked a night chorus. Max veered to head north—toward the docks and the beached riverboat, the top stacks of which he could just see over the treetops. Then he smelled something else.

The wild musk of wolves.

"You two smell that?" Max asked his friends. As if on

cue, there was a distant howl. "The wolves either came through here or are on their way."

Gizmo sniffed. "But they couldn't possibly get here before us and Boss, right? We left Dolph unconscious, and they ran off toward the city, not to the river."

"Yeah," Max said, quickening his step down the center of the asphalt road. "But there's no telling whether these wolves are the same ones as at the laboratory. If it was a big pack, Dolph may have left some down by the river in case we got away."

Quickening his step to match Max's long strides, Rocky groaned. "Now we don't just have fire-obsessed bad people to deal with, but wolves, too? This night keeps getting better and better."

Max didn't respond, just focused on running, his short-legged companions struggling to keep up. They ran beneath shallow cones of light cast from streetlamps. Small roads branched off the street to the left, leading to docks beside which bobbed shadowy boats.

They were close.

Max began to recognize buildings from the day before. A white house with peeling paint and a plastic figure of a pink bird lying on its lawn, and the small corner store with posters plastered over its windows, the biggest one showing cartoon worms writhing inside a can.

"This way," Max said.

They turned left, toward the river, and up ahead the *Flower of the South* came into view. It seemed just as they'd left it, with white lights dangling from its eaves and the flickering of a movie playing on the topmost deck. Somehow, it appeared more massive and regal than Max had remembered, with its palatial columns supporting each of the decks, the great red waterwheels resting in the waves, and the flashing lights from the casino coming through the first deck windows.

Far ahead of them on the street, running toward the sandbar that stretched out to the shore-side hole in the boat's hull, was Boss.

The old Australian Shepherd walked strangely, limping slightly as though his front right leg had been injured. The brown and white of his fur was dark with mud that caked his neck and chest.

Max opened his mouth to bark for the dog, but then he remembered—the bad people. He glanced left as he ran, across the gravel parking lot next to the red boathouse and toward the docks. The big white boat the bad people had sailed in on was still docked beyond the boathouse. Its windows were dark, and the SUVs were nowhere in sight.

Somehow Boss and Max and his friends had beaten the people there.

With a sigh of relief, Max barked out, "Boss! Hey, Boss!"

The old dog turned, then wagged his tail as he saw Max, Rocky, and Gizmo.

"I could have sworn you boys and girl would have

gone to those labs," he said as the three of them raced to his side. "How did you get here so fast?"

"We took a shortcut," Max said simply.

"We barely escaped from that lab with our hides intact," Rocky said. "We should have listened to your warnings."

"You find what you were looking for there, son?" Boss asked Max.

"We did. But that can wait for later, Boss. We know you said you don't need our help, but we're here to offer it anyway."

Boss barked, then turned back toward the boat. "To tell you the truth, I was hoping you'd come help. I ain't going to lie, it's good to see you."

Gizmo dodged forward and licked Boss's foreleg where he limped. "Oh, Boss, what happened? Are you all right?"

Boss softly wagged his tail. "It's nothing," he said. "Don't worry about it. I just saw some wolves, ran through a few trees to avoid them, and took a tumble into a ditch. My foot'll be fine."

"You saw wolves?" Rocky asked. "Coming *here*?"

"I saw a bunch of them splitting up, one bunch going somewhere, the other bunch going a different way." Boss waded through the shallows and out onto the damp, soft sand, Max, Rocky, and Gizmo following. "And their scent is on the wind. But wolves I can handle. It's those people who want to set the *Flower* on fire I'm worried about."

They leaped one by one through the smooth, small hole into the underbelly of the riverboat, their paws leaving the soft, damp sand and meeting the cold, grated metal of the walkways. In the glow of the caged red lights, they padded over the walkways, winding past the machinery and pipes until they reached the stairs. They loped up, single file, and shoved through the door into the hallway.

As they passed through the swinging doors at the other end and into the gleaming silver kitchen, Max heard muffled, anxious barks.

"What's that?" Gizmo asked.

"Sounds like they're arguing," Rocky said.

"That's not good," Boss growled. "We can't be having fights at a time like this. Come on."

Max and Boss walked side by side into the fancy dining room, Rocky and Gizmo at their heels. As they did, the voices rang loud and clear, drowning out the electronic music of the slot machines.

"The wolves will know there's food on board!" one female dog barked. "Rufus and I, we brought our boy here because we were told we'd be safe. But what's to stop the wolves from just coming up through the hull like anyone else?"

"Calm down!" a male voice yipped. "I've been running this ship long before any of you lived here. I know how to keep it protected."

"I dunno," a deep voice grunted. "I'd feel better if Boss was here."

"Boss, Boss, Boss," the second voice said. "Enough about Boss. He's not here. I am. So listen up!"

Quietly, Max, Boss, Rocky, and Gizmo padded over the carpet to stand between the booths and take in the scene.

All the dogs on the *Flower* had crowded inside the casino: the pack of Dalmatians, the burly dogs who had been trying to play card games, Gloria and her newborns, the mottled mutts Max had seen spinning a puppy in one of the game wheels, at least a dozen more of all different breeds.

They surrounded a long black table. Atop the black felt sat bushy, mustachioed Twain. The old Sheepdog sat next to a dog smaller than Max but larger than Rocky and Gizmo. This dog's body and hind legs were gray, his fur cropped short. His front legs, however, were bushy and white. Wisps of hair hung down from the cheeks of his square snout and next to his nose, making him look just as mustachioed as Twain, with a beard to boot.

There was nothing unusual about the dog at all—Max had known one of the same breed back at Vet's kennel; they were called Schnauzers. Nothing unusual, except this particular dog wore a hat between his two pointed ears that was shaped like the cap of a white mushroom with a black brim.

"Who's that?" Max whispered.

"That," Boss said, "would be Captain."

Ears perking, the young Dalmatian Cosmo jumped

to his feet and looked across the room. Catching sight of the four dogs, his tail began wagging violently. "Boss!" he cried out.

Captain sighed. "No, not Boss. *Captain.*" The dog in the cap tilted his head thoughtfully. "Unless you mean I'm the boss now, in which case, very good. Good boy."

"No," Zephyr the Dalmatian leader barked, rising and turning. "It's Boss. He's back!"

Sniffing the assembled dogs as he made his way through the crowd, Boss walked as purposefully as he could toward the center of the room despite his limp. Dogs sniffed him and panted their approval as he strode by, Max, Rocky, and Gizmo trailing behind him.

"Well, as I live and breathe," Twain said from up above. "You four look like you've been on quite the adventure. I'd love to hear the tale!"

"We don't have time for stories now," Captain barked. He looked down on Boss. "Glad to see you back in one piece. But we're in crisis."

"I know," Boss said, sitting in front of the table. "I heard. You all caught scent of the wolves outside, too."

Gloria the Golden Retriever tucked in her legs, pulling her puppies close to her belly. They squirmed over one another, mewling in confusion. "Are we in danger, Boss?" she asked softly.

"Of course we're in danger!" Captain snapped. "What we need is to stop talking over one another and figure out a plan. This is our home, and we won't give it up to those wild animals without a fight. Now, if you'll just listen to *me*—"

Max barked and sat down beside Boss, but facing the room instead of Twain and Captain.

"Sorry to interrupt," he said. "The wolves are a danger, yes, but there's something much more dangerous coming. The bad people. They're on their way back here. And they're going to set the *Flower of the South* on fire."

Several of the dogs gasped, and some got to their feet and skittered in anxious circles. A murmur of voices filled the casino.

"A fire?" Twain barked over the din of frightened dogs. "I know they're bad people and all, but why would they want to do that? This is our home! We're not hurting anybody!"

Max pointed his snout in the direction of the barred booth with the lockboxes—and at the big metal box with the dial on its front. Most of the dogs stopped speaking and looked to where he was pointing, listening.

"It's the same reason you said they were on the boat before, Twain," Max went on. "They want what's in that box—that safe, is what they call it. But they're afraid of us. They think if they burn the ship, it'll get rid of us but leave the safe behind, since it won't burn. Once we're gone, the safe will be theirs for the taking."

"They're going to burn down our home just because of what's inside that box?" the Bull Terrier named Bingo barked.

"It's not even *food*!" Cosmo shouted.

"It's money!" Rocky barked back. "It drives people *crazy*. It's like squirrels."

"So if we don't want to turn into barbecue," Boss said, "we need to evacuate this boat."

The dogs all understood that. They started barking and yapping at once, not with a murmur this time but with an unintelligible roar. The noise filled the room until Captain reared back his head and howled, "Quiet down!" As he did, the little cap tumbled off his head and landed on the felt.

The dogs fell silent, watching as Captain nudged his nose under his hat and clawed it back atop his head. Capped once more, he glared down at Boss, Max, Rocky, and Gizmo.

"As I said," Captain growled, "I lived here a long, long time. This was mine and Twain's home, but it's *our* home now. Wolves or people, it doesn't matter. We cannot abandon ship."

Next to the Schnauzer, Twain nodded in agreement.

"We won't just run off with our tails between our legs!" Captain said, his voice growing louder. "I refuse to go down without a fight!"

Twain leaped up and shouted, "They can do whatever they want to try to take our ship. If we can't have it, then they can't, either!"

Some of the bigger dogs crowding the casino barked

their approval, but others looked around nervously. Gloria whispered soothingly to her puppies.

Wincing, Boss got to his feet. "I've got me an idea about what we can do," he said.

All the dogs in the room leaned in, listening, even Captain. Boss met their eyes one by one.

"Seems to me we have some wolves and some humans both on their way to visit us," he said. "And it seems to me only proper that they have a nice meeting amongst themselves first."

CHAPTER 21

UNWANTED VISITORS

An hour later, Max found himself looking through a hatch at the scarred, snarling face of Dolph.

They'd acted quickly once Boss told everyone his plan, and the dogs who were too young or weak to stay behind had joined Gloria and her puppies and departed the riverboat for a secure hiding spot on shore.

Dolph and the few members of his pack that he'd managed to gather had shown up on the sandbar only moments after the evacuated dogs shut the door on their hiding place—the red boathouse on which the woman had painted her Praxis symbol warning. The wolves had slipped through the hole into the boat's underbelly.

Max had stood outside the stairwell door and heard

their paws stomping against the grating. But the wolves had found the door locked—and no amount of scrabbling against the metal or howling in protest would get the dogs to let them in.

That was when the dogs who had remained on board flung open the hatch above the smelly, unemptied trash bin Max had seen when first entering the ship. Their goal now: taunt and distract the wolves until the plan could go into action.

The hatch was in a room behind the kitchens, past the door to the stairs that led into the belly of the ship. It swung up on hinges, revealing the bin below that was piled with stinking, moldering trash bags.

Max stood over the open hatch, nose scrunched at the stench, with Rocky and Gizmo at his side. Captain, his cap at a jaunty angle between his ears, stood on the other side of the hatch, with Zephyr, Cosmo, Astrid, and three other Dalmatians also looking down at Dolph and five of his wolves.

"Let us up, mutts!" Dolph bellowed. He tried to climb up the mountain of trash to get closer to the dogs, but the bags shifted and he stumbled. His claws sliced through the plastic, unleashing new, rotting smells into the air.

"We want meat!" another of the wolves howled.

"Not a chance!" Rocky barked at them. "You're staying down there with the garbage, where you belong!"

The wolves were all drenched with water, and clearly

not happy about it. Max had wondered how Dolph and his wolves managed to get to the riverboat so fast, but it seemed obvious upon seeing them. Dolph must have awoken, seen Gertrude leading Max and his companions to the waterway, and then decided to take the shortcut himself.

Dolph roared from below in frustration. "We must eat! Open the door and let us in or we shall make a feast of your insides when we make it through on our own!"

"Ha!" Rocky barked. "I've heard that before. Guess what, Dolph? My insides are staying right where they belong!"

"There's plenty of food down there!" Cosmo shouted with a happy wag of his tail.

"Isn't that what you wild dogs call a gourmet meal?" Zephyr added. She and the rest of the Dalmatians burst into laughter.

Howling, Dolph tried to leap up out of the hatch. But it was too high, and the trash beneath it too unstable to get a foothold.

"Share your food with us, mutts, and we may show you mercy." Glaring at Rocky, he added, "But not the little one. He's *mine*."

"Promises, promises!" Rocky said with a dismissive yip.

Nudging Max with her snout, Gizmo whispered, "What's taking Boss so long?"

"I don't know. Let's go see what's going on outside," Max whispered back.

With a nod to Captain, Max padded away from the dogs hurling their insults, Gizmo at his side. He decided to let Rocky stay and enjoy the fun. He figured the Dachshund could use a break.

Max and Gizmo nosed past the door that opened into the hatch room, then into the hallway. Side by side, they walked quickly through the double doors into the kitchen, then out across the casino.

The gaming tables were all empty, and the noises of the flashy machines echoed through the vacated halls. It was eerie in its emptiness, considering how only an hour before it had been full of dogs.

Max shoved through the gilt door that opened onto the main deck. He let Gizmo dart through, then he walked through himself, letting the door slam shut behind him.

Dawn hadn't yet arrived, and the streetlamps and building windows still glittered from shore. Max padded up to the slatted, painted railing and stuck his head through, watching the road that led to the boathouse and dock. A flag snapped and fluttered just beneath his chin.

The two dogs didn't have to wait long.

The chirping of crickets and the lapping of the waves against the shore were soon drowned out by the revving of engines. Like twin giant, sleek predators, the two black SUVs stalked swiftly down the dark road before turning into the parking lot and coming to rest in front of the docks.

“What’s going on?” a voice whispered behind Max.

He pulled his head back through the slats and found Astrid and two Dalmatians he didn’t recognize emerging from the casino door. He shushed them, then gestured for them to come join him and Gizmo.

Car doors slammed, and Max turned his attention back to the bad people.

They had gotten out of their vehicles, and the woman, the skinny man, and one of the burly men walked around to the trunks and opened them up. The other burly man walked up the gangplank onto the big white boat, his boot steps heavy and clanking against the ridged metal, and then disappeared around the cabin into the shadows.

The three bad people still at the vehicles pulled out masks and strapped them over their faces. The masks were clear in front of their eyes but were black and ridged in front of their mouths and noses. They zipped leather jackets up to their necks, then pulled on black gloves.

Near the boat, another engine revved, this one loud and buzzing. Curious about this strange new noise, Max slung his head low and walked softly, quietly, around to the front of the riverboat nearest the bad people’s vessel.

As Max watched, a small black boat jetted out from behind the bigger vessel. It had four seats and a wide-open area in the back. The burly man who’d separated from the rest steered the boat from a wheel behind an angled windshield. He, too, was now wearing a mask and protective gear.

The roaring of the engine calmed to a smooth hum as the man steered the small boat up alongside the shore. By then, the three other humans had carted over the red-and-black containers of gasoline. They handed the jugs to one another, stacking them in the open area in the back of the boat until no more would fit.

"Here they come," Max growled.

Gizmo sat down beside him. "Why do they need the little boat?"

"They can't fit through the little hole on the sand-bar," Max said as he watched the skinny man hand one of the crates of explosives to the woman. "They're going to try to go through the big hole that we came through the first time."

Gizmo shuddered. "I still can't believe humans would do this! It's just so awful!"

"I know," Max said, turning away. "But I guess that people, just like dogs, can be bad. We'd better go get everyone ready. We'll need all the dogs together if this is going to work."

Barreling into the room with the hatch, Max shoved himself between a Dalmatian and Rocky and peered down at the garbage pit. Dolph still stood there with three of his lackeys, snarling and slobbering in rage.

"Hey!" Max barked down. "You might want to hide."

"And why is that, mongrel?" Dolph growled. "You expect you can scare me off?"

"Maybe not me," Max said. "But there are some humans coming on board any moment now."

Dolph laughed. "You lie. If there were humans, we'd smell them long before they came near."

Max wagged his tail. "Over the smell of all this trash? Why do you think we goaded you over here?"

Before Dolph could respond, there came a heavy thump behind the wolves, and then another. Max lowered his head to get a look. Just past the high walls of the garbage pit was the maintenance room, with its wall ripped open. The humans were climbing inside.

"They're here," Rocky said, casting a nervous glance at Max.

"This had better work," Captain said with a shake of his head.

The wolves had all gone still at the sounds inside the maintenance room, staring and waiting. Dolph darted his head between the small room's door and the bright hole in the ceiling above him, uneasy.

"What now?" one of the wolves snarled.

"Lead us, Dolph!" another wolf said. "We will be cornered!"

The flat handle on the maintenance closet door began to move.

"Be quiet!" Dolph hissed. "Hide now!"

Silently, the wolves filed out of the trash bin, their claws shredding the plastic as they climbed off the mountain of garbage and leaped to the grated walkways. They slunk among the pipes, disappearing into the red-lit innards of the ship. Max watched as they hid in the shadows behind machinery and ducked in the darkness behind pallets leaned up against the walls.

Max, Rocky, Gizmo, Captain, Zephyr, and the Dalmatians all crowded in around the hatch, angling their necks to get the best view possible. The horrific aroma of months-old garbage—moldy meat and spoiled milk and rotten eggs—threatened to smother them, and it didn't help that a fly was buzzing around their ears, but no one moved a muscle.

The maintenance room door opened with a creak of hinges, then flung open to slam against the wall. A human figure slipped through.

The woman.

She looked left and right, taking in the surroundings, her breaths sounding muffled, heaving from behind the mask. She took a tepid step forward, her boots clanging against the metal walkway. Then, seeing nothing, she turned and gave her companions a thumbs-up.

Two of the men came in behind her, both hefting the red-and-black containers in each fist. They stomped into the crimson underbelly of the *Flower* like they owned the place and plopped the gas jugs onto the metal floor with heavy clangs before going back for more.

While she waited for the men to return, the woman paced, her arms crossed as she studied the surroundings.

Then, glancing up at the trash bin, she caught sight of the dogs staring down from the opening above the garbage bags, their heads shadows against the bright fluorescent lights of the hatch room.

The woman's cheeks rose behind the clear portion of the mask, but her eyes were cold. Slowly she raised a gloved hand, then wiggled her fingers as though saying hello.

Or, more likely, saying good-bye.

Another heavy thump sounded from the maintenance room, and the three men emerged one by one with more of the red-and-black jugs. Once atop the grating, one of the big men slammed down his jugs, then leaned over and removed the cap from the top of one of the bigger black jugs. As gasoline glugged out of the hole, he stood back up and shoved the container forward with his booted foot, making it scoot down the grating while it splashed noxious-smelling gasoline all over the floor.

The humans laughed and spoke to one another in muffled, cheerful tones. As they did, Max felt a thrum of vibration beneath his paws.

"All right, everyone," he whispered. "This is it. Growl and bark as loud as you can. Those masks the bad people are wearing should drown out some of the noise, but it's up to us to do the rest."

"You got it, buddy," Rocky said. Then he bellowed the loudest roar that he could produce, ending in a drawn-out "Hiii-*yah*!"

All four people looked up at the grating.

Gizmo joined in, and then Captain, and all the Dalmatians. They barked and howled and yipped and yelped as loud as they possibly could. Spittle flew from their snouts from the force of their effort.

Noise filled the hold below, echoing through the machinery louder and louder until it became a thunderous din. The big bald man covered his ears and shouted something, but he could barely be heard above the noise.

Max growled and summoned up his most dangerous bark—the one he only ever used when someone was threatening his pack leaders or any of his friends. The sound that came out of his mouth was vicious—terrifying even to Max. But if anyone deserved the full force of his barks, it was these humans.

The other three humans completely ignored them. They picked up their small jugs of gasoline and busied themselves walking slowly around the pipes, splashing gasoline on the floor and walls—everywhere. Scowling behind his mask, the bald man lowered his hands from his ears and joined them.

None of the humans seemed to notice the lights blinking on the machinery, or the puffs of steam shooting from the pipes. They didn't hear—because of Max and his friends' orchestra of barks—the riverboat's engines roaring to life.

And they didn't see the six angry, hungry wolves emerge from the shadows, having decided that maybe the humans weren't so dangerous, after all.

CHAPTER 22

A PLAN REVEALED

The bald man was midsplash with his can of gasoline when his eyes went wide behind his mask. He dropped the can, sending the foul-smelling liquid splattering everywhere.

He'd seen the wolves.

Dolph and his five pack mates crept across the grated walkways, their heads slung low and their yellow fangs bared. They snarled and snapped, saliva dripping from their sharp teeth and falling to the metal floor in fat droplets.

One by one the other humans realized something was happening. The woman was the first after the bald man to catch sight of the narrowed yellow eyes and raised brown-and-gray fur, and she shouted. Her hot breath fogged up her mask, and she veered wildly backward, waving the can she held and splashing gasoline haphazardly toward the wolves.

Dolph ducked a stream of the vile-smelling liquid and roared in anger. He feigned a leap at the woman, then growled.

The barks of the dogs above the hatch still echoed through the hold, drowning out the noise of the riverboat's revving engine. So it wasn't until the woman barreled backward into the skinny man and the big man in the cap that the two men noticed the wolves, too.

All three of them dropped their gas jugs. The containers clanged and thudded against the walkway, splattering gasoline all over the machinery. The humans raised their hands as if begging the wolves to stay back, and they took small, slow steps away from the angry beasts.

Dolph didn't seem to care. He flattened his ears and growled even louder as two of his lackeys came to stand on either side of him.

And the wolves stalked forward.

Max couldn't watch any longer. He pulled his head up from the hatch and gulped in some clean air. The floor vibrated beneath his feet, and he heard the distant hum of the engines now that he no longer had his head in the bark-filled hold.

Max nudged Rocky and Gizmo with his snout, and the two small dogs raised their heads. Having gotten their attention, he led them to the door.

The three dogs raced down the hallway, through the kitchen and casino, and back outside. They stepped on deck to find the dark night sky turning gray on the eastern horizon, just past the empty city. Morning was coming.

Max had been up for almost a full day. His eyelids felt heavy, and his whole body ached for sleep. But the adrenaline rush that came with enacting Boss's plan was just enough to send a surge of energy to his limbs.

Soon this would all be over. Soon he could rest, safe from the wolves and the bad people, and then continue his journey to find his people knowing that the dogs on the *Flower* were free from harm.

"This way," Max said to Rocky and Gizmo.

They ran to the stairs that led to the second-level deck, then bounded up the steps. Rounding the railing, they veered left and headed toward the steerage cabin.

They burst through the cabin's doors and skidded across the polished wood floor, coming to a stop right beside where Twain sat. "Whoa, there!" the bushy Sheepdog said. "Careful you don't smack into anything. The levers need to be pressed in the right order." He barked a command.

Boss sat above them, perched on the leather chair, shoving his shoulder against a series of golden levers on the angled counter below the windows. A cool morning breeze swirled up off the water and blew in through the broken front window.

"Sorry!" Gizmo said. "Sometimes my legs don't stop right when I tell them to."

Boss chuckled. Eyes on the dials next to the machinery, he asked, "How is everything below?"

"It's all going according to plan," Max said. "So far, anyway. The humans and wolves are facing off in the hull, and Captain is leading the Dalmatians in being as loud as possible. The people didn't hear a thing."

"You should have seen them!" Rocky said, jumping up on his hind legs. "The wolves were all, 'We're gonna eat you!' and we were all, 'Nah, eat trash!' And then the humans were all, 'We're going to blow you up!' and then we were all—" He let out three unruly barks.

"Sounds exciting," Twain said, his bushy tail wagging. "This is turning out to be a most excellent tale—one that dogs will remember for ages."

"It ain't over yet, Twain," Boss huffed. "All right, I'm going to try it. Max, go see if it works."

"Yes, sir," Max said.

Leaving the others behind, Max shoved through the door and ran along the top deck back the way he'd come, past the stairs and around to the rear of the boat. Leaping up, he placed his paws atop the wooden railing and looked down.

The four red wheels were below. Sun-dried water weeds dangled from a few of the painted slats. He held his breath as he looked at the wheels, watching and waiting.

On the deck above Max's head, gold pipes whistled. He twisted his head back just in time to see twin plumes of steam rise into the sky.

Then he heard the wheels groan.

Max watched as they started to rotate away from him—spinning backward. This was the crux of Boss's plan. None of the dogs had ever tried to get the *Flower of the South* to go in reverse. But if Boss was right, and if they could back the boat away from the sandbar, they might be able to catch the current. Then the *Flower* would drift out into the center of the river, where the water was at its deepest.

That way, even if the boat burned down, the safe that the bad people so desperately wanted would sink into the murky depths of the giant river. They'd be deprived of their prize, just like they deserved.

Max hopped from foot to foot and barked at the giant waterwheels, anxiously willing them to keep turning. They were moving so *slowly*, and Max didn't know if they were supposed to start that way or if something was wrong.

The wheels abruptly stopped spinning, and the entire riverboat jerked backward. Max's paws scrabbled over the deck, and he almost lost his footing. But he caught himself at the last moment, bracing himself against the railing.

"What's happening?" Gizmo's voice called.

Max looked back and saw her head peeking out of

the cabin's door. Max barked, "I think the wheels are snagged on something. Keep trying!"

The four waterwheels groaned again and shuddered in their housings, then once more began to slowly turn. There was an enormous splintering and then a sharp crack as wood shattered—but then the wheels began to spin freely, churning into the water and sending up a frothy white foam. Slowly at first, and then faster and faster, the wheels tore into the gentle surface of the river—until, rumbling like an awakened giant, the big riverboat was pulled free of the sandbar and backward onto the river.

"Yes!" Max barked. He dropped down to the deck and raced back to the cabin. As he ran, he could already see the docks and the shoreline moving away. A breeze kicked up, sending the flags all along the ship flowing and snapping.

Max bounded into the cabin, his tongue hanging out and his tail a blur behind him.

"You did it, Boss," he said. "We're moving! We're going backward. It's working!"

"I knew you could do it!" Gizmo yipped as she jumped up and down in giddy circles.

"We're going to win!" Rocky barked, his spiky tail a happy blur. "I always knew we would."

Twain leaped up onto one of the empty leather chairs and bellowed, "Full steam ahead—I mean, backward!"

The bushy dog lowered his mustachioed snout and

flung up one of the golden levers. Hisses of steam and piercing whistles sounded in response, and the floor beneath Max's feet vibrated as the boat began to move faster.

"All right!" Boss barked over the roaring engines. "That's all you four can do. Now to round up the others and abandon the ship."

"Are you still sure this is what we should do?" Max asked. "Maybe there's some other way we can get rid of the wolves and the people—some way that won't make everyone lose the *Flower*."

"That's a mighty tempting idea," Twain said with a twitch of his mustache. "I would miss the old girl."

Boss leaped down from his chair, then came to stand next to the one on which Twain sat. He nuzzled the Sheepdog's flank. "We talked about this, my friend," he said. "I know what it's like to lose your home, and especially what it's like to lose your girl. But as long as bad people know there's treasure to be found here, then they'll keep fixin' to try to find a way to get it. Might as well use the sinking of the *Flower* to stop those greedy brutes—and those wolves—once and for all."

"Aw," Gizmo said. She dropped to her belly and rested her head on her paws, her tail drooping. "That's so sad. I wish those bad people had never come here."

"Me, too," Twain said with a sigh.

The boat shuddered, and everyone stumbled as they fought to stay on their feet.

"I think we need to go," Rocky said. "I don't want to be here when this boat starts going underwater!"

Twain bounded down off his chair and headed to the exit, followed by Rocky and Gizmo. Max turned back to Boss as the old Australian Shepherd jumped up in front of the controls.

"What about you?" Max asked. "You said for only the four of us to go, but the boat is moving, just like you planned. You should come with us and make sure we're all gone before anything bad happens."

Boss puffed out his chest. "Sorry, son, no can do. One of us needs to stay behind and make sure the *Flower* reaches the deep water. Since I'm the one with the lame paw"—he held up his front right foot and let it dangle there—"I'm going to let you lot get off the boat while I take care of things up here."

"Are you sure, old boy?" Twain asked from the cabin's door. "Captain and me have been watching these controls far longer than you, after all. I can stay and help, at least."

"No," Boss said. He turned his attention to the view outside the broken window. "We all agreed when I came on board: I'm the alpha now. You'll do what I say."

Twain sighed. "Aye, aye."

Max took one last look at Boss sitting atop the leather captain's chair. Even with the regal plume of fur on his chest caked with mud, the older dog looked proud, an alpha from his black nose to the tip of his mottled tail. Max had worried at times that Boss would turn out to be like Dandyclaw or the Chairman, obsessed with power. But he wasn't like that at all. Instead, he was just another dog like Max, a true and honest leader who others naturally looked up to. He was older and wiser—and a good friend.

"Good luck!" Max barked with a wag of his tail.

Boss barely glanced at him. "You still here, son?" But the old Australian Shepherd offered a wag of his tail, too.

In the hatch room, the barking wasn't as loud now, and when Max peeked his head through the door he saw the Dalmatians lounging on the floor, lazily offering a yelp or a howl. Only Captain seemed still devoted to the task. His cap had fallen down his forehead from the force of his barks, and his voice seemed hoarse, rubbed raw.

The Dalmatian leader, Zephyr, snapped to attention when Max and his companions filled the doorway.

"Is it done?" she asked. "Are we moving?"

Max nodded. "We need to hurry. The shore is getting farther away by the minute."

Captain let out one last growling bark, then jerked his head up to attention. "About time," he said, his voice raspy. "The wolves tried to attack the humans, but the humans threw jugs at them and then ran until they found a space to hide under the stairs. They've barricaded themselves in with some slatted wood pallets while the wolves growl at them, and the people keep yelling at one another."

"Then why are we still yapping?" Rocky said. "Let's get going!"

The Dalmatians raced toward the door. Max, Rocky, Gizmo, and Twain stepped to the side and let them stream through, a river of black-and-white fur.

"Way to go, you guys!" Gizmo said as they ran past. "You did an awesome job at barking!"

"Thanks, Gizmo," Cosmo said as he flitted by.

As soon as the last skinny Dalmatian tail had gone, Max, Rocky, and Gizmo raced to follow, Twain and Captain at their heels.

"I can't believe we're actually leaving this place," Captain moaned as they ran beneath the glittering chandeliers of the game room and wound between the felt-topped tables.

"I can't, either, old friend," Twain said as they followed the group of Dalmatians out the gilt door and onto the deck. "But the place served us well while it lasted. We'll always have the tales to tell."

"Aye," Captain said sadly as they reached the front of the boat. "That we will. And soon we'll have us a new home."

The dozen Dalmatians crowded around the slatted

railing, all eyes on the eastern shore. The first rays of morning were cutting through the trees now and glittering over the water that rippled in the boat's wake. The shore and the docks were already a street's width away, and the gap between boat and land was growing wider every second.

Out in the center of the river with the *Flower* properly floating on the water, the main deck suddenly seemed much higher up than before. The water was choppy and dark, surely cold, and much too solid.

It would be a long way to fall, and the distance to shore was getting farther and farther.

"Ready, firedogs?" Zephyr barked over the whoosh of the wind and the rush of water.

"Ready!" Cosmo and Astrid and the rest of the Dalmatian pack shouted back.

"Let's go!"

The skinny spotted dogs leaped atop the railing and slipped through the slats, then dove off the side. They hollered and yipped in fear as their long, skinny legs flailed beneath them. Finally they splashed into the water below, disappearing into the murk.

Max watched, holding his breath. He had no idea how prepared the dogs were for the chill of the river, or the rush of its currents. They couldn't lose anyone now, not after all they'd done to prepare.

Then, one by one, the Dalmatians' ghostly white heads bobbed up. The dogs gasped for air, splashing wildly with their front legs as they fought the river and swam toward shore.

"Oh," Rocky moaned. "That looks like no fun at all. Did I mention I've sworn off water? I've had to swim far more than any Dachshund ever should!"

Gizmo licked Rocky's snout. "That just means you've had a lot of practice."

Captain's eyes glistened as he took one last look at the boat. He turned to Twain. "Would you mind carrying my cap for me?" he said, and sniffed. "I wouldn't want to lose it."

Twain nodded his bushy head. "You got it, Captain."

Carefully, Twain grabbed the brim of Captain's cap in his jaws, then removed it from between the Schnauzer's pointed ears. With one last look around, Captain sighed, then jumped through the slats into the water below. He yipped as he fell before finally splashing beneath the waves.

Mouth full of cap, Twain couldn't speak. He winked at Max, Rocky, and Gizmo, then bounded over the railing to join the other dogs in paddling toward shore.

"See you on dry land!" Gizmo yipped, then slipped through the slats herself.

Max peered down at Rocky. "You rea—" he started to say.

But he didn't get a chance to finish. Rocky had already waddled up to the edge of the deck and, with a deep breath, he, too, jumped into the water.

Max wagged his tail. “Guess it’s down to me,” he said to himself.

Then, with his eyes aimed on shore, he bunched up his back legs and leaped high—up into the air of morning, and the breeze of the riverboat’s passage, and right over the white railing—letting out his loudest, happiest, Rocky-est “Hiiii-*yah*!”

CHAPTER 23

A BLAZE OF GLORY

Water erupted around Max as he splashed belly-first into the cold river. With a few strokes of his legs, Max's head popped out of the water and he gulped in air.

Keeping his head high, Max paddled hard. Ahead of him the Dalmatians, Captain, and Twain slogged onto shore, and a moment later, so did Gizmo and Rocky. All of them shook themselves and then lined up along the grass to watch the *Flower of the South*'s final voyage.

Max had almost reached the sandbar when a loud boom thundered behind him.

He climbed onto the soft sand and turned as a plume of flame whooshed into the sky on the back end of the riverboat. With a crack, splintered, flaming wood flung through the air in every direction, landing in the waves with sizzling thunks.

"Oh, no!" Gizmo barked as Max reached her and Rocky.

Max couldn't say anything. All he could do was watch.

The great red waterwheels on the back of the riverboat stopped churning, and the riverboat began to spin slowly, turning lazily on the water until its front end was pointed upriver and its broken wheels downriver. The large, jagged hole that Max, Rocky, and Gizmo had first used to enter the ship now faced the shore. Flames licked up the back of the boat, blackening the gold trim and white paint, and rapidly spreading along the two lower decks. The flags along the railings shriveled and turned to ash, and the windows all along the length of the boat cracked and shattered. Thick black smoke poured from the windows and billowed up to form dark clouds in the sky.

Through the windows of the cabin on the second deck, Max could make out the shadowy figure of Boss, still sitting on his chair, still nosing levers forward and back, trying to get the big spoked wheels turning again.

"Boss!" Max barked. "Boss, get out of there!"

But he knew there was no way the old Shepherd would be able to hear him.

Though the engines had died, the riverboat had reached the center of the river, and the strong current took hold. The burning vessel started to drift downriver.

"Come on!" Max shouted to Rocky and Gizmo.

The three dogs bounded along the shallows and onto the grassy shore, then joined Captain and Twain and the other dogs as they raced up the street that ran in front of the docks.

The dogs passed the boathouse with the spray-painted symbol and the dock where the bad people's big white vessel still bobbed. They howled as they ran past, calling out to Boss and condemning the humans for what they'd done.

"You'll never get what you want now!" Captain barked.

Max didn't join in. Instead, as he ran, he looked over at the burning riverboat. The orange flames undulated and danced in waves up the side of the vessel, like some sort of glowing river that flowed toward the sky. The boat itself was little more than a dark, indistinct shape behind the flames, its wooden eaves and decks flickering with embers. The last bits of gold paint caught the light and joined in the extravagant sparkle.

It was as though the sun had set directly in the calm, gray-blue waves of the river, a show of light in front of the tall green trees at the river's edge that waved gently in the morning breeze. It was almost pretty, in its own destructive way—or would have been if Max's friend weren't still on board.

A shadow moved inside the steerage cabin. Why wasn't Boss leaving?

The riverboat left a trail of glowing embers in its

wake. Suddenly the boat listed, tipping on its side toward the shore, and a waterfall of clear, chlorinated water poured over the top deck and down the side. It splashed through the flames, temporarily putting them out, but soon the pool was empty and the hungry fire roared back.

Human figures appeared in the jagged hole, silhouetted by flickering orange. Choking smoke swirled up behind them as one by one the bad people leaped out of the hole and into the water. They flung their arms wildly as they started to swim back toward their boat.

More splashes sounded, and as the blazing boat surged on the water, Max saw six dark dog heads swimming toward the opposite shore. The wolves. They must have discovered the smaller hole, he figured. He was glad to see they weren't coming back to this side of the river.

But he wasn't glad long.

There was another boom, and another huge crack echoed over the water. The top deck collapsed in a bright burst of yellow light, flames suddenly appearing where before there had been cabins. The fire burned so hot and intense that Max could feel the heat warming his fur even on the shore.

"Whoa!" Rocky yelped, eyes wide as he looked back at the riverboat.

"Come on, Boss!" Zephyr barked ahead.

"Get out of there, old boy!" Twain bellowed.

Like grasping, greedy orange claws, the flames climbed up the front of the ship, driven by the rushing river winds. Finally Max saw the wooden door to the cabin open and the proud figure of Boss come through.

He was limping toward the railing when, with a pained groan, the riverboat tilted farther on its side. The sudden shifting of the deck caused Boss to stumble and slide. The old Australian Shepherd scrabbled for purchase, but his one good front leg couldn't hold on. As Max watched in horror, the old dog slid helplessly down the angled deck, toward the flames.

"No!" Max bellowed.

But then Boss's paws caught on the railing, and he flung himself through a missing section—off the deck and away from the boat.

He tumbled and spun through the air, finally splashing into the cool waves. When Boss's head bobbed to the surface, he was already far downriver, caught by one of the currents.

"Don't just stand there," Captain ordered. "One of our pack went overboard! Find him!"

"Aye, aye!" Twain barked.

"Come on, firedogs!" Zephyr shouted.

Max didn't know how long they ran alongside the river, all eyes scanning the water for any sign of Boss. The sky grew lighter and brighter as the morning sun rose, revealing clear blue and lazy white clouds behind the plumes of black smoke. The world seemed so normal. Happy. But all Max could smell was burned wood and smoke, and his eyes watered.

Finally, one of the Dalmatians up ahead started to bark madly.

"I see something!" he called, his voice echoing through the trees. "Come quick! I think it's him!"

The white-and-black swarm of Dalmatians surged forward, then circled and crowded around something down the shore. Captain, Twain, Gizmo, Rocky, and Max arrived moments later.

"Is it...?" Max asked softly.

The Dalmatians parted to reveal the still, silent dog lying atop the rocks.

Boss lay in a puddle of water, a wet shadow of his former self.

It was the worst Max had seen any dog look since poor Madame.

Boss inhaled sharply, opened one eye, then coughed out some water. His jaws opened and shut, as though he didn't know what to say.

Max rested his head atop his paws so that he was snout-to-snout with the alpha. "It's okay," he said. "Take your time. We're not going anywhere."

Boss swallowed. "Did we do it?" he asked, his voice raw and raspy.

"Yeah," Max said. "The people swam back to their boat all afraid. And the wolves barely escaped. They won't mess with any of us again, at least not soon."

Boss chuckled, then winced. "Ow. That's good."

"Boss, why did you do that?" Gizmo asked. "Why did you stay on that boat for so long?"

"Aw, Gizmo," he said with a sigh. "I had to get that boat as far away from shore as possible to keep the pack safe."

Captain came up next to Max. "I wasn't always sure about you," the old Schnauzer said, "but I have to admit, without you leading us, we may never have escaped." He briefly turned away from the injured dog, and when he turned back around, he had his captain's cap in his teeth. He plopped it on Boss's head.

"There," Captain said with a wag of his tail. "I think you earned that. Sir."

"Thanks, Captain." Silently, Boss lowered his head to rest back against the smooth pebbles. The cap tumbled off his head, but no one moved to replace it. The old dog took in a deep, shaky breath that made his side tremble.

Boss looked up at the clear blue sky. When he spoke again, his scarred voice was distant, wistful. "I think this is the end of the road for me, pups," he said. "My trail was long and winding. Led me to friends I never thought I'd meet." His tail thumped once, twice. "I can't complain that it's ending now. I have no regrets about reaching the final bend."

Twain sniffed, his bushy mustache trembling. "That's downright poetical, Boss."

"Actually, there's one thing I wish I could do again," Boss whispered. "I wish I could have made my pack leaders take Belle with us when we came here. I always meant to go and find her one day. I wish . . . I just wish she knew I never wanted to leave her behind."

"We'll find Belle for you," Max said. "We'll tell her that you loved her and missed her and never meant to abandon her."

Boss raised his singed brows in surprise. "You'd do that for me?"

"Of course we will!" Rocky said.

Gizmo wagged her tail but didn't say anything.

"I promise, Boss," Max said. "It would be an honor."

"You'll find Belle down south in Baton Rouge," Boss said. "She'll be the most beautiful and kind Collie for miles around. Did I tell you that? I must have." He wheezed. "And fun. We used to run through the tall grass, chasing firebugs and bullfrogs, and in the summer we'd laze about the old pond and swat at the fish. Sometimes . . . Sometimes we . . ."

Max waited for the dog to finish. But Boss didn't speak again.

His open eye had glossed over, gone dim. It reflected back the light from the bright morning sky, but the old Australian Shepherd was gone.

"Good-bye, Boss," Gizmo whispered. "We'll never forget you."

They buried Boss at the base of a tall, sturdy tree with a view of the river. It was what Boss's pack-leader humans would have done if they were around. But they weren't, and so it was up to the dogs themselves to give him a proper burial.

The Dalmatians worked together to dig a great hole, and then everyone worked as one to nose him gently inside. They covered his still body until he was completely enveloped by the earth, where he could rest peacefully.

With Captain's blessing, Max set the captain's cap atop the mound of dirt. Last he saw, it was still there.

CHAPTER 24

LOOKING AHEAD

Max dreamed.

He floated in the small rowboat that he had lost long ago.

He lay on his side and looked up at the sky. The boat bobbed and rocked beneath him, and the crystal tinkling of a gentle stream met his ears. Birds called to one another and flew overhead, each one a different color of the rainbow.

Birds from the zoo, he thought. *I'm so glad they're happy. They sound nice.*

Fluffy white clouds drifted across the blue canvas of the sky. They shifted and transformed into familiar shapes—a squat pig with her nose in the air, an elephant the size of a mountain trumpeting as he floated by.

Other, smaller clouds drifted between them, one like a gorilla slowly chasing a cackling hyena across the sky, two red pandas laughing behind them.

The clouds parted, revealing the sun—the single, solitary sun. He couldn't look at it, of course. But he enjoyed the warmth of it against his golden fur.

Max, a voice echoed in his head.

Max tilted his head up to look at the back of the small boat. Two dogs sat there atop plush red pillows. One was an old black Labrador with wise, kind eyes and a golden collar. The other was a weary Australian Shepherd with mottled brown, tan, and white fur, who nonetheless smiled down at Max.

Max wagged his tail, thumping against the wooden floor with wild abandon. "Hi, Madame," he said. "Hi, Boss. Are you enjoying the ride?"

Madame looked to Boss, and Boss met her eyes. Neither opened their jaws to speak, but their words entered Max's mind anyway.

I'm doing well, son, Boss's voice said.

We've weathered the darkness, Madame added, *and we're none the worse for the wear.*

"Mmm," Max moaned. "That's nice to hear."

Closing his eyes, he stretched out in the bottom of the rowboat, then flopped onto his back and let the sun heat up his belly.

Your journey isn't over yet, Max, Madame said.

"But I'm tired," he said. "I want to rest for a while

more. Bad things happened to good animals, to my friends. I'm not ready for more. Not yet."

Boss chuckled. *Well, sleep up, pup. You earned it. But don't forget to look ahead.*

Max blinked his eyes open and then got to all fours. He spun around and faced the front of the rowboat.

Ahead of him, on the gentle stream that wound lazily between bright green trees, was another rowboat. A human with white hair sat on a bench in the back, leaning over and petting some dog who Max couldn't see. Rocky and Gizmo sat on either side of her, their eyes wide and adoring.

"Hi!" Max barked, his tail wagging again.

The woman turned around in her seat to look back at Max. Catching sight of him, she offered him a warm smile that crinkled the pale skin around her lips and eyes, then raised a hand in a friendly wave. Floating in the air on either side of her were two round orange plastic discs with *X*s etched in their middles.

Something glimmered around her neck. A gold necklace with the same three-ringed symbol that was on Madame's collar.

It was Madame Curie's pack leader, Max remembered. The woman who would help him find his family. She looked exactly as she did in the photo he had seen, right down to the strands of hair falling free from her loose bun. The discs must have been the beacons Gertrude told him about.

And the unseen dog in front of the old woman, the one she'd been treating with such a loving petting session, was Boss's lost love, Belle. Max wasn't entirely sure how he knew this. He just *knew*.

The stream curved around a bend, and the woman, Rocky, Gizmo, and unseen Belle disappeared through the dangling branches of a willow tree. Max turned back to look at Madame and Boss, who still sat clean and healthy atop their plush pillows.

"What about you?" Max asked. "Sometimes, when I dream, I see darkness in this place. I don't want it to hurt anyone."

Don't worry about us, Madame's voice said as she smiled down at him.

Always keep looking ahead, Boss said.

Max turned back toward the stream just in time for the willowy branches to envelop him, brushing against his fur like the friendly, energetic hands of his lost pack leaders, Charlie and Emma. He closed his eyes and lay down once more on his belly, letting the trees pet him as he drifted past, feeling safe and comfortable for the first time in as long as he could remember.

🐾

Max awoke to the sound of lapping waves and the cool splash of water against his face. A charred wood plank clattered over the rocks, buffeted endlessly against the shore by the waves. And though Max had collapsed into sleep in the scrub on shore after burying Boss in the morning, somehow it was morning again. He'd managed to sleep through an entire day and an entire night.

He'd rested there, claiming to be taking watch to make sure that no wolves or bad people would come back to try to hurt them. Not that there was much risk of that. The bad people's black SUVs and their big white boat were gone by the time Max, Rocky, Gizmo, and the rest of the dogs who'd buried Boss stepped back onto the roads in front of the docks. Max hoped he never saw the bad people ever again. And he hoped they'd learned their lesson about messing with dogs and their homes.

The wolves, meanwhile, were trapped on the opposite shore far across the river, and their scent had faded away. With no easy way across, it didn't seem likely they'd be offering up more trouble, for a little while, at least.

The other dogs who had been hiding in the boathouse near where the *Flower* had crashed were devastated to learn of Boss's death. But as the now capless Captain told them, he gave his life to save theirs, and it was up to them to find a new safe place to live so that all of them—old dogs and young, like Gloria's puppies—could stay well fed and sheltered from harm.

Yawning, Max padded up off the slick rocks and onto the road. He made his way down the docks until he found the boathouse and, inside, Rocky and Gizmo.

Captain asked if they might like to stay with the riverboat pack for a while. To live in comfort for a little longer once they found a new home before they set out to find Belle.

Max remembered his dream. Remembered the images of Madame's pack leader and Boss's words to always keep looking forward.

"Sorry," Max told the Schnauzer. "But my friends and I made a promise."

Max, Rocky, and Gizmo set out later amid a chorus of farewells from their new doggy friends and a flurry of parting licks from Twain, Zephyr, Cosmo, Astrid, and a few of Gloria's rapidly growing Golden Retriever puppies. But soon the boathouse and the docks were dots on the horizon behind them, and the three friends walked swiftly over the grass and rocks next to the wide, surging river.

🐾

Several days passed as the three dogs followed the river, so many that Max soon lost track of how often the sun rose into the sky and then descended to bring the darkness. For the first time in a long time, the three dogs managed to travel without running into trouble—no other dogs or crazed wild animals or bad people.

Some days, rain pounded on them, a gray murk descending over the river and causing it to churn and thrash in complaint. Most days it was muggy and hot. They took shelter when they needed to, raided stores for kibble as they passed, but mostly just kept one another company. Rocky cracked jokes, Gizmo told more tales of her adventures, and Max led them with his singular focus.

But even he was beginning to think the river would never end. And so far, he hadn't seen any sign of the small barriers and the glowing orange beacons that Gertrude had promised Madame's pack leader would leave behind.

One morning, they passed by a tall, metal gate painted green. It was locked with a padlock and chains, blocking a road that entered into the thick forest of trees and ferns. Next to the gate was a large sign as tall as a house. On the sign, at the bottom, was a light that blinked red over and over.

Only Max noticed the sign at first. They hadn't eaten since the night before, and Rocky was twisting his head and snapping at the air.

"I know, buddy," he yowled. "I know, Giz. You think I'm spoiled. But when you tore open that bag of kibble a few days back and it came down like a meaty, pebbly rain—well, I can't think of anything else." He nipped at the sky as though the kibble were streaming down on him once more. "We get water to drink from the sky, don't we? Why not food, too? It's just not fair."

Gizmo giggled. "But wouldn't that make a huge mess? Water dries up or goes down drains, but kibble would just cover everything!"

Rocky winked at her and wagged his spiky tail. "Not if I'm around. I'll eat it all up. I'll probably get chubby again, but hey! More of me to love!"

Chuckling, Max looked down to say something, but the blinking light caught his eye. The sign. Something inside him told Max to investigate.

"Hey, guys," he said, already padding off the shore and onto the craggy road that led up to the locked gate. "Let's go take a look at that sign."

"Oh, what help will that do?" Rocky grumbled. "It's a people sign; it won't make much sense."

"Don't be so grumpy, Rocky," Gizmo said as she darted ahead, her tuft of a tail wagging. "Looking can't hurt."

As they neared the gate, the sounds of chirping insects and the rustling of small animals met Max's ears. Somewhere beyond, he could barely hear the trickling of a smaller stream over the sound of the surging river behind them. The whole place smelled like damp leaves and grass and moss; despite the road, it seemed as though this place was all natural.

High above, a tree branch creaked as it gently bounced up and down. The leaves rustled, then fell still.

Max stopped in his tracks, angling his head back to look up at the branch. Rocky and Gizmo came beside him to look up, too.

"Something's up in that tree, isn't there, big guy?" Rocky whispered.

"Ooh!" Gizmo said. "Is it a squirrel? Can I chase it? Maybe I can get it to play fetch with a nut!"

Whatever it was shifted again, and Max could barely

make out a mound of orange fur. Whatever it was, it was large—definitely not a squirrel.

"Hello?" Max called up. "Who's there? Don't worry, we're friendly. We'd just like to look at this sign, is all."

The flat green leaves flapped as the creature tried to crawl its way back up the branch. Its stripes of orange and tan fur were clear now.

"It's just the wind," a high voice whispered from the branch. "Blowing leaves around. This voice is in your head. Pay it no mind."

Gizmo snorted. "Uh, we can see you; we know it's not the wind. Unless your name is Wind! Then that would be kind of clever, I think."

The creature stopped its climb. It sighed, loudly, the sound echoing through the trees. A moment later, a fat, fluffy orange face peered through the tree branches.

It was a cat. One with a face squashed so that it looked like it had run into a wall at high speed. What Max could see of her body was fat and plump—or maybe that was just her puffed-out fur. Still, she was big for a house cat, and he was surprised she could maneuver her way in a tree so stealthily.

"My name isn't Wind," the cat yowled. Her puffy tail rose up behind her and flicked back and forth. "It's Lucille. This is *my* area, and I don't want visitors today."

Gizmo hung her tongue out and wagged her tail. "Don't worry, we're just passing through."

"We're not interested in dealing with any cats, anyway," Rocky said.

The cat licked her paw and swiped it over the whiskers on her flat cheeks. "That's good, then. We understand one another."

"Actually, maybe you can help us," Max called up. "We're trying to get to a place called Baton Rouge to find a dog named Belle. You heard of either?"

The cat meowed a laugh. "Baton Rouge? Oh, honey, you've got a ways to go. You'd best keep following the river."

Max nodded, already weary at the thought of how much farther they'd have to walk. But he had made a promise.

"Well, may we look at the sign here in your territory before we continue on, at least?" he asked. "Once we're done, we'll be on our way."

Lucille's whiskers twitched as she looked up at the blue sky, considering the notion. Then she said, "All right, have at it. Though I agree with your friend there—I'm not sure what good a people map is going to be for some dumb dogs."

Max bristled at being called dumb, but he didn't have the energy to press the matter. Instead, he bowed his head and barked, "Thanks, Lucille. Sorry to have disturbed you."

The squash-faced orange cat meowed dismissively, then backed away until she was once more hidden by a shroud of broad green leaves.

"She seemed nice," Gizmo said as Max led them toward the green gate. "At least we know we're on the right path to get to Baton Rouge."

Rocky snorted. "Nice enough for a cat, I guess. I'm glad she so graciously allowed us to look at this sign that doesn't even really belong to her."

Max didn't respond to them. He padded over wet leaves that plastered the road, the sensation cold and slimy beneath his paws. Reaching the sign, he leaped up and pressed his front paws against the glass-covered base and studied the thing.

The red blinking light was inside a red arrow on the bottom of the map that pointed to the winding path of blue that Max recognized as the river. Strange blocky symbols were written beneath the arrow in black, and Max scrunched his eyes as he studied them.

"I think this light means this is where we are," he said. Following the path of the river with his eyes, he saw the blue open up into a fan-shaped delta before spilling farther into an ocean.

He gestured with his nose. "Up at the top there is the Gulf of Mexico—that's what that part of the ocean is called. There's a big red dot on the top right portion of the map where it's green—that's Baton Rouge. That's where we're supposed to go."

"Wow!" Gizmo said as she jumped up and down at Max's side, trying to get a look. "You can tell all that from this map?"

"Yeah, that's crazy, big guy," Rocky said. He peered up at Max with wary brown eyes. "What, can you understand the people symbols now?"

Max looked at the bold black symbols—the slashes of lines in different patterns that made up letters, which in turn made up words. Max had seen them everywhere in people homes and at Vet's office and on signs, in various sizes and colors, but of course he'd never understood them.

Only now, somehow, when he looked at the symbols beneath the arrow he knew it read YOU ARE HERE. The words made sounds in his head like what his people used to say, and suddenly it all made sense. He knew what the words next to each dot on the map read. He knew that Baton Rouge was to the east of the river, and the ocean to the south, because the legend in the corner of the map showed the different directions.

Shaking, Max dropped down from the slick glass and plopped to all fours on the gravel and leaves next to the gate. Slowly, he turned and met Rocky's and Gizmo's waiting stares.

"Rocky," he whispered. "I *can* read the human symbols. They're words."

"Wow, really?" Gizmo asked. "That's amazing!"

"That doesn't make any sense, buddy," Rocky said. "What does that mean? Have you gone smart on us all of a sudden?"

Swallowing, Max turned and looked back up at the

map again. He blinked once, twice. But the symbol didn't change back to illegible scrawls. They were still words. Words he knew.

"Oh, Rocky, I think I can read it, too," Gizmo said. "Try it out."

Rocky blinked as he looked up at the map, then his eyes went wide. "I think I *can* understand those words! How is that possible?"

"Maybe whatever it was that Gertrude was trying worked, guys," Max said after a moment. "You remember how the Mountain described the Praxis process with the room that exploded with electricity. Maybe we didn't get out of that room fast enough. Maybe... maybe we were hit just enough that it changed us somehow."

Tail wagging in a blur, Gizmo jumped up and down. "Oh, Max!" she cried. "Oh, this is wonderful!"

"What's so wonderful?" Rocky asked as he plopped onto his belly and rested his head on his paws. "I was already plenty smart. I didn't need no Praxis to come and mess with my brain."

Gizmo bounced over to Rocky and nudged his side. "I'm not talking about that, Rocky," she said as she licked his fur. "Remember, Gertrude was trying to cure the virus that made the people go away. So if we're smart now, maybe the virus in us was cured, too!"

Perking up, Rocky rose to his four squat legs and met Max's eyes. "You think so, buddy?"

"I don't know," Max said with a shake of his head. "It's a possibility. But first things first, guys. We need to get to Baton Rouge and find Belle—and we also need to find the beacons that will lead us to Madame Curie's pack leader."

Max walked back onto the road, and Rocky and Gizmo came to match his stride on either side of him.

"We know exactly where to go now," Gizmo said, "and when we find the people, they'll be able to hug and pet us, and they won't get sick from the virus."

"Let's not get ahead of ourselves," Max said as they left the asphalt and came back to the river's edge.

"Oh, Max," Rocky said, running out in front to splash at the water while his spiked tail wagged. "Don't be such a downer, big guy. This is great news."

Max raised his head and laughed, the sound echoing over the rushing waves and through the trees. "All right, all right, I'll say it," Max said. "Things are looking up!"

Max knew they still had a long road ahead of them. Danger was surely around every corner, waiting to cause trouble for Max and his friends.

But for the first time in a long while, Max felt like he knew exactly what he was doing. His friends were safe, they had a place to go, and there was a woman somewhere out there who, once they found her, could take them back to their people.

And that thought was enough to keep Max going, at least for one more day.

ACKNOWLEDGMENTS

The continuing adventures of Max, Rocky, and Gizmo in *Dark Waters* wouldn't have been possible without the insight, patience, and assistance from many exceptional people. I must first give a giant thank-you to Michael Stearns and Ted Malawer of the Inkhouse, who not only worked with me to develop this exciting story, but also helped mold the manuscript into something resembling an actual book during what proved to be quite a time crunch.

Special thank-yous must also go to my fantastic editors, Julie Scheina and Pam Garfinkel, who saw the potential in this book even when it was bare-bones and whose notes helped flesh out the final product, as well as the entire Little, Brown Books for Young Readers team, who have worked tirelessly to produce the finished books and get them into the hands of our readers.

I am in awe of the talents brought to the Last Dogs series by artist Allen Douglas, who creates such a fun and energetic view of our cast of canines in his gorgeous illustrations, and by voice actor Andrew Bates, who, along with ListenUp Audiobooks, gives life to my animal creations in the exceptional audiobook productions of the stories.

Finally, a thank-you to all the kids and kids-at-heart who are reading this series. Max's long journey only gets more exciting in the books ahead, and I can't wait for you to read all about it!

DON'T MISS THE NEXT ADVENTURE

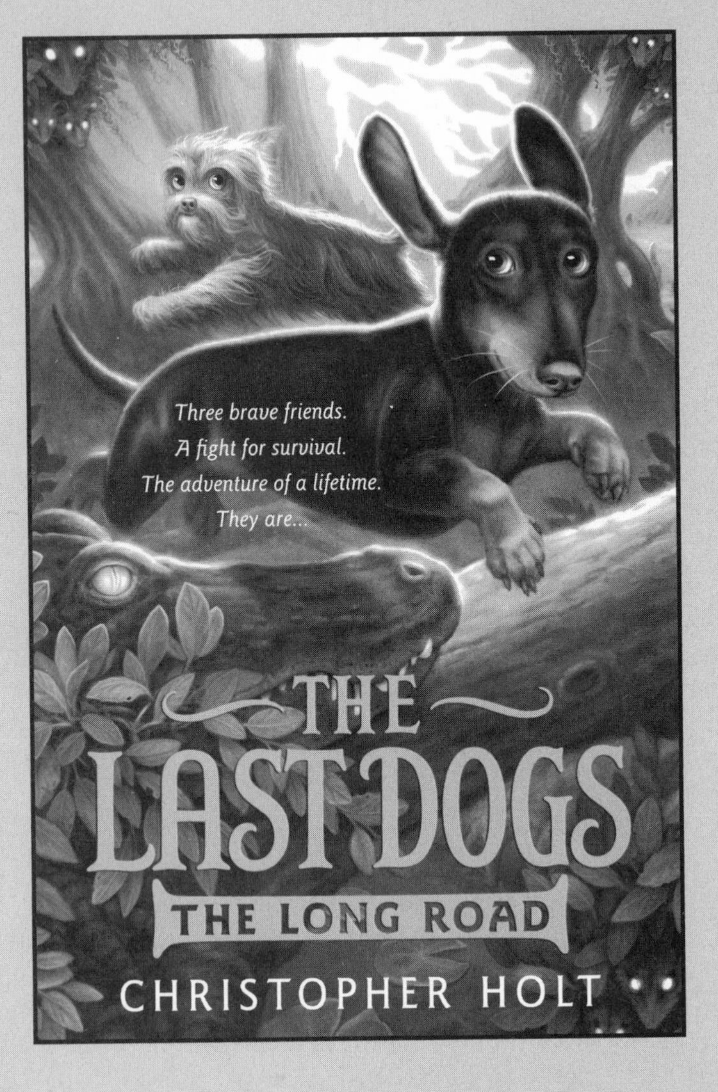

COMING NOVEMBER 2013